The World of
Fairy Tales

The World of Fairy Tales

Retold by
Vladimír Kovářík

Translated by
Stephen N. Finn

Illustrations by
Daniela Benešová

CATHAY BOOKS

First published 1982 by
Cathay Books Limited
59 Grosvenor Street
London W1
Reprinted 1984

Retold by Vladimír Kovářík
Translated by Stephen N. Finn
Graphic design by Naděžda Bláhová
Illustrations by Daniela Benešová
This edition © Artia, Prague 1982

ISBN 0 86178 180 5

Printed in Czechoslovakia by Svoboda, Prague
1/20/04/51—02

Contents

Preface

In olden times, there were no books of fairy tales. But for hundreds of years such tales had been known. People told them to each other. Grandfathers and grandmothers, especially, were wonderful storytellers. Many of their tales had been passed down from generation to generation. They were repeated so often that they became changed in the telling. Sometimes, something new was added to them, or something was taken away. Sometimes, a single story was made into two!

It was not until much nearer our own time that scholars began to collect these wonderful tales and write them down. They put them together in the first books of fairy tales. And other writers began making up their own stories which were based on folk tales. But into their own, original stories, they introduced new ideas, which sometimes made their stories more exciting. But their stories always had something in common with the old folk tales. Good always triumphed over evil. The greedy man was always outwitted by the simple, generous man. And the honest man always won his just reward!

Fairy tales by those writers who, a century ago in many different lands, put them in their first storybooks, are contained in the book you are about to read. They recall their childhood years and the dream world they loved so much. That is why we have called this book THE WORLD OF FAIRY TALES.

The Magic
Fishbone

Once upon a time there was a king and queen. The king was the most handsome of men, and the queen the most beautiful of women.

The king and queen had nineteen children: the oldest was seven years old and the youngest seven months, and the family was growing larger all the time. Seventeen of the children looked after the baby, while the eldest, Alicia, looked after all of them.

Now our story may begin.

One morning, the king, on his way to the office, called at the fishmonger's to buy a pound and a half of salmon, not too close to the tail, and have it sent home, as the queen, a careful housekeeper, had instructed. Mr. Pickles, the fishmonger, said, 'Certainly, sir! Will there be anything else? Delighted to be of service!'

The king went off to his office in a melancholy mood. It was, you see, a long time till the next pay-day, and some of the little children were growing out of their clothes.

He hadn't gone far, when Mr. Pickles' errand-boy caught up with him and said, 'Sir, did you notice that old lady in the shop?'

'What old lady?' asked the king. 'I didn't see one.'

He hadn't seen the old lady for the simple reason that she was only visible to Mr. Pickles' errand-boy. This may have been because the errand-boy was so busy splashing and spraying water about the shop, and was slapping down the sole so energetically, that if she had not been visible to him, her clothes would have been ruined!

At that moment, the old lady came tripping up to them. She was dressed in best quality shot-silk, which smelt of dried lavender.

'You are King Watkins the First, are you not?' the old lady said.

'Watkins is my name,' replied the king.

'Father, if I am not mistaken, of the beautiful Princess Alicia?' the old lady continued.

'And of eighteen other children,' replied the king.

'And now you are on your way to the office!' said the old lady.

At this, the king decided she must be a fairy; otherwise how could she have known where he was going?

'You are quite right,' she replied, reading his thoughts. 'I am a fairy godmother. Listen! When you get home, you must ask Princess Alicia to share the piece of salmon you have just bought.'

'It might not agree with her,' the king objected.

So enraged was the old lady at this ridiculous suggestion that the king lost his nerve entirely and humbly begged her pardon.

'One hears a little too often how this or that does not agree with one,' said the old lady, with as much contempt as she could muster. 'Don't be such a miser. I do believe you want to eat the whole salmon yourself!'

During this scolding, the king hung his head, and promised to say no more of anything not agreeing with anyone.

'Be so good as not to speak of it,' said the fairy godmother. 'If the princess takes the salmon and eats it, and I think she will take it,

she will leave the fishbone on her plate. Tell her to dry it, then to rub it and polish it till it shines like mother-of-pearl, and to cherish it as a present from me.'

'Is that all?' asked the king.

'Don't be so impatient, sir,' returned the fairy. 'Don't interrupt! How trying you adults are! Always the same!'

Again the king hung his head, and promised not to do it again.

'Be so good as never to do it again!' the fairy godmother went on. 'Give my regards to

9

Princess Alicia, and tell her that the fishbone is a magic gift, which may be used once only, but when it is used, her wish shall be fulfilled — *if she wishes at the right time.* That is my message. Please give it to her.'

The king was just about to say, 'And might I ask why?' when the fairy godmother really did lose her temper. 'When are you going to behave yourself, sir?' she shouted, stamping her foot. 'Why do you always want to know the reason? I am sick and tired of you grown-ups always asking why, why, why!'

The king was quite shaken to see how angry the old lady was, and he told her he was most sorry to have offended her, and that he wouldn't ask any more questions.

'You won't get the chance,' said the old lady, and she ended the conversation by disappearing into thin air.

And the king went on and on and on, until he reached the office. There he wrote and wrote

and wrote, until it was time to go home. When he got home, he offered Princess Alicia some salmon, just as the fairy godmother had instructed. When she had eaten it, with great relish, the king saw that she had left the fishbone on her plate, just as the fairy had said, so he gave Alicia the fairy's message. The princess dried the bone, then rubbed and polished it till it shone like mother-of-pearl.

The next morning, as the queen was about to get out of bed, she said, 'Oh dear me, my head, my poor head!' and fainted.

Just by chance Princess Alicia was peeping through the door of the bedchamber to ask what was for breakfast. When she saw what a state her mother was in, she became quite upset, and called Peggy, the head chambermaid.

But suddenly remembering where the bottle of smelling-salts was kept, Alicia climbed up on a chair to get it; then she climbed on another chair by the bed and held the bottle of smelling-salts under the queen's nose. After that she jumped down and went to fetch a little water, and then climbed back on the chair to moisten the queen's brow with it. In short, when the head chambermaid arrived, there was nothing for her to do.

'What a clever little thing you are!' Peggy said. 'I couldn't have done better myself!'

But that was not the worst of the queen's illness. Oh no! She was very ill indeed for a long time. Princess Alicia saw to it that the seventeen little princes and princesses kept quiet. She dressed and undressed and generally pampered the baby, and made sure that the water in the tea-kettle was always ready; warmed the soup and cleaned the stove, and nursed the queen and poured her medicine. She did all she was able, and had quite as much work as she could manage. There weren't many servants in the palace, for three reasons. First, the king didn't have much money. Second, it looked as if he would never be promoted at the office, and third, pay-day was so far off that it seemed as far away as the littlest star.

But where was the magic fishbone that morning the queen fainted? It was, of course, in Princess Alicia's pocket! She had been on the point of pulling it out to bring the queen round, but she had thrust it back again, and looked for the bottle of smelling-salts instead.

As soon as the queen had come round from her faint and dropped off to sleep again, Princess Alicia had rushed upstairs to her room

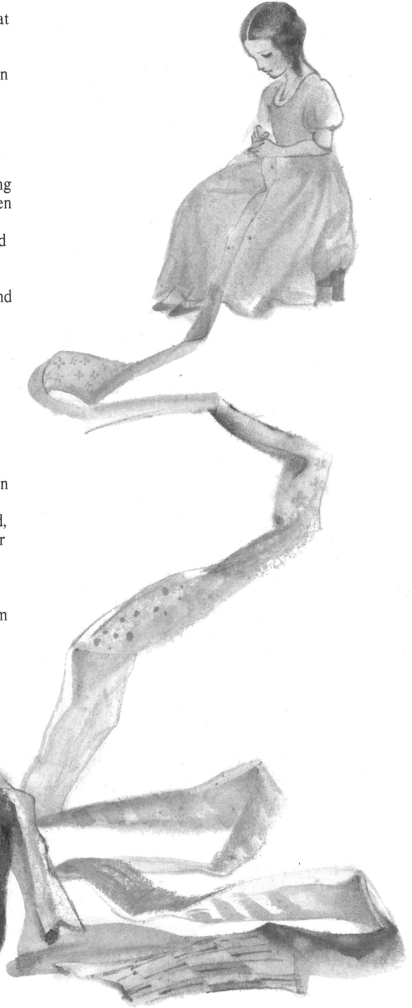

to share her secret with her most intimate friend, the duchess. People used to think the duchess was a doll, but she really was a duchess, even if the princess was the only one who knew that!

That most wonderful secret Alicia had ever had to share with the duchess was the story of the magic fishbone, which lay hidden in her pocket. Princess Alicia ran on, knelt down by the bed where the duchess lay, awake and fully dressed, and whispered her secret to her. The duchess smiled and nodded her head. Perhaps people thought the duchess never smiled or nodded her head, but in fact she did it often, even if no one knew except the princess!

Then the princess ran quickly downstairs again to look after the queen. In the daytime, she was often quite alone in the queen's bedchamber. But since the queen had been taken ill, the king would sit at the queen's bedside with her in the evening. And every evening the king sat and looked at Alicia sideways, and wondered why she didn't pull out her magic fishbone. Whenever Princess Alicia noticed this, she would run upstairs, whisper her secret again to the duchess, and add, 'Grown-ups think we children never have any sense!'

And the duchess, though she was the most majestic duchess the world had ever seen, would wink at the princess.

'Alicia, dear,' the king said, one day, as the princess was saying goodnight.

'Yes, father?'

'What has happened to the magic fishbone?'

'It's in my pocket, father.'

'You haven't lost it, have you?'

'Oh no, father!'

'Or forgotten about it?'

'Oh no, father!'

One morning, the fierce little terrier next door charged at one of the little princes, who had stopped on the front steps on his way home from school, frightening him to death. The prince stuck his hand through the glass door panel, and bled and bled and bled. As soon as the seventeen other little princes and princesses saw how he was bleeding, they too were frightened to death, and began to wail until their seventeen little faces turned black and

blue. But Princess Alicia put her hand over their seventeen mouths, one after the other, and made them stop crying, because of the queen being so ill. Then she put the wounded prince's hand in a bowl of cold water, while seventeen pairs — twice seventeen is thirty-four — of little eyes gazed on; then she examined the hand to make sure there were no splinters of glass in it, and luckily there were none. Then she told two small, but sturdy, chubby-legged princes: 'Bring me the royal remnant-bag. I must stitch and sew, and somehow put together some sort of bandage.'

So the two little princes heaved at the royal remnant-bag and pulled it and dragged it in. Princess Alicia sat down on the floor, took a big pair of scissors and a needle and thread, and cut and stitched and patched until she had sewn together a bandage. She tried it on, and it was a perfect fit. When she had quite finished, she spied her royal father standing by the door looking at her.

'Alicia!'

'Yes, father?'

'What were you doing?'

'I was cutting and stitching and patching, father!'

'Where is the magic fishbone?'

'In my pocket, father.'

'You haven't lost it, by any chance?'

'Dear me, no, father!'

'Or forgotten it?'

'No, indeed, father!'

Then she ran upstairs to the duchess to tell her what had happened, and again confided her secret to her. The duchess shook her golden locks and smiled with her rosy lips.

Another time, the baby fell into the fireguard. The seventeen little princes and princesses were used to this, for they were nearly always falling into the fireguard, or falling downstairs, but the baby hadn't got used to falling into fireguards, and its face swelled up and its eye went black.

How did the poor baby come to fall there? It slipped off Princess Alicia's knee while she was sitting in front of the kitchen fire in a big rough apron that was miles too big for her, peeling turnips for the vegetable soup. And how did Princess Alicia come to be doing this work? Well, that very morning the royal cook had run off with her true love, a very handsome but very drunken soldier! When the baby fell into the fireguard, all seventeen little princes and princesses, who cried about everything that happened, began to weep and wail. But Princess Alicia, though she couldn't help shedding the odd tear herself, told them sharply to be quiet, so as not to aggravate the queen's condition, for she was making a very rapid recovery upstairs. Then she said, 'Silence, you scallywags, while I take a look at him!'

So she had a look at the baby, and found that nothing was broken; she held a cold iron to his poor eye and cuddled his poor cheek, and the baby fell asleep in her arms. Then she told the

seventeen little princes and princesses, 'I'm afraid to put him down now in case he wakes up and it hurts him. Just you be good, and you can all be cooks!'

When the princes and princesses heard this, they jumped with joy and made themselves chef's hats from old newspapers. Princess Alicia gave one the salt cellar, and another the pearl

the baby clap its hands too, and when the little princes and princesses saw it clapping and looking as if it had a rather comical toothache, they burst out laughing. So Princess Alicia said, 'Laugh if you like, but be good! After lunch we'll make the baby cosy in the corner and he shall sit there and watch the dance of the eighteen cooks.'

barley, and another the greens, and another the turnips, and another the carrot, and another the onion, and another the spice jar, till they were all cooks, and all running to and fro working, while she sat in the middle, scarcely to be seen in the great rough apron, and nursed the baby. After a time, the vegetable soup was ready and the baby woke up and smiled like an angel, and Alicia gave him to the quietest of the princesses. The rest of the princes and princesses crowded into the far corner because they were afraid of being splashed and scalded, for something was always happening to them, and from there they watched as Princess Alicia poured the soup from the brimming pot.

As the soup bubbled and steamed, and smelt like a bouquet of flowers, all the little princes and princesses clapped their hands. This made

The little princes and princesses were so pleased at this that they ate up their vegetable soup, and washed all the plates and all the pots and pans, and tidied up everything. Then they pushed the table into the corner. And in their tall chef's hats, and Princess Alicia in the rough apron — which was miles too big for her, and which belonged to the cook who had run off with her true love, the very handsome but very drunken soldier — they danced the dance of the eighteen cooks in front of their baby brother. And the baby forgot his swollen cheek and black eye and beamed with joy and chortled with glee as he watched.

Then Princess Alicia again spied King Watkins the First, her father, standing in the doorway looking at them and he asked, 'What have you been doing, Alicia?'

'I have been cooking and keeping house, father.'

'And what else have you been doing, Alicia?'

'I have been keeping the children amused, father.'

'Where is the magic fishbone, Alicia?'

'In my pocket, father.'

'You haven't by any chance lost it?'

'Oh, no, father.'

'Or forgotten it?'

'No, indeed, father.'

Then the king sighed most deeply and sat down most sadly. He rested his head in his hand and leant his elbow on the kitchen table, which was pushed away into the corner, and he looked so dejected that the seventeen little princes and princesses crept quietly out of the kitchen and left him alone with Princess Alicia and the baby.

'What has happened, father?'

'I am terribly poor, my child.'

'Have you no money at all, father?'

'None at all, my child.'

'And have you no way of getting any, father?'

'No way,' answered the king. 'I have done all I could and tried everything!'

No sooner had he said this than Princess Alicia began to slip her hand into the pocket where she kept the magic fishbone.

'Father,' she asked, 'if someone has done all he can and tried everything, he must really have done all that was in his power, mustn't he?'

'Without a doubt, Alicia.'

'If we have done all that is in our power, father, and that is not enough, then I think the time has come to ask others for help!'

This was the true secret of the magic fishbone, which she had found out for herself, and which she had so often whispered to her beautiful and noble friend, the duchess.

So now she drew from her pocket the magic fishbone, dried and polished it till it shone like mother-of-pearl, kissed it gently, and wished that it might be pay-day. And in a trice it really was pay-day, and the king's quarterly salary came crashing down the chimney and thudded into the middle of the room.

But that was not the half of it — nor even a quarter! Right away the fairy godmother arrived in a coach pulled by four peacocks, and at the rear stood Mr. Pickles' boy, dressed in

silver and gold, with a cocked hat, powdered hair, and pink silk stockings, and holding a cane set with precious stones, and a bouquet of flowers. Mr. Pickles' errand-boy then leapt down from the coach with his cocked hat in his hand — all charm and politeness — the magic had quite changed him — and helped the godmother to alight. The fairy stood there in her rich shot-silk, smelling of dried lavender, and fanned herself with a sparkling fan.

'Alicia, dear girl,' said the charming old fairy, 'how are you? I trust you are quite well. Give me a kiss.'

Princess Alicia embraced her, and then the fairy godmother turned to the king and said to him, a little sharply, 'Are you being good?'

The king said that he hoped so.

'I suppose you know now why my godchild here,' said the fairy, kissing the princess again, 'did not use the fishbone sooner?'

The king bowed his head shyly.

'Ah, but you didn't know then, did you?' continued the fairy. 'You would have had her use it much sooner!'

The king bowed even more shyly.

'No more 'whys'?' asked the fairy.

The king answered that there were none and that he was very sorry.

'Then be good,' said the fairy, 'and live happily ever after.'

Then the fairy godmother waved her fan, and the queen came in, beautifully dressed; then the seventeen little princes and princesses came, no longer in clothes they were growing out of, but in new clothes from head to foot. Then the fairy tapped Princess Alicia with her fan, and the rough apron that was miles too big for her flew off, and Alicia appeared, gorgeous as a young bride, with a garland of orange blossom and a silver veil. Strangely, the kitchen dresser turned itself into a handsome wooden wardrobe, decorated with gold and mirrors, and this was filled with all kinds of clothes, all for Alicia, and all fitting her perfectly. Next came the smiling infant, toddling up on its own, and its face and eye much, much better. Then the godmother asked to be introduced to the duchess, and when they brought her downstairs the two of them exchanged numerous compliments.

The fairy godmother and the duchess went on whispering together for a while, and then the fairy said aloud, 'Yes, I thought she would have told you!'

The fairy godmother turned to the king and queen and said, 'I am going to find Prince

Certainpersonio. In exactly half-an-hour you will honour us with your presence at church.'

After that, she got into the coach with Princess Alicia, and Mr. Pickles' errand-boy passed the duchess to them, who sat by herself on the seat opposite. When Mr. Pickles' boy had raised the steps and stood at the rear, the peacocks, with their long tails, flew off.

Prince Certainpersonio was sitting at home by himself, eating barley sugar and twiddling his thumbs. When he saw the peacocks draw the coach up to the window, he knew at once that something unusual was about to happen.

'Prince,' said the fairy godmother, 'I bring you your bride.'

As soon as the fairy godmother had spoken these words, Prince Certainpersonio stopped twiddling his thumbs. His ordinary jacket and corduroy trousers changed into a velvet suit the colour of peach blossom, and his hair curled, and a feathered hat flew into the room like a bird and landed on his head. At the fairy's invitation he stepped into the carriage, where he renewed his acquaintanceship with the duchess, whom he had already met.

In the church there were the prince's relations and friends and the relations of Princess Alicia, and the seventeen princes and princesses and the baby and a crowd of neighbours. Words cannot describe how beautiful the wedding was. The duchess was matron-of-honour, and she watched the ceremony from the pulpit, where she leaned on its upholstered rail.

Then the fairy godmother gave a fine wedding breakfast, where there was everything you can think of and more to eat, and everything you can think of and more to drink. The wedding cake was finely decorated with white satin sweets and silver and white lilies, and was twenty-four yards around.

When the fairy had toasted the young couple and Prince Certainpersonio had made a speech, and they had all shouted 'hip, hip, hurrah!', the fairy godmother told the king and queen that from now on they would draw a quarterly salary eight times a year and ten times every leap year. Then she turned to the prince and Alicia and said, 'My dears, you will have thirty-five children, and they will all be handsome and good. Seventeen will be boys and eighteen will be girls. All of them will have curly hair by nature, they will never have measles, and they will get over whooping cough before they are born.'

When they heard the good news, everyone shouted once more, 'hip, hip, hurrah!'

'Now,' concluded the fairy godmother, 'we have only to make an end of the fishbone.'

So she took it from Princess Alicia's hand, and the bone at once flew into the throat of the terrible snapping little terrier next door, and choked it. And it passed away in a fit of convulsions.

The Ginger-haired Manikin

There was once a miner who had three sons and was very poor. One day the eldest son said he would go out into the world to seek his fortune. And right away he packed up his bundle, put a little food in it, and set off.

He walked and walked until he came to a deep forest, and since he was tired after his long walk he sat down on a large stone by the wayside, unwrapped his bundle and began to eat some bread and cheese he had brought with him. As he was eating, he heard a thin little voice, and, looking around, spied a ginger-haired manikin coming out of the trees, no bigger than his little finger. When the manikin reached the eldest son he said, 'Be so kind, dear boy, as to give me a piece of bread and cheese. I have not eaten for three days.'

'Certainly not. Go back where you belong! I haven't enough to share,' the eldest son cried in a rough voice, and swung his staff at the little man.

The manikin said nothing, and hobbled off into the forest. When the eldest son had eaten his fill he went on his way. But he sought his fortune in vain, and after some months he returned home just as poor as when he had left.

Now the eldest son had returned, the middle son said:

'Now it's my turn to go into the world. Perhaps I'll make my fortune there, and we shall all be rich!'

And he, too, packed his bundle, put a little food in it, and set off into the world. When, at last, he came to the same deep forest where his brother had rested, he too was tired from his long walk, and sat on the stone. Then he unwrapped his bundle and began to eat. As he was eating, he suddenly saw in front of him a ginger-haired manikin, no bigger than his little finger, who said, 'Be so kind, dear boy, as to give me a little of your food. None has passed my lips for three days.'

But the middle son went on eating and did not even bother to answer the manikin. When he had eaten everything, he threw the ginger-haired little man the last few crumbs that were left in his bundle. The manikin accepted the crumbs, and advised the middle son to seek his fortune in a mine he would find in the middle of the forest.

The middle son continued his journey, but now he searched for the mine, and when he found it, he said to himself, 'But this is only an old, abandoned mine, long since worked out! The little man has tricked me. I'll not waste my time exploring it.'

And he went on his way. After a long time, having sought his fortune in vain, he returned home, just as poor as when he had left.

In the meantime the youngest son, who was called Jack, had grown up, and when the middle son came home penniless, Jack said to his father, 'Now I shall go into the world and try to make my fortune.'

He put his few possessions in a bundle, took a little food for the journey, said goodbye to his father and brothers, and strode off into the world. He walked and walked until, like his brothers, he came to the deep forest, and on seeing a large stone by the wayside, he sat down on it, unwrapped his packet of food, and began to eat the bread and cheese. After a little while, he spied the ginger-haired manikin. And the manikin, no bigger than his little finger, said, 'Dear boy, give me just a crumb of food, I have eaten nothing for three days.'

Jack did not hesitate. He cut the little man a generous slice of bread and a hunk of cheese to go with it, and said, 'Eat what you will, little man, and if you have not enough I'll cut you some more.'

At this the little man drew close to Jack, and said to him, 'I only wished to find out if you have a good heart. Now I know that you would share your last morsel with me, and in return I'll help you to find your fortune. You need only do as I say.'

Then he told Jack to go deeper into the forest, where he would come across a mine. Jack followed his advice, and when he came to the mine, the manikin was already waiting for him.

The way into the mine led from an old hut, built over the shaft, with a hoist over it. The manikin told Jack to get into the bucket, and when he had done so, he began to lower him down. The bucket with Jack in it went lower and lower. Down, down, down! When Jack reached the bottom of the shaft, he found

himself in the most beautiful countryside.

Amazed at the beauty of his surroundings, Jack forgot all about the ginger-haired manikin. But, suddenly, there he was! And holding out a sword to him!

'Take this sword, and put on the armour you see here,' said the little man. 'You must free the princess who is held prisoner by a giant in his copper castle.'

The manikin then showed Jack a little copper ball. When it began to roll away from them, he told Jack to follow it. The ball led him to the copper castle. He shook the gates until the giant came out. Jack fought with him until he killed him. Then he freed the princess, who returned home to her father's kingdom.

The little man appeared to Jack immediately afterwards, and told him that he must free another princess, who was held prisoner in a silver castle by an even bigger giant.

This time he threw in front of him a silver ball. The ball began to roll, and Jack followed it until it stopped before a silver castle. Jack shook the gates so violently that the giant woke up. He rushed out of his castle to see what was happening, and Jack fought with him, killed him, and set the princess free. A few days after he had freed the princess from the silver castle, the ginger-haired manikin, no bigger than his little finger, appeared in front of him again and said, 'Now you must free a third princess, who is imprisoned in a golden castle by the biggest giant of all. She is the most beautiful of all the princesses, and she will be your fortune!'

And the little man threw a golden ball to the ground in front of Jack. Away it rolled, and Jack followed it until, all at once, he saw in the distance a golden castle, gleaming like the sun. The ball began to roll faster and faster, until it crashed into the gates of the golden castle. When the giant heard the noise, he came out to see what was happening. Jack attacked the huge giant, and the fight was on! On and on they battled, from morning till night, until Jack finally defeated the giant. Then he entered the golden castle and found there a beautiful maiden. As soon as he saw her, he fell in love

with her, took her by the hand, and led her to the ginger-haired manikin, who made them man and wife. Then he gave Jack and the princess as much gold as they could carry, and led them out of the mine shaft. After he had taken his leave of them, he disappeared as if the ground had swallowed him up, and Jack took his bride home to his father's cottage.

With the gold, Jack built himself a fine house, and another for his father. But his elder brothers were so jealous of his good fortune that they set off for the old mine so that they too might bring home gold. But when they got to the hut which stood over the shaft they began to argue as to who was to go down first. They tugged so violently at the bucket that the rope broke, and both of them fell to the bottom of the shaft.

After a long time, Jack and his father went to look for the two brothers. But when they reached the mine, they found the shaft caved in, and the hut fallen down. The mine was closed for ever, and the two selfish, jealous brothers were never seen again.

Little Ragamuffin

There once lived, in a great castle on the edge of the sea, a rich old count. He no longer had a wife or children — just one little granddaughter whom he had never even seen. The count hated her because her birth had cost the life of her mother, his eldest daughter. So when the nurse had brought the newborn baby to show him, the old count had turned away from the child, declaring that he would never look upon his granddaughter as long as he lived.

The baby was taken away, and the old man spent his time looking out to sea, and mourning his dead daughter. His white hair and beard, which he refused to cut, grew down to his shoulders, and onto his chest. It grew so long that it twisted around his chair, and reached down into the cracks in the floor. And the count's tears ran down over the stone window-sill until they made a deep channel in it. Through this, his tears ran like a river into the wide ocean.

Meanwhile, his granddaughter grew up on her own, with no one to look after her. There was no kind mother to give her food and proper clothes. Only her old nurse would give her a plate of scraps from the kitchen from time to time, or a torn frock from the closet when no one was looking. The count's servants in the castle drove her from the house with blows and jeers, shouting after her 'Little Ragamuffin', and pointing their fingers at her bare feet and bare shoulders, until she ran off in tears, and hid in the bushes.

So the little Ragamuffin grew up cold and hungry, and spent all her days in the fields and meadows with her only friend, the goose-boy. When she was hungry or shivering with cold, the goose-boy would play his pipe for her so gaily that she would at once forget her troubles and begin to dance. And the geese would dance with her.

One day, people began to talk of how the king himself was to visit their part of the

country, and that in the nearby town he was to give a grand ball for all the counts and countesses, and that the prince, the king's only son, would choose his bride at the ball.

The king's invitation arrived at the castle by the sea, and the servants took it to the old count, who was seated at the window, wrapped in his long white beard, his hot tears running like a river into the wide ocean.

But when the count saw the king's invitation, he dried his eyes, and ordered the servants to bring scissors and cut his beard, in which he was so entangled that he could not move. When this was done, he dressed himself in his finest clothes and jewels, and had his white charger decked out in gold and silk, so that he might go to the king.

Meanwhile, little Ragamuffin had also heard the news of the grand ball. The poor girl sat by the kitchen door and cried bitterly because she could not go to the ball and see all the grand ladies, and the noble prince.

When the old nurse heard her crying, she went to the count and begged him to take his granddaughter with him to the royal ball. But the count only frowned fiercely, and told the old woman to be silent.

And the servants laughed and whispered, 'Ragamuffin is happy in her rags. She only wants to play with the goose-boy. Just leave her alone, she's good for nothing!'

The old nurse begged the count a second and a third time to take his granddaughter with him. He always made the same reply — with evil looks and harsh words, and in the end the scornful servants drove her from the chamber with jeers and blows.

The old nurse returned in tears to the kitchen door, but Ragamuffin was no longer there. The cook had driven her out, and she had fled into the fields to tell her friend, the goose-boy, how much she longed to go to the royal ball.

The goose-boy listened to Ragamuffin and then comforted her, 'Don't cry. We'll go together to see the king, and we'll see all the wonders of the ball for ourselves.'

When Ragamuffin looked sadly at her torn frock and bare feet, he played two or three tunes on his pipe, so gaily and with such spirit, that she at once forgot her tears. And the goose-boy took her by the hand and they both danced off, geese and all, towards the town.

They hadn't gone far when a finely dressed young man overtook them. He pulled up his horse and asked them the way to the castle where the king was staying. When he heard that they were going there too, he dismounted and walked along with them.

The goose-boy took out his pipe and played a soft, merry tune, and as he piped, the stranger looked at Ragamuffin's beautiful face, and almost at once, fell in love with her with all his heart, and asked her to marry him.

But Ragamuffin only laughed, and shook her golden head.

'Oh, a fine match a goose-girl would be for you!' she answered. 'You would do better to take one of the beautiful ladies you will see tonight at the royal ball, and not make fun of me, a poor little ragamuffin.'

But the more she refused to take the proposal seriously, the more sweetly the pipes played, and the more the stranger fell in love with her. He told her to come to the royal ball at midnight with her goose-boy and his geese, just as she was, barefoot and in rags, and he promised to dance with her before the king and all the noble guests, and to present her as his dear and honoured bride.

Night came and the whole castle was flooded with brilliant light, and the high-born gentlemen and ladies danced with each other before the king himself. At the stroke of midnight, the great doors flew open and Ragamuffin and her goose-boy came into the hall with their flock of cackling geese. The dancers parted, the beautiful ladies whispered among themselves, the gentlemen laughed, and the king, at the far end of the hall, was amazed.

But when Ragamuffin and her companion came before the king's throne, the king's son stood up, for he was the handsome young man who had walked to the castle with them.

He took the girl by the hand, kissed her three times in front of the grand company, and said to his father, 'Sire, I have already chosen my bride; here she is. She is the dearest and most beautiful girl in the whole land!'

Before the prince had finished speaking, the goose-boy put his pipe to his lips and played a tune as charming as the song of a bird. Scarcely had he finished, when Ragamuffin's rags changed into a gorgeous dress, set with sparkling gems, a golden crown gleamed on her golden head, and the flock of geese all at once became a line of page-boys, carrying her long train.

Overcome by her grace and beauty, the king rose from his throne to welcome Ragamuffin as his daughter. The trumpeters sounded a fanfare in honour of the new princess, and the crowds in the streets murmured among themselves: 'The prince has chosen as his bride the most

beautiful and dearest girl in the whole land!'

Strange to say, the goose-boy was never seen again, and no one knew what had become of him. As for the old count, he returned to his castle by the sea. He could not have remained at court if he had wanted to, for he could not break his solemn vow that he would never look upon his granddaughter.

And, to this day, he sits by the window, gazing out to sea, and weeping great rivers of tears.

The
Selfish
Giant

Every afternoon, when the children came home from school, they went to play in the giant's garden.

The garden was big and full of delights, with grass that was soft and green, dotted here and there with flowers, like little coloured stars. There were twelve peach trees in it; in spring they burst out into rosy and pearly-white blossom, and in autumn they were laden with fruit. The birds in the trees sang so sweetly that the children would stop playing to listen to them. 'How blissful it is here,' they would say to themselves.

Then, one day, the giant came home. He had been to see a friend of his, a Cornish ogre with whom he had stayed for seven years. In seven years he had said everything he had to say, and had decided to go home to his castle. When he arrived, he saw the children playing in his garden.

'What are you doing here?' he shouted, so harshly that the children ran away. 'My garden belongs to me,' the giant said, 'everyone should realize that, and no one may play here except me!'

And he built a high wall around the garden, and put up a notice saying, 'Trespassers will be prosecuted'. He was a very selfish giant!

After that, the poor children had nowhere to play. They tried playing on the road, but that was dusty and stony, and they didn't like it at all. After their lessons they used to walk round the high wall and talk about the beautiful garden. 'How happy we were there!' they would say to each other.

Spring came, and the whole country was covered in flowers and the trees filled with small birds. Only in the giant's garden did the winter remain. The birds didn't want to sing there now that the children no longer came.

One pretty little flower did push its head out of the grass, but when it saw the warning notice, it felt so sorry for the children that it slipped into the earth and went back to sleep. The only ones who were pleased were the Snow and the Frost. 'Spring has forgotten this garden!' they cried. 'And we shall live here the whole year round!'

The Snow covered the ground with its heavy white coat, and the Frost painted all the trees white. Then the two of them invited the North Wind to come to stay, and he did. He was dressed in a fur coat, and he howled up and down the garden the whole day long, hurling down the chimney tops. 'What a fine place this is!' he roared. 'We must invite the Hail.'

And so the Hail came too. Three hours a day it beat down on the castle roof, till nearly all the slates were broken, then it swept round and round the garden as fast as it could. It was dressed all in grey, and its breath chilled like ice.

'I can't think why Spring is so late in coming,' said the giant, as he sat by the window and gazed out on to his cold, white garden. 'I hope there will be a change in the weather.'

But neither Spring nor Summer came. Autumn brought its golden fruit into every garden, but to the giant's garden it brought nothing at all. 'That one is far too selfish,' it said to itself. And so only Winter stayed in the garden, and the North Wind, the Frost and the Snow danced among the trees.

One morning, the giant was lying in bed when he heard beautiful music. The sound was so sweet to his ears that he thought the royal musicians must be passing by. In fact it was just one little linnet singing beneath his window. It was so long since he had heard the song of

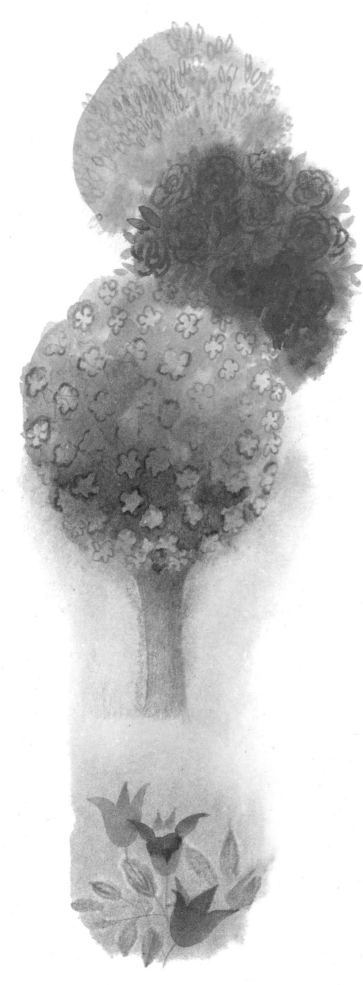

a bird in his garden that it seemed to him the most beautiful music in the world. Then the Hail stopped dancing above his head, the North Wind ceased to howl, and a delicate perfume drifted in through the bow windows.

'I do believe Spring is here at last,' said the giant, leaping out of bed, and he went to look out of the window.

And what do you think he saw?

The children, who had crept in through a hole in the broken-down wall, were sitting on the branches of the trees. In every tree he looked at, there was a little boy or girl. The trees were so pleased to see the children again that they covered themselves with blossom, and waved their boughs gently over the children's heads in greeting.

The birds flew around them, twittering with delight, flowers peeped out of the green grass and smiled at them. It was a charming sight; but there was just one little corner of the garden where Winter still remained. There, on the far side, beneath a tree, stood a little boy. He was too small to reach the branches, and he walked round and round the tree, complaining bitterly. The poor tree was still covered with ice and snow, and the North Wind roared and howled above it.

'Come on, lad!' called the tree, bending its branches as low as it could, but the boy was too small.

The giant's heart melted when he saw this. 'How selfish I have been!' he exclaimed. 'Now I know why Spring did not come here. I will lift that poor little boy to the very top of the tree, then I will knock down the wall, and my garden will be a playground for ever more!' He was truly sorry for what he had done.

He went quietly downstairs into the garden. Alas, when the children saw him, they were so scared that they ran off, and Winter came back into the garden. Only the very small boy did not run away, for his eyes were full of tears, and he didn't see the giant coming. The giant stole up to him, took him gently by the hand, and lifted him up into the tree. It burst into flower immediately and the birds flew up and sang among its branches. The little boy threw his arms around the giant's neck.

When the rest of the children saw that the

giant was no longer evil, they came running back. And with them came Spring. 'It's your garden now, children,' the giant told them, and with that he picked up a huge axe and knocked down the wall. And when the people went to market, what did they spy but the giant playing with their children, in the most beautiful garden they had ever seen!

The children played all day, and when evening fell they came to say goodbye to the giant.

'Where's your little friend?' he asked. 'The boy I lifted up into the tree?' The giant liked him best of all, because he had kissed him.

'We don't know,' said the children. 'He's gone.'

'Just tell him to be sure to come tomorrow,' the giant told them. But they replied that they didn't know where he lived, that they had never seen him before. This made the giant very sad.

Every afternoon, after school, the children came to play with the giant. But the smallest of them all, the little boy he was so fond of, never appeared. The giant was very kind to the children, though he longed to see his little friend again, and often spoke of him.

'How I should like to see him again!' he used to say.

The years went by, and the giant grew very old and weak. He couldn't even play any more, so he would sit in his giant armchair watching the children play, and admiring his garden. 'I have many beautiful flowers,' he used to say, 'but the children are the most beautiful flowers of all!'

One winter morning, as he was getting dressed, he glanced out of the window. He no longer hated Winter, for he knew that it was only sleeping Spring, and that the flowers were resting. Suddenly, he rubbed his eyes in astonishment, then stared and stared. It was truly a wonderful sight. There, in the farthest corner of the garden, stood a tree covered in soft white blossom. Its branches were all of gold, it was hung with silver fruit, and beneath it stood the little boy the giant loved so much.

Filled with delight, the giant ran downstairs into the garden. He hurried across the grass to the child. As he drew near, his face grew red with anger, and he cried out: 'Who has dared to hurt you so?'

For the child's hands and feet bore the marks of nails.

'Who has dared to hurt you so?' he cried again. 'Tell me, and I shall take my great sword and kill him!'

'That you must not do,' replied the child, 'for these are the wounds of love.'

'Who are you?' asked the giant, and he was filled with such awe that he knelt down in front of the little boy.

At this the child smiled at the giant and said: 'You once let me play in your garden, and today you shall go with me to my garden, which is Paradise.'

And when the children came running along that afternoon they found the giant lying dead beneath the tree, covered all over with white flowers.

The Two Daughters

There was once a man and his wife who had a daughter as pretty as a picture. The wife died, and the man married again, a wife who bore him a daughter as ugly as sin. When the two girls grew up, the stepmother, who hated the beautiful daughter, and beat her several times a day, said to her husband, 'Take your daughter into the forest and get rid of her.'

The man was sorry for his pretty daughter, but he was so afraid of his wife that he said, 'Wife, I shall do as you ask.'

But the pretty daughter was listening through the keyhole and heard everything. Right away she went to tell her godmother.

'My godchild,' said her godmother, 'fill your pockets with ashes and drop them on the path. Then you can find your way home again.'

The pretty daughter hurried back to her father and filled her pockets with ashes. She had only just done this when her father said to her, 'Come, my poor child, we shall go into the forest to pick mushrooms.'

So they set off together into the forest to pick mushrooms. As they went deeper into the forest, the pretty daughter scattered the ashes from her pockets on the path as her godmother had told her. Then, as darkness began to fall, her unhappy father hid himself in a thicket when she wasn't looking. As the girl wandered on, the poor man returned home without her.

'Well, husband, have you got rid of your daughter?'

'Yes.'

'Good! Now, for your trouble, you shall have a dish of millet gruel with us.'

As he was eating the gruel, he thought of the

pretty daughter he had left in the forest, 'Oh, if only the poor child were here to share the gruel!'

'Here I am, father,' answered the pretty daughter, who had found her way home by the ashes, and had been listening outside the door.

Her father was glad that his daughter had returned, and pleased to see her enjoying her share of the gruel. When she and her sister had gone to bed, her stepmother said to the man, 'What a fool you are! You did not take her far enough. Tomorrow you must take her into the forest again, but take care she doesn't return this time!'

The man was sorry for his daughter, but he was so afraid of his wife that he said, 'I shall do as you ask.'

The pretty daughter had got out of bed and was listening through the keyhole, and heard everything. Right away she ran to tell her godmother.

'My godchild,' said her godmother, 'fill your pockets with linseed and drop it on the path. Then you can find your way home again.'

The pretty daughter hurried back to her father, filled her pockets with linseed, and went back to bed.

Early the next morning her father came into the parlour and said, 'Come, my poor child, we shall go to the forest to pick mushrooms.'

So they went together into the forest. The father, however, was not interested in mushrooms. Nor was his pretty daughter, for she was dropping the linseed on the path as her godmother had told her. Finally, her father again jumped into the thickest thicket when she was not looking, leaving her alone in the forest. And, towards evening, he arrived home.

'Well, husband, have you got rid of your daughter?'

'Yes.'

'Good! Now, for your trouble you shall have a plate of millet gruel with us.'

As the man was eating his gruel, he thought of his pretty daughter, whom he had left in the forest, and sighed, 'Oh, if only the poor child were here to eat her share of gruel!'

'Here I am, father,' answered his daughter, who had found her way home by the linseed, and had been listening outside the door.

The father was glad that his pretty daughter had returned, and pleased to see her enjoying her share of the gruel. But when she and her sister had gone to bed, the stepmother said to her husband, 'What a fool you are! Again you did not take her far enough. Tomorrow you will take her to the forest again, but make sure she does not return this time!'

The man was sorry for his pretty daughter,

So the two of them went off into the forest. Of course, the man did not want to pick mushrooms. The pretty daughter dropped the millet on the path as her godmother had told her. Finally her father jumped into the thickest thicket when she was not looking, leaving her alone in the forest, and arriving home towards evening.

But when the pretty daughter tried to find her

but he was so afraid of his wife that he said, 'Wife, I shall do as you ask.'

But the pretty daughter had got out of bed, was listening through the keyhole, and heard everything. Away she ran to tell her godmother.

'My godchild,' said the godmother, 'fill your pockets with millet and drop it on the path. Then you can find your way home.'

So the pretty daughter hurried back to her father, filled her pockets with millet, and went back to bed.

Early the next morning, her father came into the parlour and said, 'Come, my poor child, we shall go into the forest to pick mushrooms.'

way home by the millet, she found none. The magpies had eaten it all. The poor girl walked and walked through the forest till she came to a great castle. And she knocked at the huge door.

'Who is knocking?' cried a voice from within.

'A poor girl who is lost and begs for her supper and a bed for the night!'

The mistress of the castle invited her inside, and sent her to the kitchen to eat with the servants. Then she ordered a good bed to be made up for her.

The next day she called the pretty girl to her chamber and opened the doors of a wardrobe full of the most beautiful clothes.

'Pretty girl, take off your rags, and choose what clothes you wish to wear.'

The pretty girl selected the ugliest robe. But the mistress of the castle made her take the most beautiful and put it on at once. Then she opened a great chest full of gold, silver, pearls and all manner of other treasures.

'Pretty girl, take out what you wish.'

The pretty girl took out two plain rings and a copper bracelet. But the mistress of the castle loaded her with gold coins, rings, silver chains, ruby ear-rings, and took her to the stables.

'Pretty girl, choose the horse you wish, and a bridle and saddle to go with it.'

But the pretty girl chose only a donkey, a hempen halter and a poor blanket. The mistress of the castle then made her take the most beautiful horse, the most beautiful bridle, and the most beautiful saddle.

'And now, sit on the horse and go home. Do not look back at the castle until you reach the top of yonder hill. Then raise your head and wait.'

The pretty girl thanked the mistress of the castle, sat on the horse, and rode homeward without turning her head. When she got to the top of the hill she lifted her head and waited.

Three stars fell from the heavens. Two of them landed on her head and the third on her chin.

When she set off again she met a young man astride a great horse, returning from the hunt with nine greyhounds: three as black as coal, three as red as fire, and three as white as the finest linen. When he saw such a beautiful rider, he took off his hat. 'Pretty maid, I am the son of the English king. For seven years I have wandered the world and not found a man as strong or as courageous as myself. If you agree, I will be your guide, and protect you from evil men.'

'Son of the English king! I am on my way home. But I am afraid to return, for I fear my stepmother, who hates me because her own daughter is as ugly as sin. Three times she forced my father to leave me in the forest.'

At this the son of the English king became terribly angry. He drew his sword and whistled to his greyhounds.

'Pretty maid, show me the way to your home. I shall order my pack of hounds to tear your father, stepmother and sister apart!'

'Son of the English king, your hounds will obey your order, but do not do this. Unless God wills it, neither my father nor my stepmother nor my sister must suffer on my account.'

But the son of the English king would have none of this, and he roared like a lion, 'Listen! I shall say to my judge: sentence them to death. I pay him, and he must earn his keep.'

'Son of the English king, your judge obeys your command, but do not do this. Unless God wills it, neither my father nor my stepmother nor my sister must suffer on my account.'

'Well, if you want me to forgive them, you must become my wife.'

'Son of the English king, if you forgive them I shall be your wife.'

So the son of the English king married the pretty girl, who was happy with him, and became the greatest lady in the whole country.

Shortly after her wedding, her sister who was as ugly as sin learnt what had happened and said, 'I too shall go into the forest, and the same will happen to me.'

She went off into the forest, and walked and walked. At last she came to the great castle. And she knocked at the huge door.

'Who is knocking?'

'A girl who is lost and begs for her supper and a bed for the night.'

The mistress of the castle sent the ugly girl to the kitchen to sup with the servants, and ordered a good bed to be prepared for her to sleep in.

The next day she called her to her chamber and opened the door of the wardrobe full of beautiful clothes.

'Take off your rags, my dear, and choose what clothes you wish.'

The ugly girl, ugly as sin, chose the most beautiful clothes. But the mistress of the castle forced her to take the most ragged and soiled and to put them on at once. Then she opened the trunk full of gold, silver, pearls and all manner of other treasures.

'My dear, take from the trunk what you will.'

The ugly girl, ugly as sin, chose a hundred golden ducats and a hundred golden rings. But the mistress of the castle let her take only two plain rings and a copper bracelet. Then she took her to the stables.

'My dear, choose what horse you wish, and a bridle and saddle to go with it.'

The ugly girl, ugly as sin, chose the most beautiful of the horses, the most beautiful bridle, and the most beautiful saddle. But the mistress of the castle let her take only a donkey, a hempen rein, and a poor blanket.

'Now sit on the donkey and go back home. Do not turn towards the castle until you reach the top of yonder hill. Then lift your head and wait.'

The ugly girl, ugly as sin, did not even thank the mistress of the castle. She got on the donkey and set off for home. But, before she got to the hilltop, she turned to look at the castle, raised her head and waited. Then, three pats of cow dung fell on her, two on her head, the third on her chin.

When she set off again, she met an old man as dirty as a pig and as drunk as a lord.

'I like you, my girl, you must be my wife, and if you will not, I shall kill you.'

The ugly girl, ugly as sin, had to go with the drunkard to his house and marry him. From that time on, her husband has drunk more than ever, and beaten his wife several times a day!

The Fairies

There was once a widow who had two daughters. The elder had the nature and looks of her mother, like peas from the same pod. Both were ill-natured and proud, impossible to live with. The younger daughter, who took after her father in her kindness and good heart, was in addition exceptionally beautiful. Birds of a feather flock together, and the mother worshipped her elder daughter and hated the younger one. She made her eat in the kitchen and work till she dropped.

Among other things, the poor child had to go for water twice a day and bring back a full jug. It was half-an-hour's walk to the well. One day, when she was standing by the well, a shabby woman came up and asked her for a drink.

'But of course, mother,' said the graceful young girl. At once she rinsed the jug and took water from the cleanest part of the well. And she gave the woman the jug, holding it so that the woman could drink from it more easily. When the poor woman had drunk, she said,

'Since you are so good and kind I shall make you a gift.'

For the woman was a fairy. She had taken the form of a shabby, peasant woman to find out if the girl was really good and kind. She went on, 'I shall give you a special thing. For every word you speak a flower or a precious stone will fall from your mouth.'

When the pretty girl arrived home, her mother began to scold her for taking so long.

'Forgive me, mother,' said the poor girl, and as she said this, a rose, a pearl and a large diamond fell from her mouth.

'What is this I see?' cried the surprised mother. 'Pearls and diamonds falling from her mouth? What has happened, daughter dear?' This was the first time she had spoken kindly to her.

The poor girl told her what had happened and diamonds continued to fall from her mouth as she spoke.

'Upon my soul,' said the mother, 'I must send

35

my elder daughter too. Look, Fanny, see what falls from your sister's mouth when she speaks. You, too, would like such a present, wouldn't you? It is enough for you to go to the well and, when a poor woman asks you for a drop of water, willingly give her a drink.'

'You won't catch me going for water,' was the rude reply.

'I want you to go right away,' said the mother.

So Fanny obeyed, but she continued to grumble, and she took a silver bowl, the most beautiful in the house. She had only just arrived at the well when she saw a lady in gorgeous clothes come out of the forest. The fine lady went straight up to her and asked for a little water. It was the same fairy, but now she was transformed into a royal princess. She wanted to see if the girl was really as wicked and rude as she had been told.

'I am here to give you a drink!' said the girl rudely. 'I brought a silver bowl just to give you a drink. So there you are! Get on with it! But don't expect me to help you.'

'You are not too polite,' replied the fairy, but she was not angry. 'Well then, since you are so unobliging, I shall give you this gift: with every word you speak a toad or snake shall fall from your mouth.'

As soon as her mother saw her coming, she called to her, 'Well, dear daughter, how did you get on?'

'See for yourself, dear mother!' replied the rude child, and two snakes and two toads fell from her mouth.

'Mercy upon us!' cried the mother. 'What is this I see? This is your sister's doing. She will pay for this!' And at once she rushed away to beat the younger daughter.

The poor girl ran away and hid in the woods nearby. A royal prince was out hunting in the woods that day. When he saw her grace and beauty, he asked her why she was in the woods alone and why she was crying.

'Alas, sir, my mother has driven me from my home!'

The royal prince saw several pearls and diamonds fall from her mouth. He asked her to tell him why this was so. And she told him the whole story. The royal prince listened, and fell in love with her at once. He considered her gift more precious than a dozen kingdoms, and he took her to the royal palace.

Her sister did not fare so well. Since snakes and toads fell from her mouth whenever she spoke, her mother could bear her no longer. She too was driven from the house. But no one wished to take in the hapless girl; she wandered to and fro, until she perished.

That is the way of the world; whoever is polite and obliging and behaves pleasantly to others will, sooner or later, be rewarded, even if he does not expect it!

The Princess of the Shining Star

On a certain river, long ago, there lived a miller. He once took his gun and went to shoot swans and wild ducks on the millpond. It was December, and very cold, and the countryside was covered with snow.

He came to the banks of the pond, and saw a duck in the water, and, raising his gun, he aimed and fired. But scarcely had he done so when a beautiful princess appeared beside him, and said to him, 'Thank you, good man. I have long been here under the spell of three evil spirits, who will not leave me in peace. You have returned my human form to me, and you might set me free entirely, if you have a little courage and patience.'

'What am I to do?' asked the astonished miller.

'Spend three nights in a row in the ruins of the old castle you see up on the hill.'

'Is there some demon there?'

'Alas, not one but twelve demons will afflict you there. They will throw you from corner to corner of the great hall, and then they will fling you on the fire. But whatever happens to you, do not fear; have faith in me, for I have an ointment that will save your life and make you well again even if you are torn limb from limb. Even if they kill you, I can bring you back to life. If you endure this for me for three nights, without a word of complaint, you will not be sorry. Beneath a stone in the fireplace of the old castle there are three casks of gold and three of silver, and these will be yours. And I will be yours, if you want me! Have you the courage to try?'

'Even if there were not twelve, but a hundred demons, I would try!' replied the miller bravely.

At that, the princess disappeared, and the miller returned to his mill, thinking of what he had seen and heard.

When night fell he went to the old castle, taking with him firewood, apple juice and tobacco, so that he would be warm, and have something to drink and smoke.

Towards midnight, he heard a great noise in the chimney and, though he was no coward, he hid under an old bed. From there he saw eleven demons come out of the chimney. They were surprised to find a fire in the hearth.

'What does this mean?' they asked themselves.

'And where has the lame demon got to? He is always late,' said another demon, who seemed to be the leader of the band.

'Here he comes,' said a third.

And the lame demon arrived by the same route as the others, down the chimney.

'What is new, my friends?' he asked.

'Nothing,' they replied.

'Nothing? I think there is a miller here, come to try and take our princess. We must search for him.'

So they searched everywhere, until the lame demon looked under the bed, and saw the miller crouching there.

'Here he is, under the bed,' he cried.

And he caught the miller by the foot and hauled him out.

'So, dear miller, you would take our princess from us?' he chuckled. 'They say you like pretty girls.'

'First we shall play a game you will not like too much, my friend. But it will cure you of wanting to take away our princess,' said the leader of the demons.

And they began tossing him about like a ball, from one corner of the hall to another. But the poor miller did not make a murmur. When the demons saw he would not speak, they threw him out of the window into the courtyard, and because he did not move or cry out, they thought that he was dead. At that moment the cock crowed, and the demons left as they had come, through the chimney.

At once the princess came, with a pot of ointment in her hand, and rubbed the miller with it. Soon, he was able to stand. He felt as hale and hearty as before.

'Did you suffer much, my friend?' asked the princess.

'Yes, I suffered much, princess,' replied the miller.

'You have before you another two such nights, if you are to free me from these evil demons.'

'I fear it is none too pleasant a business, setting princesses free, but I shall see it through, nonetheless!'

When night fell, the miller went up to the old

castle again and hid beneath a pile of faggots at the back of the hall. At midnight the twelve demons came down the chimney again.

'I smell human,' said the lame demon.

So they began to search, and soon found the milller.

'Ah, it is you again, miller!' cried the demons' leader. 'How do you come to be alive after yesterday's game? But do not worry, this time we shall make an end of you, and it will not take us long.'

And they threw him in a great cauldron filled with boiling oil. When the cock began to crow at the break of day, the demons left.

At once, the princess arrived and pulled the miller out of the cauldron. He was well boiled, and in a sorry state. But she brought him back to life with her ointment.

The third night the demons came again and were surprised to find the miller alive.

'This is the last night, and if we don't get rid of him this time, we shall lose the princess,' said one of them. 'He must be protected by some magician. What are we to do?'

Each gave his opinion, and finally the lame demon decided.

'We must make a big fire, roast the miller on it, and eat him.'

'Very well, we shall roast him and eat him,' agreed the others.

But they had wasted much time in discussion and preparation, so that at the moment they were about to impale the miller on the spit and put him on the fire, the cock crowed, and they were forced to leave in a hurry. They made a great noise as they went, and hurled down the spire from the main tower.

Again the princess came with her ointment, but this time she did not need it. She was radiant with joy, and she embraced the miller, and said to him, 'All is well! You have set me free, and the treasure is yours!'

They raised the stone by the hearth, and found three casks of gold and three of silver.

'Take the gold and silver, and do with them what you will,' said the princess. 'As for me, I cannot yet stay with you. First I must go on a journey which will last a year and a day; then I will come to you.'

And the princess disappeared. The miller was a little disappointed, but thoughts of the treasure soon comforted him, and he left the mill to his servant and set off with a friend on his travels, as a means of filling in time until the princess came back to him. The two friends visited far-off lands, and since they had money enough, they wanted for nothing.

After eight months of such a life, the miller said to his friend, 'Let us return to our own country. We are now far from it and I should not wish to be late for my appointment with the princess, which was to be in a year and a day.'

So they set off for home.

On the way, they met an old woman with a basket of beautiful apples.

'Buy my apples, you fine fellows,' said the old woman to them.

'Do not buy her apples,' said the miller's friend.

'Why not?' asked the miller. 'I should like an apple.'

He bought three apples, ate one of them at once, and felt ill right away.

The next day the princess was to arrive, and the miller and his friend went into the forest to the meeting-place. Since they had arrived early, they had to wait, and the miller ate another of the apples he had bought the day before. He was immediately overcome by sleep and he sat on the grass beneath a tree and fell into a deep sleep.

Soon after this, the princess arrived in a fine coach, the colour of the stars, drawn by two horses of the same colour. When she saw the sleeping miller, she grew sad, and asked his friend why he slept.

'I do not quite know,' answered the miller's friend, 'but he bought three apples from an old woman we met by the roadside. It was after eating one that he fell asleep.'

'Alas! It is so, for the woman from whom he bought the apples is a witch, who wishes us ill. I cannot take him with me as he is, but I shall come twice more, tomorrow and the day after. If he is awake, I will take him with me in my coach. When he opens his eyes, give him this golden pear and handkerchief, and tell him I will come tomorrow at the same time.'

And the princess and her starry coach rose into the air and disappeared.

A moment later the miller woke up. His friend told him what had passed while he was asleep, gave him the pear and the handkerchief, and said the princess would come again the next day, and that if he slept she would come the day after.

The miller was sad, and said, 'Tomorrow I shall not sleep.'

As soon as he got home he went to bed, so that he would be wide awake the next day.

The next day the miller and his friend went early to the forest. But, tired of waiting, the

miller ate the third apple, which he had in his pocket, and again fell fast asleep.

The princess arrived in a coach with horses the colour of the sun, and when she saw the miller, she cried, 'Alas! Again he sleeps!'

And she said to his friend, 'I shall come again tomorrow, but for the last time. Here is another golden pear and another handkerchief. Give them to him when he wakes, and tell him that if he sleeps again tomorrow he will never see me again, unless he seeks me beyond three kingdoms and three seas!'

And again she rose into the sky in her coach, the colour of the sun, and disappeared.

When the miller woke up, his friend told him how the princess had come again and found him asleep, and how she had said that she would come the next day for the last time. If she found him asleep, he would not see her again unless he crossed three kingdoms and three seas to find her. And he gave the miller the second golden pear and the second handkerchief.

The poor miller was uneasy, and said to his friend, 'For the Lord's sake, do not allow me to sleep tomorrow; talk to me, so that I may stay awake.'

But in spite of all his friend's efforts, he slept the next day too, and the princess came in a coach and horses the colour of the moon.

'Alas, again you sleep, my hero!' she cried in anguish, 'and I may not come again. Tell him,' she said to his friend, 'that if he wants to see me, he must seek me in the kingdom of the shining star, and to get there he must cross three kingdoms and three seas, which will not be easy for him. Give him this third golden pear and

third handkerchief, which will be of great
service to him.'

And she took off into the air in her
moon-coloured coach, and disappeared.

When the miller awoke and found that the
princess had again left and was not to return, he
began to weep and tear his hair in despair. It
was a sad sight to see.

'I shall go and seek her. I must find her, even
if it means a journey to hell itself!' he said at
last.

And he set off at once to find the kingdom of
the shining star. On and on he went, day and
night. At length, he passed through a deep
forest, from which he could find no way out.
When he had wandered several days and nights,
he chanced to climb a tree in the night, and saw
a light in the distance. He went towards it until
he reached a poor hovel made of branches and
dried grass. He opened the door, which was
ajar, and inside he found an old man with a long
white beard.

'Good evening, old man,' he said to him.

'Good evening, young friend,' replied the old
man, surprised, 'I am glad to see you, for I have
been here eighteen hundred years and seen no
human face. You are welcome. Come inside, and
tell me a little about the world, for I have long
had no news of it.'

The miller came inside, told the man his
name, where he came from, and the purpose of
his journey.

'I should like to help you, young man,' the old
man said, 'here are some golden spats, which
I found most useful when I was your age, but
which are of no use to me now. If you put them
on you may go seven miles in one stride, and so
you can reach the castle of the shining star
without great trouble, for it is still a very long
way from here.'

The miller slept in the old hermit's hovel and,
as soon as the next day broke, he took the
magic spats and went on his way.

Now he travelled swiftly, passing quickly
over river, lake, mountain and forest. At sunset
he saw another hovel, like the one before, at the
edge of the forest, and because he was hungry
and a little tired, he said to himself, 'I must ask
for my supper and a place to sleep, and I may
get some good advice.'

At the back of the dwelling an old woman sat on her haunches in the ashes on the hearthstone. She had teeth as long as fingers. 'Good evening, old woman,' he said to her. 'Would you be so kind as to give me shelter for the night?'

'Alas, young fellow,' she replied, 'you should not have come here, and you had better leave at once. I have three sons who are terrible boys, and if they find you here I am afraid they will eat you. Be off, for they will soon return!'

'And what are the names of your sons, old woman?'

'They are called the January Wind, the February Wind and the March Wind.'

'So you are the mother of the Winter Winds?'

'Yes, I am the mother of the Winter Winds. But go now, and do as I say, for they will soon be here.'

'For pity's sake, old woman, I beg you, give me shelter, and hide me where they will not find me.'

At that moment there was a great noise outside.

'Here comes my eldest son, the January Wind,' said the old woman. 'What am I to do? Very well, I shall tell him that you are my nephew, my brother's son, that you have come to visit me, and would like to meet your cousins. I shall tell them you are called Ivan Pharaoh, and you must be friendly to them.'

And straight away a great giant with a white beard flew down the chimney. He was shaking with cold, and he cried, 'Brrrh, mother, I am cold and hungry. Brrrh!'

'Sit by the fire, son, I'll prepare you some food.'

But the giant saw the miller crouching in the corner, and asked, 'Mother, what is that earthworm there? I'll swallow him up while I am waiting for my supper...'

'Son, sit quietly on your stool, and do not dare to hurt the child. It is little Ivan Pharaoh, my nephew and your cousin.'

'Mother, I am very hungry, and I shall eat him,' replied the giant, baring his teeth.

'Sit quietly, and do not harm the child, or it's the sack for you!'

And she pointed to a large sack hanging from a beam. So the giant sat quietly and said no more.

The old woman's other sons, the February Wind and the March Wind, then came, one after the other, with a terrible noise. The trees creaked and fell, stones flew in the air, and wolves howled. It was frightful! The old woman was hard put to protect her charge from the hungry giants, and she only saved him by threatening them with the sack.

At last they all sat down to the table good friends, and they devoured three whole oxen and in a trice drank three buckets of wine. When the giants had eaten their fill they were calmer and began to speak quietly to their supposed cousin.

'Now tell us, cousin,' asked the January Wind, 'if you have come only to visit us, or if your journey has another goal.'

'Indeed so, dear cousins, I wish to go to the castle of the Princess of the Shining Star. If you can tell me the way, you will do me a great service.'

'I have never heard of the castle of the Shining Star,' said the January Wind.

'I have heard of it, but I do not know where it is,' said the March Wind.

'I know where the castle is,' said the February Wind, 'indeed, I passed by it only yesterday, and saw them making ready a grand wedding for the princess for tomorrow. They killed a hundred oxen and calves and lambs and chickens, more ducks than I can say, all for the great feast which is to be held there.'

'The princess is to marry?' cried the miller. 'I must get there before the ceremony. Tell me the way, cousin February Wind.'

'Gladly,' answered the February Wind, 'I am going there tomorrow, but you will not be able to keep up with me.'

'Indeed I shall, for I have spats which take me seven miles at a stride.'

'Very well, then, we shall go tomorrow.'

Towards midnight the January Wind was the first to leave, with a great noise, and an hour later the February Wind left with the miller. The miller kept up with him without trouble till

they came to the sea, but there he had to stop.

'Carry me across the sea, cousin,' said the miller to the February Wind.

'We must cross not one, but three seas,' replied the February Wind. 'I am afraid I cannot carry you so far on my back.'

'For pity's sake, cousin, take me on your back.'

'I shall take you as far as I can, but I tell you now that when I grow tired I will let you fall.'

The miller sat on the February Wind's back and found himself at once above the great sea. They flew across one sea, and then another, but in the middle of the third, the February Wind said, 'I am tired, and can carry you no further; I must drop you in the water.'

'For pity's sake, dear cousin, do not do that. We are near the land, for I can see it already, and soon we shall be there.'

Finally the February Wind reached the land, but he was at the end of his strength, and he put down his burden at the gates of the city where the princess's castle stood.

Soon afterwards the March Wind flew by, and the miller said to him, 'Cousin March Wind, cousin dear, hear me awhile.'

'What do you want, cousin Ivan Pharaoh?' asked the March Wind.

'February Wind put me down before these high walls, which I cannot scale. Take me on your back and carry me to the other side.'

'Gladly! Sit on my back,' said the March Wind.

So the miller sat on the March Wind's back, and the wind took him to the far side of the walls. The miller was then able to continue his journey.

He lodged at an inn, and after lunch struck up a conversation with the innkeeper's wife.

'Good lady, what is new in your town?' he asked her.

'They speak only of the wedding of the Princess of the Shining Star, which is to take place today,' answered the innkeeper's wife.

'Indeed? Then she has found the man she wants?'

'They say she does not love the prince she is to marry, that she marries against her will. Soon the wedding procession will pass by our house on its way to church.'

The miller placed the first pear and the first handkerchief the princess had left him on a table in front of the inn door, and waited.

Soon the procession came by, with the princess and her bridegroom at its head. The princess saw the pear and the handkerchief, and recognized the miller standing nearby. At once she stopped, saying that she felt ill, and asked for the ceremony to be put off till the next day. This was agreed without anyone suspecting.

The procession returned to the palace, and when the princess reached her chamber, she sent one of her chambermaids to the miller to buy the pear and handkerchief. The chambermaid brought them to her.

The next day the procession set off for the church by the same route. The miller put the second pear and handkerchief on the table in front of the inn. When the princess saw them, she again pretended to be ill, and again the procession returned to the palace. Again she sent her chambermaid, to buy the second pear and handkerchief.

Finally, on the third day, the whole thing was repeated, but the princess told the chambermaid to bring the man who was selling the pears and handkerchiefs. And so it was. The miller and the princess embraced each other warmly, and wept with joy at their reunion.

The princess's bridegroom, however, declared that since his bride-to-be always felt ill on the way to church, the wedding feast should take place before they went to church, and only then was the procession to set off.

The princess, when she heard this, brought the miller fine clothes and told him to wait in her chamber till she came for him.

When all the guests were seated at the table in their grandest clothes, the feasting began. The princess was so beautiful that she shone in the hall like the sun. As the meal drew to a close, the guests laughed and chattered and sang in a merry fashion.

'Now it is your turn, my beautiful Princess of the Shining Star, to entertain us,' said her future father-in-law.

The princess nodded and spoke as follows,

'Listen, father-in-law, to my dilemma. I should like your opinion. I have a pretty casket, to which I had a lovely golden key, and I was very fond of the key. I lost it and had a new one made. I have just found the old key, before I had time to use the new. The old key was good, and I do not know what the new one is like. Tell me which of these keys I am to prefer, the old or the new?'

'We should always honour and cherish old things,' replied the old man. 'But still, I should like to see both keys before deciding on one of them.'

'That is wise,' said the princess, 'I shall show you both of them.' And she rose from the table and went to her chamber. She returned at once with the miller and introduced him to the assembly.

'This is the old key,' she said, 'which I lost and have just found again. The new key is this young prince, to whom I am betrothed. But the wedding ceremony has not yet taken place, so I am still free to offer my hand to whomsoever I wish. As you said so wisely, my lord, what is old deserves to be honoured and cherished. I shall keep the old key, which has been found again, and leave you the new. The old key is this courageous and faithful man' — she pointed to the miller — 'who released me from a castle where a wicked magician had imprisoned me. He followed me here, and endured a thousand trials. The new key, as you know, is your son! I return him to you. He will soon find another bride.'

The princess and the miller left the hall immediately, and no one tried to stand in their way. When they came to the castle courtyard, a beautiful golden carriage, drawn by four exquisite horses, was waiting for them. And they drove away at high speed. When they reached Brittany, with its great and beautiful capital city, they were married in church, and there followed such celebrations, public rejoicing and feasting as I have never seen and scarcely dreamed of.

The Animal Husbands and the Enchanted Castle

There was once a father who had three daughters and a son. The son grew up and went to war. The father, who was very poor, went every day to the forest for a load of firewood, which he sold in the market.

One day he took his donkey into the forest and was gathering firewood when a stranger appeared and said, 'If you give me your eldest daughter I will give you a donkey laden with gold.'

'Very well, if she is willing,' answered the father. 'When I get home I will tell her.' And he went home in good spirits, and told his eldest daughter what had happened in the forest.

'Just fancy, daughter, when I went for the firewood a stranger appeared before me and told me that if I gave him my eldest daughter he would give me a donkey laden with gold. I said that if you were willing I should not object . . .'

The daughter agreed. She would have agreed to anything for the sake of having enough to eat.

The next day, her father returned to the forest to say that his daughter agreed, and the stranger handed over the gold, and took the woodcutter's eldest daughter.

It is said that greed knows no bounds. The next day the father went again to the forest for another load of firewood. And there he met another stranger who said to him: 'If you consent to give me your middle daughter, I will give you a donkey laden with silver.'

'Very well, if she is willing. When I get home I shall tell her,' said the woodcutter.

When he got home he told his daughter and she replied: 'Very well, father, so long as it means we have enough to eat.'

The next day the father gave this second stranger his answer. The stranger handed over a donkey laden with silver, and led the middle daughter away.

Soon after this, the father went again into the forest to gather firewood, and met a third stranger who said to him: 'If you will give me your youngest daughter I will give you a donkey laden with copper.'

And the father gave him the same answer, saying that if his daughter were willing, he would have no objection. When he got home he told her of the meeting, and she agreed. The

next day the stranger gave the father a donkey laden with copper and led off the youngest daughter.

When the wars were over, the woodcutter's son came home. He saw that they were exceedingly rich when once they had been poor. He asked them where his sisters were, and was told that three strangers had come and taken them off, and they had vanished as if the earth had swallowed them up.

The boy was surprised that his parents should not know where his sisters were and he was indignant that they could have given them to men they did not know. But his father told him, 'For our eldest daughter we got a donkey laden with gold, for the middle one a donkey laden with silver, and for the youngest a donkey laden with copper. You can see for yourself how much better off we are.'

'Well, I will go and look for them,' said the youth. The father tried to make his son change his mind, but the young man was determined, saying that nothing would stop him. And the next day he set out, taking plenty of money with him.

He had gone quite a way when he came to a ravine, where he saw three shepherds fighting fiercely. He shouted to them, 'Why are you fighting so, my lads?'

The shepherds told him that they were fighting over the three things they had found, a napkin, a pair of cork slippers and a hat.

'But what is so special about them that you must fight over them?' he asked.

'See here,' said one of the shepherds, 'the napkin is such that if you lay it on the ground and say: "Napkin, be laid!" it is laid with the finest food you can imagine. And the hat has a different power: if you put it on your head you become invisible. And if you put the slippers on and say: "Slippers, take me to . . .", they will take you anywhere you wish!'

'Then it is easily settled. Run to that hilltop over there. Whoever gets there first shall have first choice of these three things,' said the woodcutter's son.

As soon as the shepherds were some distance away, the youth put on the cork slippers, and ordered them: 'Slippers, take me to my eldest sister!'

And the slippers set off, carrying him along until they suddenly stopped at a cliff-face. The boy did not know what to do. At length he struck the ground with his stick. From a great depth he heard a voice say, 'Who is it?'

'I am the woodcutter's son, at your service!' replied the boy.

At this, his eldest sister suddenly stepped out from the cliff. When they saw each other, they exchanged greetings, embraced, and his sister asked, 'What brings you here?'

'I came to look for you. Do you not know where our other sisters are?'

'Each went with her husband, as I went with mine,' his sister told him. 'He gave father a donkey laden with gold, and then led me here. Our middle sister was taken away by a man who gave father a donkey laden with silver. And the youngest sister was exchanged for a donkey laden with copper. I imagine you have seen how rich father and mother are now. But, brother, you must leave before my husband comes!'

'Why?' the youth asked in surprise.

'Because when he comes he will eat you if he finds you here!'

'And who is your husband?'

'The King of the Rams!'

'Don't be afraid, he won't hurt me, because if I put this hat on he won't see me,' laughed the young man, putting on the magic hat.

'He will smell you,' the girl cried. 'And if I try to hide you, he will kill and eat me as a punishment.'

Scarcely had she spoken when her husband arrived: 'Wife, I can smell human flesh!' he grunted. 'If you do not show me the man, I'll kill you!'

'Husband, it is only my poor brother, who has come to look for me and my sisters. He so wanted to see us!' cried the girl.

'Then let him show himself, I shall not harm him!'

The boy made himself visible, and paid his respects to the King of the Rams.

'Brother-in-law,' the King said, 'you have come at a bad time. I have no money. But take a strand of wool from my head, and when you are in need, call: "King of the Rams, help me!"'

The woodcutter's son did this, and then set off to find his middle sister. He ordered the slippers to take him to her. And they carried him along until they stopped before a cliff-face just as before. And since he had struck the ground with his stick the first time, the youth did so again. A voice from the deep asked, 'Who is it?'

And he replied, 'I am the woodcutter's son, at your service!'

As it had been with his eldest sister, so it was with his middle sister! She appeared and they embraced. And then his sister asked what had brought him to the cliff.

'I came to look for you,' the youth replied.

'Brother,' said his sister, 'you must leave

At that moment the King of the Eagles returned.

'I can smell human flesh. If you do not hand the man over to me, I shall kill you!' he cried.

'Husband, it is only my poor brother, who has come to look for me and my sisters, and is happy that he has found us.'

'Then let him show himself, I shall not harm him!'

The youth showed himself and greeted the King of the Eagles, who said, 'Brother-in-law, you have come at a bad time. I have no money. But take a feather from my head and when you are in need, call: "Let the King of the Eagles appear!"'

Then the woodcutter's son set off to find his youngest sister. He put on the magic slippers, and ordered them: 'Slippers, take me to my youngest sister!'

They carried him along until he was so hungry that he stopped and ordered the napkin: 'Napkin, be laid!'

The napkin laid itself with all manner of food, and the boy ate all he wished. Then he put the napkin away, and set off again. When he had walked for a long time, the slippers stopped at the bank of a river. The boy did not know what to do. Finally he bent down and struck the water. A voice from deep down asked, 'Who is it?'

And he replied, 'I am the woodcutter's son, at your service!'

And his youngest sister appeared. They greeted each other lovingly, and his sister asked what had brought him. He told her that he had been looking for her, and after they had spoken together for a time, his sister said, 'Brother, you must leave before my husband returns. He will make trouble for you.'

'Who is your husband?' he asked.

'The King of the Fishes,' his sister replied. 'And he will eat you.'

'He will not,' said her brother, 'for I have a hat which makes me invisible when I put it on.' And he put on his magic hat.

'But he will smell you, and I shall have to hand you over!'

'That is what our sisters said when I found them, but their husbands did not harm me. Indeed, they were glad to see me.'

before my husband returns. If he finds you here he'll kill and eat you.'

'Who is your husband?' asked the youth.

'The King of the Eagles,' replied the girl.

'Well, our eldest sister told me her husband would kill me. But I have a hat which makes me invisible when I put it on!' laughed the youth, and he put on his magic hat.

'But he will smell you, and I shall have to hand you over!'

'Our sister said the same,' the young man told her. 'Her husband did not harm me — in fact, he was pleased to see me!'

Just then the King of the Fishes appeared.

'Wife, I smell human flesh. If you do not hand the man over, I'll kill you!'

'Husband, it is only my poor brother, who has come looking for us.'

'Then let him show himself, I shall not harm him!'

The boy showed himself and the King of the Fishes said, 'Brother-in-law, you have come at a bad time. I have no money. But take a scale from my head and when you are in need, call out: "King of the Fishes, help me!"'

The youth took his leave, and he ordered the slippers:

'Slippers, take me to my fortune or misfortune!'

And the slippers took him along a narrow, dark street.

After he had walked and walked, he saw a light, and went towards it until he came to a castle. He stepped inside, and in one of the bedchambers he came upon a girl. A giant was just bringing her supper.

The youth quickly put on his hat so that no one could see him and he began to eat some of the supper. He ate from the girl's plate and drank from her cup.

When the girl had finished, she called to the giant, 'Giant, you did not bring me enough supper!'

'The same as every evening . . .' the giant protested.

'No, it couldn't have been!' replied the girl, 'for I am still hungry.'

'Indeed, I brought the same as always,' protested the giant.

'There is no more!'

When the girl had lain down, the youth crept up to her bed, and she cried out in fright, 'Giant, there is someone here!'

The giant came to look, but saw no one. 'No, it is impossible that anyone is here besides ourselves!' he said, and went away.

Hardly had he gone when the girl called out again, 'Giant, there is someone here!'

And the giant came again to look. 'But I have told you that there can be no one here besides ourselves. If you call me again, I shall kill you!'

As soon as the giant had lain down, the boy

returned to the girl's bed. She was now too scared to speak, and he whispered to her, 'Do not be afraid. Tell me, why are you here?'

The girl replied, 'This is an enchanted castle, and I may not leave.'

'Why may you not leave?'

'Because someone must first kill the giant, and there is no one who can!'

'Why not?'

'Listen! In a certain sea there is a rock, and in that rock a dove. The rock must be taken from the sea. And when it is out of the sea, it must be broken open. Then the dove will fly out, and she must be caught. She has an egg, and the egg must be taken from her without killing her! That is the enchantment which protects the giant!'

The youth said, 'All this can be done! I will bring the egg, you'll see! Then you can do with it what you will!'

And he ordered his magic slippers to take him over the sea to the rock of which the girl spoke. When he reached the rock, he cried, 'King of the Fishes, help me! I would take this rock from the sea!'

And the fishes pushed against the rock until they brought it to the shore. As soon as the rock was ashore, the youth called, 'King of the Rams, break the rock open for me!'

Then rams came and battered the rock until it was broken to pieces. The dove flew out, and the boy cried, 'King of the Eagles, help me! Catch the dove and bring her to me!'

And the eagles flew up, caught the dove, and brought her to him.

Again the youth put on the cork slippers and ordered them, 'Slippers, take me back to the girl I left in the enchanted castle!'

When he found himself in the castle again, the dove laid the egg. At that instant, the giant began to feel ill, and he said to the girl, 'You were right when you said someone was here!' And he went to lie down.

The woodcutter's son then showed himself to the girl and asked her what he should do with the egg to kill the giant.

'When the giant is asleep,' she said, 'you must strike him on the forehead with the egg. That will kill him. Then the spell will be broken and I may leave this place. But be careful! The giant is only asleep when both his eyes are closed. If one eye is closed and the other open, he is awake. Try to hit him with the egg right in the middle of his forehead, otherwise you will not kill him and he will devour both of us!'

The youth put on his magic hat and waited for the giant to go to sleep. His aim was true, and he hit the giant right in the middle of the forehead with the egg and killed him.

The enchanted castle changed into a beautiful mansion and the captive maid and all three enchanted sisters were set free. The woodcutter's son married the girl, and a great wedding feast was held. The sisters came too, and I was there myself, to eat and drink with them!

The Soldier

There was once a soldier who came home from the war. He was a brave soldier, who did not limp, whose back was not bent, and who still had all his arms and legs. But the war was over, so they sent him home.

He was a seaman's son, and his name was Johann van Deulen, according to a village in Flanders. But people soon began to call him Kinglet, which is a Flemish name for the chiff-chaff. They either called him that because he was as thin as a rake, something quite unusual among the Flemings, or because he was supposed to become a king one day. Or maybe it was because he looked so innocent! I really don't know, and he himself would be pleased to find out the real reason for his nick-name!

At that time the stove in his cottage was cold and empty, which meant that no one at home was expecting him, not his father or his mother, or his brothers or his sisters. And so, though he had a long journey before him, he went on his way slowly and steadily, and did not hurry at all. He stepped out proudly, left right, left right, his knapsack swinging on his back, left right, left right, his sabre dangling by his side, left right, left right, till one evening he came into a strange forest, where he decided to have a smoke of his pipe. He began looking for his tinderbox to light it, but much to his annoyance he found that he had lost it on the journey.

So he went on a bow shot further, till he suddenly caught sight of a light beyond the trees, and he made his way towards it. Soon he was standing in front of a big, old house — its gate swinging open wide.

The soldier went into the courtyard and, through one of the windows, saw a low chamber with a great hearth full of glowing coals. He filled his pipe, knocked gently, and

But the dragon said, 'Do not dare to draw your sword! I have been waiting for you! You shall set me free!'

'And who are you?'

called out, 'May I come inside and light my pipe?'

No one answered. Johann knocked louder, but there was no reply. So he lifted the latch and went in. The chamber was empty.

The soldier went straight over to the hearth, grasped a pair of tongs, and was bending down to take a piece of coal, when suddenly, thwang! The sound was like the twanging of a mighty spring, as a terrible dragon emerged from the fire.

Strange to say, the dragon had a woman's head. Now, most of us would have taken to our heels at such a sight, but our soldier was a real soldier. He just took a step backwards and closed his hand on the hilt of his sabre.

'My name is Ludovina, and I am the daughter of the King of the Netherlands. Set me free from here and I will marry you and make you happy!'

Most men would have asked for time, to think matters over — but not Kinglet! He had not the slightest notion that prudence is the better part of valour. And besides, Ludovina was fixing him with her eyes, and he was fascinated by them. They were beautiful, green eyes, but not round like a cat's, rather almond shaped, with a peculiar glint in them. They shimmered like will-o'-the-wisps over the marshes, and they shone in an enchantingly lovely face, framed by long golden hair. It looked like an angel's head on a dragon's body.

55

'And what am I to do?' asked Kinglet, at last.

'Open that door over there. Go into the passage. At the end of the passage there is a hall just the same as this one. Go through it, open the wardrobe which stands there, and bring me a stomacher from it!'

The soldier set off boldly. He went through the passage without difficulty, but when he entered the hall he saw in the starlight that there were eight fists waving in front of his nose. No matter how hard he peered, he could not make out the owners of the fists.

With his head bowed, he dashed bravely through the hail of blows, answering them with his own fists. When he reached the wardrobe, he opened it, took down the stomacher from its hook, and returned with it to the first chamber.

'Here you are!' he cried, a little out of breath.

Ludovina again emerged from the flames with a dreadful hissing. This time she had a human body down to her waist. She took the stomacher and put it on. It was an exquisite garment of orange velvet, set all over with pearls.

'But that is not all!' she said. 'Go back along the passage, mount the stairs on the left to the first floor, and there in a second chamber you will find another wardrobe with my skirt inside. Bring it to me!'

Kinglet did as he was told. When he entered the chamber, he saw, instead of fists, eight outstretched arms with enormous clubs. But our soldier did not turn a hair, drew his sabre, and dashed through as before, swinging his sword so fiercely that only a couple of blows caught him. In a flash, he was back with the skirt, a beautiful silk skirt, blue as the bluest sky.

'Here is the skirt,' he cried, and at that moment the dragon again appeared, this time with a human body down to the knees.

'Now I need only my stockings and shoes,' said the dragon. 'Fetch them for me. They are in a cupboard on the second floor!'

The soldier set off down the passage, and when he reached the second floor, he saw before him eight goblins. They had hammers in their hands, and their eyes were filled with fire. When Johann saw this, he stopped in the doorway.

'My sabre is of no use to me now,' he said to

himself. 'These goblins with their hammers will smash me to smithereens, and if I can't think of anything to do, it will be the end of me!'

He looked at the door and saw that it was made of oak, very thick and strong. He threw his arms about it, forced it from its hinges, and raised it over his head. Then he strode straight up to the goblins, hurled the door at them, and ran to the cupboard to take the stockings and shoes. He found them, took them to Ludovina, and at once she was a woman from head to foot!

If there was still anything of the dragon about her, Kinglet did not even notice. He had eyes only for the beautiful Ludovina. She put on the white stockings and the blue shoes, and said to her liberator, 'You cannot stay here any longer. Whatever happens you must enter this place no more. Here is a purse with two hundred ducats. Sleep tonight at the Three Lime Trees Inn, on the edge of the forest, and tomorrow morning be prepared. At nine o'clock in the morning I shall pass by the door and take you into my carriage.'

'Why do we not leave at once?' inquired the soldier.

'Because the time is not yet come.'

As she said this, Ludovina gave Kinglet a queenly glance, which enchanted him.

In fact, she was a great and proud princess. Her form was slender and stately. But there was something snakelike and arrogant in her movements which Kinglet failed to notice!

As he turned to leave, the princess seemed to have second thoughts, and said, 'Wait! You have at least deserved something good to drink.'

A soldier, especially a Flemish one, never spurns a drink for the road. Kinglet stopped, and Ludovina took down, from a dusty old shelf, a crystal decanter with sparkling liquid, in which specks of gold appeared to swirl. She poured out some of this liquid and handed the glass to Johann.

'To your health, beautiful princess!' cried Kinglet. 'And to our happy wedding!'

Then he drained the glass, without seeing how Ludovina's mouth had twisted itself into a grimace, until it looked like a lizard's tail disappearing down a hole!

Just make sure you know where we are to

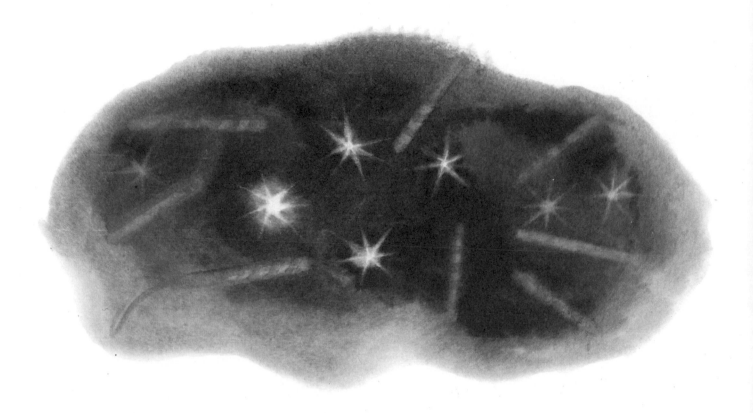

meet tomorrow,' the princess reminded him.

'Don't worry, I shall be on time!' Johann lit his pipe, saluted, and set off.

'It is clear,' he said to himself, as he walked along, 'that I am called Kinglet purely and simply because one day I am to be a king!' And he did not think to ask himself what such a beautiful princess might have done that she had been three-quarters turned into a dragon!

When Johann reached the Three Lime Trees Inn he ordered a big supper. But though he struggled against it, he had scarcely sat down at the table when such a weariness came upon him that he began to fall asleep over his plate.

'I must be terribly tired,' said Johann to himself. 'I had no idea!'

And he asked to be roused at eight as he went to his room.

All through the night, the soldier slept like a log. When the servant came at eight in the morning to knock at his door, he called out, 'Present and correct!' and slept on like a baby. At half-past eight, and again later, at a quarter-to-nine, the girl knocked at his door again, but Johann always went back to sleep. In the end, she decided to leave him in peace.

When he finally did wake up, noon was

striking. He leapt straight out of bed, roughly threw on his clothes, and ran to ask the landlord if anyone had been looking for him.

'A beautiful princess in a golden coach was here,' replied the landlord. 'She said she would come again tomorrow at eight o'clock sharp, and asked me to give you this bouquet.'

The soldier was upset at what had happened, and cursed his sleepiness over and over. In the end, it occurred to him that he should go to the big house and make his apologies. Then he remembered that Ludovina had forbidden him to enter it again, and he was afraid that she would be angry. He was comforted by the bouquet she had left him, which was of everlasting flowers.

'It is a bouquet of remembrance,' he thought to himself. He had no idea that the dried flowers are found on graves!

When night came he slept with one eye half open and woke up ten times an hour. Scarcely had he heard the dawn chorus when he leapt out of bed, climbed out of the window of the inn, and clambered up one of the lime trees which shaded its door. He pulled himself on to a bough of the tree where he could see his precious bouquet sparkling in the half-light

58

like a cluster of stars in the night sky.

He stared at it so long and so hard that he finally fell asleep. Nothing woke him! Neither the glare of the sun nor the twittering of the birds, nor the rattle of Ludovina's golden coach, nor the shouting of the landlord as he searched the place for him!

Again he slept on until midday, and was quite amazed to look through the window of the inn and see the tables being laid for lunch.

'Was the princess here?' he asked when he entered the inn.

'She was indeed. She left you this scarlet ribbon and said that she would return tomorrow at seven, but that it will be for the last time.'

'Someone must have cast a spell on me,' thought the soldier to himself. He took the ribbon, which was made of silk, the princess's embroidered monogram shining upon it in gold, and a strong, sweet perfume coming from it. He tied it around his left arm near his heart and said to himself that the best way to keep awake was not to go to bed at all. He paid his bill, bought himself a sturdy horse with the remaining money, and when evening came swung himself into the saddle and stayed by the door of the inn, firmly determined not to move from there the whole night.

Every so often, he bent over to smell the ribbon. And he bent over for so long that in the end he let the ribbon fall upon the neck of his steed and both of them, horse and rider, fell fast asleep. They slept right through to the next day.

When the princess arrived, all the innkeeper's guests shouted at him. They tugged at the soldier, slapped him, but to no avail. The soldier only awoke after the carriage had disappeared down the winding track.

Johann put his horse into a gallop. It was strong and swift, and it ran like the wind. But the carriage moved like lightning. A whole day and a whole night Johann chased after the carriage and, in all that time, his horse drew not an inch nearer to it!

Through towns, townships and villages they rode at such a rattling pace that the people came out of their houses to see what was going on. In the end they reached the seashore.

Johann hoped that the coach would stop, but strange to say it drove straight into the waves

jar. I took it from the net, opened it, and in it there was a red cloak and a purse containing fifty ducats. The cloak is over there on my bed, the bottle is on the stove, and the purse is in the table drawer.'

And she pulled out the drawer.

'I put away the fifty ducats for a dowry, for I do not always wish to be alone,' she said.

'You have no father or mother?' Johann interrupted.

'My mother died when I was born, and my father and two brothers have lain a year or more on the sea bed along with our barque.'

'Poor child,' said Johann. 'Marry as soon as you can!'

'Alas, I have no suitor. What if you were to take the purse? When you have rested, go to the nearby port, take ship, and when you have

and dashed across the surface of the water just as it had passed over the roads. Johann's brave horse fell exhausted to the ground and did not rise. The soldier sat on the shore and gazed sadly at the coach as it disappeared over the horizon.

When he had rested himself a little, he set off on foot along the coast to see if he could find a boat so that he could row after the princess. He did not want to give up. But he found neither ship nor boat, and, at the end of his strength, he sat down in the doorway of a fisherman's cottage.

Inside the cottage, a girl was mending a fishing net. When she saw Johann she invited him inside, offered him her stool, and placed in front of him, on a table of whitest wood, a jug of wine, two roast fish, and a slice of rye bread. Johann began to eat and drink, and he told the fisher-girl all that had happened to him.

The fisher-girl was very pretty, and beneath her suntan her skin was as white as a teal's wings against a black sky. She was called Sarcelle. But Johann noticed neither her white cheeks, nor her eyes, the colour of violets. He could think only of the green eyes of his princess.

When he came to the end of his story, Sarcelle said to him sympathetically, 'Last week, while I was fishing on the ebb tide, I found something besides shrimps. It was a big copper

become the King of the Netherlands, bring me back my fifty ducats. I shall be waiting for you.'

As she said this, she sighed; the soldier had taken her fancy, and she would have been pleased if he had stayed to become her husband. But Kinglet did not notice the sigh.

'When I become King of the Netherlands,' he said, 'I will make you a lady of the court beside the queen, for you are just as worthy as she.'

The girl only smiled, and replied, 'I must go about my work. If you wish, put my cloak around you and have a sleep. And if I don't see you, fare-you-well and may you have good fortune!'

'May we soon meet again,' said Johann, and

he wrapped the cloak around him and lay down on a pile of hay. All that had happened, from the moment he began to look for his tinderbox, went through his mind, and inwardly he cried, 'Oh, if only I could be in the capital of the kingdom of the Netherlands.'

And lo and behold! In an instant he was standing in a large square in front of a beautiful palace. He stared, rubbed his eyes, felt himself all over, and when he had made sure he was not asleep, he went up to a merchant who was smoking a pipe in a doorway, and asked, 'If you please, where am I?'

'Heavens, man, can't you see! You are standing before the king's own palace!'

'If you please, which king?'

'Why, the King of the Netherlands, of course,' replied the astounded merchant, shaking his head over the strange fellow.

You can imagine how amazed Johann was. He suddenly knew that the cloak had magic powers and, being an honest man, he was upset that he still had it. He decided to return the cloak along with the purse of ducats, as soon as

he could. But first he must try out its magic powers.

And right away he wished, under his breath, to be in the best inn of the royal city. In a flash, he was there, and ordered a good supper and two bottles of the best wine, and since it was late, he went to bed.

In the morning, when he put his head out of the window, he saw that the houses were hung with flags and decorated with sprigs and chains of flowers, hung across the street from roof to roof. Amid the great bustle, he could make out the soft tinkling of glass ornaments hanging from the wreaths of flowers used as decorations.

The soldier called out, asking if some prince was expected or if there was some procession in the street.

'We await the king's daughter, the beautiful Ludovina,' came the reply. 'She was lost and now she is found, and today she is to return with great ceremony. Listen! Can you hear the trumpets? The procession is here!'

'What a piece of luck!' thought Kinglet to

himself. 'I shall go and stand in the doorway and see whether the princess recognizes me!'

He hurriedly finished his dressing, took the stairs in two leaps, and stood in front of the door just as the princess's golden carriage was passing by. Ludovina was dressed all in brocade, with a gold tiara on her head, and her long flaxen hair over her shoulder. At her side sat the king and queen, and courtiers in silk and velvet hung about the doors. She had a haughty look, but when her glance fell upon the soldier she grew pale and turned away her head.

'Can she have failed to recognize me?' wondered Kinglet. 'Or is she angry that I did not wait for her?'

Without delay, he joined the joyous train, and when the procession went inside the palace, he followed it, and asked to speak with the king. He asked in vain, though he declared that he had rescued the princess. The guards thought he was off his head and shut the gate on him.

This enraged the soldier. And he went into a nearby tavern, and downed a tankard of beer.

'This is all because I am dressed like a common soldier,' he thought. 'Until I shine with gold and silk, like those overdressed

dummies, no one will even speak to me. I must count how many ducats I have left.'

He took out the purse and began to count. To his surprise, he found that he had still fifty —

though he knew he had already spent a good few.

'Sarcelle must have been mistaken,' he said to himself. 'There must have been more than fifty in the purse!'

And he paid for the tankard of beer from the purse, and counted again. Fifty! He put five ducats aside and counted for the third time. And again there were fifty ducats in the purse! So he tipped all the ducats out of the purse, tied it up again, and when he opened it, he again counted fifty ducats. Now he understood: the purse was magic, it was always full!

'Good Lord, I am a rich man,' said Johann to himself. 'Now let the courtiers throw me out like a miserable dog!'

And he went to the court tailor, and had a tunic and cloak of blue velvet made up, set all over with pearls. He chose blue because the princess liked the colour. Then he went to the carriage-maker, and bought a golden coach, just like the one the beautiful Ludovina rode in.

A few days later, the soldier drove through the streets of the city in his fine coach, drawn by six white horses, and driven by a tall coachman with a long beard. At the rear stood four liveried footmen. In his hand, the soldier held the bouquet of dried flowers, and across his left shoulder, he threw the princess's scarlet ribbon.

Twice he drove through the city, and twice he dismounted and walked beneath the palace windows. As he was driving through the city for the third time, he took the purse from his pocket and threw handfuls of ducats into the street. All the children and beggars ran behind the coach, shrieking with delight. There were more than a thousand of them when the coach reached the palace courtyard for the third time.

The next day, a rumour spread through the city that some foreigner was throwing handfuls of ducats from a bottomless purse. Even the royal court was talking about it and the queen, who was very inquisitive, wished to see the magic purse.

'I can easily fulfil your wish,' said the king. 'Invite this man to come and play cards with me this evening.'

Kinglet did not refuse the invitation. He found the king, the queen and the princess awaiting him in their small red drawing-room.

The king was smoking a pipe, while the queen and the princess were at their spinning. The tomcat sat by the fireside and purred. The king sent for some cards and invited Johann to sit at the table. Johann lost once, he lost twice, a third time, a sixth time. True, it seemed to him that the king was cheating a little, but he did not care; he was losing on purpose.

They played for fifty gold pieces, and as soon as the soldier had emptied the purse, it filled itself again.

The sixth time the king said, 'How peculiar.'

The queen said, 'How strange!'

And the princess said, 'How amazing!'

'But not so amazing,' the soldier piped in, 'as your being turned into a dragon!'

'Shhhh!' interrupted the king, who did not like to hear such things.

'I only mention it,' continued Johann, 'so that you might know that I am the one who set your daughter free from the goblins' claws, and that in return she promised me her hand.'

'Is this true?' the king asked the princess.

'It is,' answered Ludovina. 'But I bade my deliverer wait for me at an appointed hour when I would pass by in my coach. Three times I came, and each time he was sleeping so soundly that he could not be wakened!'

'I could not help myself!' the soldier said, with a smile, 'but it was all on account of your kindness!'

'What is your name?' asked the king.

'I am Johann van Deulen, but people call me Kinglet.'

'You are a king, or a king's son?'

'I am a soldier, and a sailor's son.'

'You are not exactly a rich bridegroom for our daughter. But if you give us your purse, the princess is yours!'

'The purse is not mine, so I cannot give it to anyone.'

'But you can lend it to us till the wedding,' said the princess, pouring him coffee with her lily-white hand, and looking at Johann with that strange look which he could not resist.

'And when shall the wedding be?'

'At Whitsuntide,' said the king.

'Which Whitsuntide thou witst not,' muttered the princess, under her breath.

The king sent for a bottle of vintage wine to close the bargain, invited the soldier to fill his pipe and have a smoke, and then sat over the wine so long that it was two hours after curfew when Johann staggered from the palace.

The next day, he went again to the palace for a round of cards with the king and a word or two with the princess. But they told him at the gate that the king had left for the country to collect taxes. When he called the day after, the soldier got the same reply. So he asked to speak to the queen. But she had a headache. He came a third time, a fourth, a fifth, a sixth, to the palace, but each time, he saw no one of importance. Finally, the soldier understood.

'They have deceived me! They have made me a laughing stock,' he said to himself. 'What a fine king! He should be ashamed of himself!'

And as he fretted and fumed, his eyes fell on his red cloak.

'By all the stars,' he said aloud. 'What a fool I am. I can get into the palace quickly and easily, whenever I want!'

That evening he took the red cloak and went for a walk in front of the royal palace. All was

dark except for a light in one window on the first floor. Johann, who had eyes like a hawk, made out the princess's shadow at the window.

'I wish to be in the Princess Ludovina's room at once,' the soldier said to himself, and there he was!

The royal daughter was sitting at a table, counting the ducats she was taking from the bottomless purse.

'Eight hundred and fifty, nine hundred, nine hundred and fifty . . .'

'A thousand!' cried Johann, and then added, 'Good evening to you!'

The princess turned, and cried out softly: 'You are here? What are you doing here? How did you get here? What do you want? Go away at once, or I shall scream!'

'I came only to remind you of your promise that our wedding is at Whitsuntide. That is the day after tomorrow, and so it's time to make preparations!'

Ludovina began to laugh.

'Our wedding!' she said. 'What a fool you are to believe that the daughter of the King of the Netherlands would take the son of a common sailor for her husband!'

'In that case give me back my purse,' said Johann, but the princess retorted, 'The purse? Never!' and hid it in her pocket.

'It's like that, is it?' shouted the soldier. 'But cheats sometimes get what they deserve!'

And he took the princess in his arms, threw a corner of his red cloak around her, and cried, 'I wish to be at the very end of the earth!'

And so it was!

Johann put the princess down under a tree and said, 'Now, what have you to say? We are farther from your kingdom than you can imagine!'

The princess realized that the time for laughing was over. She was confused by the sudden turn of events, and was at a loss for words.

She was so spoilt and selfish that she could think only of herself. That was why she had been turned into a dragon!

When the soldier had set her free, she had
thought only of how to trick him. The wine she
had given him to drink, the bouquet of flowers,
and the ribbon she had given him, all had the
power to put him to sleep!

When she spoke at last, she hid her true
feelings.

'I see that you are not such a worthless fellow
after all,' she said, in a voice like honey. 'Now
I see that you are more powerful than a king.
Here is your purse. But tell me if you still have
my ribbon and my bouquet.'

'Here they are,' answered Kinglet, enchanted
by the change in her, and he pulled the bouquet
and the ribbon from his breast. Ludovina put
the nosegay in Johann's buttonhole, and tied the
ribbon around his arm.

'Now you are my lord and master,' she said,
'and I will take you for my husband whenever
you wish.'

'You have a better nature than I thought,'
answered Johann, touched by her humility. 'I
promise you will be happy with me, for I love
you dearly.'

'Do you speak truly?'

'I do,' answered Johann.

'Then tell me, Johann, tell me how you were
able to take me in your arms and carry me so
quickly to the very ends of the earth?'

Johann scratched his head. Could he trust
her? Was she trying to fool him again? Would
it not be wiser to keep the secret of the red
cloak to himself?

But again Ludovina asked, 'Tell me, tell me,
my dear one!'

She spoke in such a sweet and pleading voice

and looked at him so innocently that the soldier was lost!

'I will tell her my secret,' he thought to himself, 'but I will not part with the cloak!'

And so he told her the secret of the red cloak's power.

'I am so tired,' sighed Ludovina, when she had heard him out. 'What if we were to sleep a little? Then we shall think of what to do!'

She lay down on the grass and Kinglet lay down beside her. As he lay there, he breathed the scent of the ribbon, and he could not keep awake. Soon he was in a deep sleep.

This was just what Ludovina expected. Quickly she unfastened his cloak, put it on, took the purse from the sleeping soldier's pocket, and said, 'I wish to be in my room!'

And so it was!

You can imagine Johann's surprise, when he awoke after a day and a night, and found neither purse nor cloak nor princess! He tore his hair, beat himself with his fists, kicked the treacherous bouquet, and tore the red ribbon to a thousand pieces.

'Surely they call me Kinglet because I am as silly as a bird!' he sighed.

But it was no use lamenting. He was now very hungry and there was no sign of an inn.

What would he do — if he could not find anything to eat?

Suddenly he raised his head and saw that the tree under which he lay was hung with beautiful yellow egg-plums, shining like gold. Thankfully, he climbed the tree and began to feast on the fruit. But wonder of wonders! He had eaten but two of the plums when there was something pressing on his forehead. He touched his head and found that he had a pair of horns! Alarmed, he leapt from the tree and ran towards the stream in the distance. And what did he see? There were indeed two fine horns. These would have looked marvellous on some deer's head, but were not exactly suitable on a soldier's!

Despair and fear filled his heart.

'Isn't it enough that I am robbed?' he cried. 'Now the devil himself has given me these horns. How can I ever turn to my friends looking like this?'

But since the horns were there, and the plums had not filled his stomach, there was nothing for it but to climb another tree, where red plums were growing. As soon as he had eaten two, the horns vanished from his forehead!

The soldier, surprised and pleased by this new magic, decided he had been foolish to complain.

'These yellow and red plums may help me to

get back my purse and my cloak, and to punish that good-for-nothing princess,' he told himself. 'She has the eyes of a gazelle already, so let her have the horns! I'd like to see a princess with horns!'

In order to satisfy himself that the fruit really had the magical powers, he tested them once more. Then he made himself a basket of willow twigs from the trees beside the stream, filled it with yellow and red plums, and set off on his journey.

He walked for many days, living on berries and roots. He was afraid that the plums might go bad on the way, but luck was on his side. His most precious possession remained without a blemish, and he bravely endured hunger and thirst, heat, cold and danger, being several times attacked by wild animals. Nothing daunted him. The thought of getting his own back gave him strength.

'I'll show them!' he said to himself. 'The Kinglet may be small and trusting, but he is no more stupid than the cunning fox!'

Finally he came to a port. In return for a few ducats, which he had managed to save, he boarded a ship to the Netherlands. It was exactly a year and a day since he had left that country's capital.

Once in the capital city, he put on a false beard, placed a black patch over one eye, and dressed himself as a food vendor. It was Sunday, and he took up a position by the church gates. He spread his yellow egg-plums on a wide cloth, and they looked fresh and very inviting.

When the princess and her ladies of the court came out of church, he began to shout in a hoarse voice, 'Plums for the ladies! Plums for the ladies!'

'I have heard of plums for gentlemen, but never of plums for ladies,' said the princess. 'How much are they?'

'Fifty golden ducats each.'

'Fifty golden ducats? What is so special about them? Do they make one wise? Or increase one's beauty?'

'Beautiful princess, how could they increase something which is itself so perfect? But they can add to your beauty a remarkable ornament.'

The deft compliment flattered the princess.

'What kind of ornament?' she asked with a smile.

'You shall see, beautiful princess, when you have eaten them. It will surely be a surprise for you!'

Ludovina was filled with curiosity at such a rarity. For each of the yellow plums in the

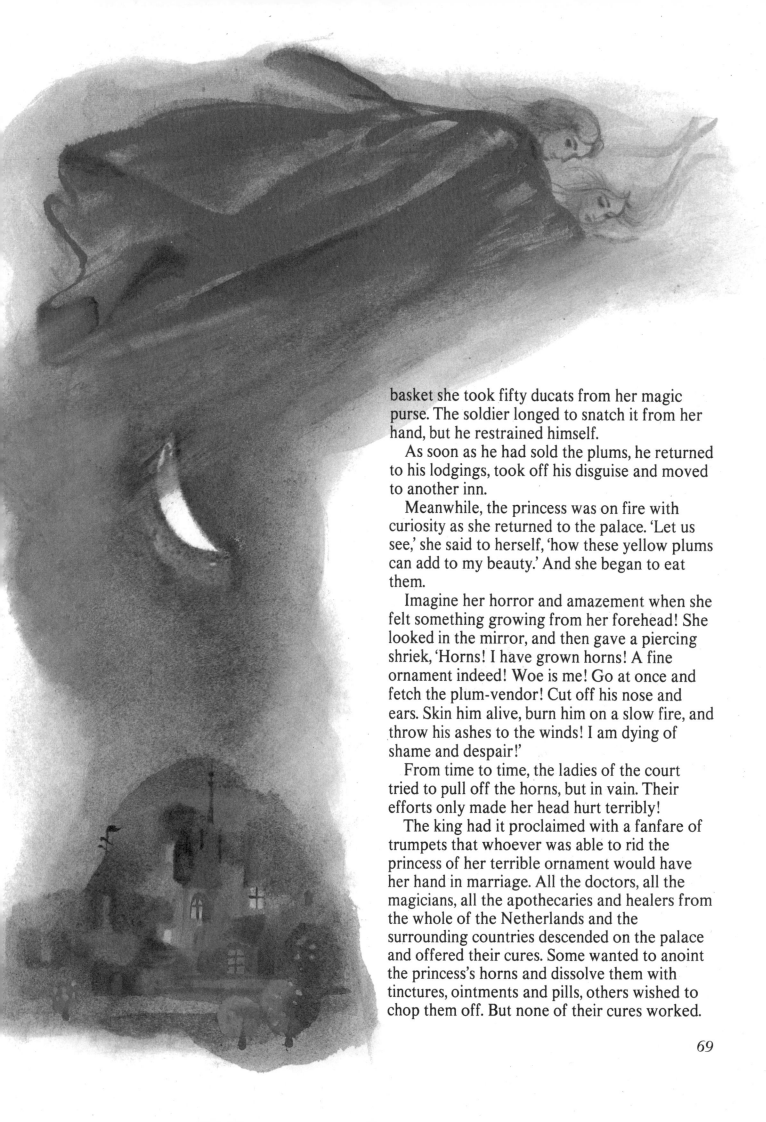

basket she took fifty ducats from her magic purse. The soldier longed to snatch it from her hand, but he restrained himself.

As soon as he had sold the plums, he returned to his lodgings, took off his disguise and moved to another inn.

Meanwhile, the princess was on fire with curiosity as she returned to the palace. 'Let us see,' she said to herself, 'how these yellow plums can add to my beauty.' And she began to eat them.

Imagine her horror and amazement when she felt something growing from her forehead! She looked in the mirror, and then gave a piercing shriek, 'Horns! I have grown horns! A fine ornament indeed! Woe is me! Go at once and fetch the plum-vendor! Cut off his nose and ears. Skin him alive, burn him on a slow fire, and throw his ashes to the winds! I am dying of shame and despair!'

From time to time, the ladies of the court tried to pull off the horns, but in vain. Their efforts only made her head hurt terribly!

The king had it proclaimed with a fanfare of trumpets that whoever was able to rid the princess of her terrible ornament would have her hand in marriage. All the doctors, all the magicians, all the apothecaries and healers from the whole of the Netherlands and the surrounding countries descended on the palace and offered their cures. Some wanted to anoint the princess's horns and dissolve them with tinctures, ointments and pills, others wished to chop them off. But none of their cures worked.

But the reward was so tempting that there were still those daring enough to try. And as they failed, they ended their lives on the gallows. In order to comfort her, the gentlemen and ladies of the court began to assure the princess that they suited her immensely. They even ate the rest of the plums, and the world has never seen such a strange set of horned courtiers as those who attended the court of the king of the Netherlands!

Since there were not enough plums to go round, many of the lords and ladies had false horns made. This particular form of ornament was soon generally considered exceedingly beautiful, and the ordinary people saved up to have horns made!

Though the king had given strict orders for the plum-vendor to be caught and brought to him, none of the soldiers managed to find him.

And when Johann thought that he was now safe from pursuit, he squeezed the juice from the red plums into a bottle, bought a doctor's white coat in a second-hand shop, put on a wig, placed some glasses on his nose, and set off, in his disguise, to see the King of the Netherlands. He told the king that he was a learned doctor from a foreign land, and he promised to cure the princess, providing he could be alone with her.

'Another madman for the gallows,' said the king, 'but let it be as he asks!'

They took the soldier to the princess and left him alone with her. Johann poured a few drops of juice from his bottle into a glass. The princess had scarcely drunk it when the ends of her horns disappeared.

'They would have disappeared altogether if something had not interfered with my elixir,' declared the false doctor. 'My medicine cures only those patients who have a soul as pure as a lily. Have you done some wrong? Try to remember!'

Ludovina knew perfectly well she had done wrong. But she hesitated for a while between the humbling confession and the desire to get rid of her horns. In the end the latter won.

'I stole a leather purse from the soldier Johann van Deulen,' she said, with downcast eyes.

'Give me the purse!' she said. 'While you

There were so many who tried to cure the princess, and she suffered so much from their attempts, that the king was obliged to give further orders that anyone who tried unsuccessfully to cure the princess would be hanged without so much as a trial!

keep it, the medicine will not work.'

The false doctor held out his hand to take the purse from Ludovina, but she still hesitated. What use was the purse! The gold gave her no pleasure now. She sighed, and then gave the doctor the purse, and he poured a few more drops into her glass, and when Ludovina drank, her horns shrank by a half.

'Listen,' said Johann, 'you still have something on your conscience. Did you not take anything else from the soldier, apart from the purse?'

'I took his cloak.'

'Give it to me!'

'Here you are!'

Now it had just occurred to Ludovina that after her cure and the disappearance of the horns, she could call the soldiers, and force the doctor to give everything back to her! But her hopes were short-lived. While she was secretly smiling at her idea, the false doctor wrapped himself in the cloak, threw off his wig and glasses, and there before the treacherous princess stood Johann van Deulen!

She was speechless and frozen with horror.

'I could leave you to suffer for the rest of your life,' said Johann, 'but I have a kind heart, and I once loved you. Now, I know how greedy and selfish you are!'

He poured the rest of the bottle into the glass and disappeared. The princess drank eagerly. She did not leave a drop for the ladies of the court, who had suffered as she had!

Meanwhile Johann had wished himself back in Sarcelle's cottage, and in a trice he was there.

Sarcelle was seated by the window, mending a net, and looking now and then towards the sea as if searching for someone. When she found the soldier in the parlour, she turned and blushed a pretty pink.

'You have come back!' she cried. 'How did you get here?' And then she said, wistfully, 'But where is your princess? Did you marry her?'

Johann told her all that had passed, and when he had finished he offered Sarcelle her purse and her cloak.

'What would I do with them?' said Sarcelle. 'They are rare things indeed, but your misfortunes have convinced me that such treasures do not bring happiness.'

'Happiness is nothing more than honest work and a good wife,' said Johann, who noticed for the first time how her eyes shone! 'Dear Sarcelle, will you take me for your husband?'

'I shall be glad to marry you,' answered the fisher-girl, blushing even more, 'but on condition that we put the purse and the cloak back into the copper bottle and throw it into the sea.'

And so they did. Then Johann married the wise Sarcelle, and they were as happy together as if they had been royalty.

And do you know — this story must be true, because Johann himself told it to me!

The Ugly Duckling

The countryside was in its full glory. It was summer; the rye was turning yellow and the oats green; down in the meadows the hay had been raked into heaps, and the stork was strolling up and down on his long red legs and speaking in Egyptian, because he had learnt that tongue from his mother.

All around the fields and meadows were great forests where deep lakes lay hidden. Yes, how glorious it was! There, bathed in sunshine, stood an old mansion, surrounded by a deep moat; from the walls down to the water the banks were covered in colt's-foot — its leaves growing so high that a small child could stand beneath the largest of them.

It was a complete wilderness, like in the deepest of deep forests. And it was there that a mother duck had built her nest; she wanted to have a family of little ducklings, but she had had just about enough of sitting on her eggs, because the whole business took too long altogether, and she so rarely had any visitors! The other ducks much preferred to swim in the moat rather than climb all the way up the bank to sit under a leaf and have a quack with her.

At long last the eggs began, one by one, to hatch out. 'Peep, peep, peep!' All the chicks came to life and stuck out their little heads.

'Quack, quack!' said the mother duck, and the ducklings waddled away from the nest as fast as their little legs could carry them, peering all around them beneath the green foliage. Their mother let them look to their hearts' content, since green is good for the eyes.

'How big the world is!' cried the ducklings in wonder — now having, as you can imagine, much more room than when they were lying in their eggs.

'Do you suppose this is the whole world?' said their mother. 'My dears, the world stretches right to the other side of the garden, all the way to the parish field! Mind you, I've never been that far. Well, that must be the last of you,' she

added, standing up. 'Dear me, no! The biggest egg of all is still to hatch. How much longer will it take? I have really had enough of all this sitting!' And she returned to the nest, and went on sitting.

'Well now, how is it going?' asked one of the old ducks, who had come visiting.

'This one is taking a terrible time!' said the mother duck. 'It just won't hatch! But look at my other children. They're the prettiest ducklings I ever saw! They all take after their father — the rogue! He never even came to see me.'

'Show me the one that won't hatch,' said the old duck. 'It could be a turkey's egg! I was once caught out that way, you know, and what a time I had with those chicks! Afraid of water, would you believe! Couldn't get them off the bank at all — quacked at them, nipped them, but all to no good. Show me the egg! 'Pon my soul, it IS a turkey's egg! Let it be, I tell you, and teach the rest to swim!'

'I'll sit on it just a little longer,' said the mother. 'If I've sat on it this long, then I might as well keep it up for a little while yet!'

'As you like, dear!' replied the old duck, and went off.

At last the big egg hatched out. 'Peep, peep, peep!' chirped the chick, and rolled out onto the grass. It was big and ugly, and the mother duck looked it up and down. 'My, what a big duckling!' she exclaimed. 'None of the others looks like that! What if it is a turkey after all? Well, we shall soon see! Into the water it shall go, if I have to push it in myself!'

The next morning the weather was a delight to see, with the sun beaming down on the green-grown bank, and the mother duck set off with her family for the moat. Plop! Into the water she flopped. 'Quack, quack!' she called. And, one by one, the ducklings splashed in after her. At first the water covered their heads, but they came straight up again, and were soon swimming around as if they had been doing it for years. Their little feet paddled back and forth quite without trying, and there they were, the whole family, even the ugly grey chick.

'That's no turkey, dear me, no!' the mother duck said with satisfaction. 'Look how nicely he paddles, how well he moves along! Why, he's not such an ugly little thing, after all, when you take a proper look at him. Quack, quack! Come along with me, now, I'll show you the world and introduce you in the duck-yard. But mind you stay close to me, so no one treads on you, and watch out for the cat!'

And so they came to the duck-yard. There
was a fine row going on there, because two
families of ducks were fighting over an eel's
head — which, in the end, the cat made off with
anyway.

'There you are,' said the mother duck, 'that's
the world for you,' and she licked her beak,
because she wouldn't have said no to an eel's
head herself. 'And now, get moving!' she
ordered. 'You must go and curtsey to that old
duck over there. She's the most noble of all the
ducks. She's got Spanish blood in her veins —
that's why she's so fat; and do you see that red
ring on her leg? That's something very special,
the highest honour a duck can receive! It means
that she is to be left in this world, and both
animals and men are to know her by it. So, get
along with you, and no shuffling, now, properly
brought-up ducklings keep their feet well apart
when walking, like their mothers and fathers!
Well, then — curtsey nicely, and say quack!'

So the ducklings curtseyed and said 'quack'.
But the other ducks looked them over and said,
quite out loud, 'Well, look at that, now we're
going to have this tribe to put up with too! As if
there weren't enough of us here already! And
just look at that one over there! Ugh! We don't
want THAT one here!' And straight away one
of the ducks bent over and nipped the ugly
duckling on the neck.

'Leave him alone,' said his mother, 'he's not
hurting anyone!'

'But he's too big by far, and there's something
funny about him,' retorted the duck who had
done the nipping, 'and that means he should be
kept in his place!'

'You have lovely children, dear,' proclaimed
the old duck with the ring on her leg, 'they are
all lovely, except that one — you didn't make
such a good job of him! If you would carry out
a few improvements, I should be much
obliged!'

'I'm afraid that is not possible, ma'am,' said
the mother duck, 'I know he is not beautiful, but
he is a very good duckling, and he can swim
quite as well as the others — I venture to say,
better. I suppose he may grow into beauty, or
that he will get a little smaller in time! He was
too long in the egg — that's why he hasn't quite
the figure he should have!' And she ruffled the
down on the duckling's neck with her beak,
arranging it to look as pretty as possible. 'And
anyway,' she added, 'he's a drake, so looks aren't
so important. I think he's going to be strong,
and that he'll make his way in the world all
right!'

'The other ducklings are charming,' the old
duck said, 'so just you make yourselves at home
here, and if you should find an eel's head, be
sure to bring it along to me!'

And the ducklings did make themselves at home.

But the poor duckling who had hatched last, and who looked so ugly, had a hard time of it; the ducks and hens nipped him, pushed him, and made fun of him. 'It's far too big!' they all said. And the turkey, who had been born with spurs, and so thought he was the cat's whiskers, would puff himself up like a frigate in full sail, charge at the duckling, and gobble away till he was blue in the face. The poor duckling didn't know which way to turn, and he was ashamed of being so ugly, and unhappy that he was laughed at by the whole of the duck-yard.

So the first day passed, and from then on things went from bad to worse. Everyone picked on the poor duckling; even his brothers and sisters were nasty to him. 'Hope the cat gets you, you freak!' they used to say, and even his mother would say: 'If only you were somewhere far away!' And the ducks nipped him, and the hens pecked him, and the girl who fed the poultry used to kick him.

One morning, the duckling took a run, flapped its wings, and flew up over the fence. The birds in the bushes flew off in alarm.

'That is because I'm so ugly,' thought the duckling to himself, and he closed his eyes in shame. But then he went on running, until at last he came to the marshes where the wild ducks lived. There he lay all night, sad and exhausted.

In the morning, the wild ducks flew up and caught sight of their new companion. 'Who are you?' they asked, and the duckling turned in every direction and greeted them as politely as he knew how.

'How ugly you are!' said the wild ducks. 'But we don't mind, as long as you don't marry into the family!'

Poor thing — he had no thoughts of marrying; he was quite content to lie in the rushes and take an occasional drink of the muddy water.

Two whole days the ugly duckling lay there. Then a couple of wild geese, or better to say wild ganders, came flying along. They weren't long out of the egg, so they spoke rather coarsely.

'Hey, friend,' they said, 'you're so ugly that we like you. How would you like to fly with us and

edge of the marshes, and some of them were even sitting in the branches which reached over the rushes right down to the water's edge.

Small clouds of blue smoke wafted slowly from the dark line of trees and drifted far out over the water. Game dogs sloshed around the swampy ground, and the rushes swayed from side to side. The poor duckling was terrified; he turned his head to hide it under his wing, and at that moment an enormous dog stopped right next to him. Its tongue hung right down from its mouth, and its eyes gleamed maliciously. It thrust its muzzle right up to the duckling — then dashed off again without so much as touching him.

'Thank heavens,' sighed the duckling, 'I'm so ugly that not even a dog will bite me!'

And he lay there without moving a muscle, as pellets whizzed through the rushes, and shot after shot cracked away all around him.

It was late in the day before silence again fell. But the poor duckling didn't dare to move, and he waited several more hours before taking a look around, and then hurrying away from the marshes. Through field and meadow he ran, and it was hard going for him, for there was a strong wind blowing.

Towards evening he arrived at a ramshackle cottage. It was in such a poor state that it didn't know which way to fall down, which was the only reason it was still standing. By now the wind was blowing against the duckling so hard that he had to sit back on his tail so as not to fall over. And the storm was getting worse and worse. Then he noticed that the cottage door was off one of its hinges, so that it hung askew, leaving a gap through which he was able to slip inside.

In the cottage there lived an old woman, a tomcat, and a hen. The tomcat, whom the woman called 'son', knew how to arch his back and purr, and could even give off sparks, though only if you stroked him the wrong way. The hen had very short legs, and for that reason she was known as Squawky Shortshanks; she laid fine eggs, and the old woman loved her like her own child.

When morning came they soon spotted the strange duckling; the tomcat began to purr and the hen to squawk.

be a bird of passage? There are some more marshes just across the way, with some lovely little wild geese on them, all of them young ladies, and how they cackle! You're so ugly, you should be all right there!'

'Bang, bang!' Two shots cracked out from above; the two young ganders fell dead in the rushes, and the water darkened with blood. 'Bang, bang!' More shots snapped out, and a whole flock of wild geese rose from the rushes. More shots followed; a great shoot was on. The shooters were spread out all along the

'What's the matter?' asked the old woman, and looked around the parlour. But she was short-sighted, so she thought the duckling was a fat duck who had wandered in. 'A fine catch,' she said, 'now we shall have duck's eggs — as long as it's not a drake! We must try it and see.'

So the duckling was given a three weeks' trial period, but no eggs appeared. The cat, who was master of the house, and the hen, who was mistress, would speak of 'We and the world', since they considered themselves to make up a half of the latter, and the better half at that. The duckling said to himself that one might think otherwise, but the hen would have none of it.

'Do you know how to lay eggs?' she inquired.

'No.'

'Then keep your beak shut!'

And the cat said, 'Do you know how to arch your back, and purr, and give off sparks?'

'No.'

'Then keep your opinions to yourself, when sensible folk are talking.'

The duckling sat in the corner feeling miserable. Then he remembered the fresh air and the sun's rays, and he was seized with a strange desire to glide across the surface of

the water. In the end he could contain himself no longer, and he told the hen.

'Whatever are you thinking of?' the hen asked, sharply. 'You have no work to do, which is why you are getting such ideas. Lay some eggs or purr, and you will soon put such things out of your head!'

'But it is so nice to swim in the water,' said the duckling. 'If only you knew what a lovely feeling it is when the water closes over your head and you dive right down to the bottom!'

'A fine way to pass the time, indeed!' retorted the hen. 'You must be mad. Why, ask the cat — the cleverest creature I know — if HE likes to swim in the water or dive. To say nothing of myself. Or ask her ladyship, the old woman, who is the cleverest in the whole world! Do you suppose she ever takes it into her head to swim and to dive?'

'But you don't understand,' said the duckling.

'If we don't understand you, then who is to understand you! Surely you don't think yourself cleverer than the cat or the old lady, not to speak of myself? Just you take care not to get ideas above your station, child, and be thankful for what you have! Have you not come by a warm room and company in which you may learn something? But you are never satisfied, and sharing a roof with you is no fun, I tell you.

Believe me, what I say is for your own good; it may not be pleasant, but that's just how you may know your real friends! So get on with laying eggs, and learn to purr or give off sparks!'

'I think I shall go out into the wide world,' said the duckling.

'Then be off with you!' snapped the hen.

So the duckling went. He swam in the water and dived, but all the animals ignored him because he was so ugly.

Autumn came. The leaves of the forest turned yellow and brown, then they were taken up by the wind and swirled about. A chill descended from the skies, clouds heavy with hail and snow hung close to the ground, and a raven stood on the fence and called out with the cold: 'Owh, owh. Brrh!' The very thought of winter was enough to freeze you. And the duckling, of course, was far from comfortable.

One evening, as the sun was setting in glorious shades of orange and red, out of the bushes flew a whole flock of great birds. The duckling had never seen such beautiful creatures; their feathers were lily-white and their necks long and graceful. They were swans; they gave out strange cries, spread their brilliant white wings, and flew far away from the coming winter to warmer lands, where the lakes do not freeze. They climbed up and up, and some sort of strange longing filled the ugly duckling's heart. He turned right round in the water, thrust out his neck towards the departing birds, and finally gave a cry that was so strange and strong that he was himself quite taken aback.

He couldn't forget those beautiful birds, those
blissful birds, and as soon as they were lost from
sight, he dived down to the very bottom of the
lake; when he came up again, he was quite
beside himself with excitement. He didn't know
what the birds were called or where they were
flying to, he only felt that he loved them as he
had never loved any creature. He was not
jealous, not in the least — for how could he
even envy such beauty! He would have been
satisfied if only the ducks had been prepared to
put up with him. Poor, ugly thing!

And the cold came, bitter cold. The duckling
had to keep swimming up and down so that the
water would not freeze around him. All the
same, night by night, the hole in the ice where
he swam grew smaller and smaller — the frost
deepened, until the sheet of ice began to creak.
The duckling had to keep moving his feet to
stop the ice from closing, but in the end he
could paddle no longer, and he was left frozen,
motionless in the ice.

Early the next morning a passing farmer saw
the duckling, stepped onto the ice, hacked out
the duckling with his wooden shoe, and took
him home to his wife. In the warm kitchen, they
slowly brought him back to life.

The children wanted to play with him, but
the duckling thought they were going to
hurt him, and in his fright flew right into a
milk-jar. The milk splashed out onto the floor,
the farmer's wife gave a shout and clapped
her hands in dismay — and the duckling
flew into a trough of butter, then straight into
the flour-bin, and out again. What a sight

he was! And the farmer's wife flailed at him with the poker, and the children stumbled over each other trying to catch him, laughing and yelling! A good thing the door was open — the poor duckling ran out and hid among the bushes in the fresh-fallen snow. And there he lay, as if sleeping out the winter!

It would be too sad to tell of all the misery and misfortune the duckling went through during that cruel winter. He was lying among the reeds in the marshes when at last the sun began to warm the earth. The larks sang; spring was come in all its splendour.

Suddenly, the duckling lifted its wings — they hummed more strongly now, and thrust him forward powerfully. In no time at all he found himself in a great garden, where apple trees stood in full blossom and lilac bushes scented the air, casting long green branches down to a bend in the moat. How beautiful it was there, filled with the freshness of spring. Right opposite the duckling, three lovely white swans appeared from the bushes. Their feathers were puffed out, and they glided lightly across the water. The duckling recognized the splendid birds, but he was filled with a strange sadness.

'I shall fly to those majestic creatures! And they will nip me for even daring to go near them, an ugly thing such as I! But I don't care if they do! Better to be killed by them, than to be nipped by the ducks, pecked by the hens, and kicked by the poultry-girl, or to go through another such winter!'

So the duckling flew onto the water, and swam towards the beautiful swans.

'Go ahead, kill me!' said the poor creature, bowing his head towards the water and waiting for the swans to do as he asked.

What should he see reflected in the clear water?

There beneath him, he saw a strange sight! Not the clumsy, unsightly, dirty-grey bird he had been, but the lovely swan he had grown into!

After all the trials and troubles the young swan had known, he was now happy beyond all his dreams. At last he knew how great was his good fortune, and what beautiful things were in store. The big swans circled round him and stroked him with their beaks.

Some small children came into the garden; they threw bread and corn onto the water, and the smallest of them called out, 'There's a new swan!'

And the others jumped for joy, and shouted, 'Hurray, there's a new swan!'

They clapped their hands and danced, then ran off to fetch their mummy and daddy. They threw more pieces of bread and buns into the water, and cried, 'The new one is the most beautiful of all! So young and so lovely!' And the old swans bowed their acknowledgement.

The young swan hid his head shyly beneath his wing, and somehow didn't know what to do. He was so happy, but not proud, for a good heart knows no pride. He thought of how he had been mistreated and scorned, and here he was being called the most beautiful of beautiful birds! The lilacs bowed their branches right down to where he lay in the water, the spring sun shone warm and pleasant — and the young swan ruffled his feathers, raised his slender neck, and called out joyously with all his heart, 'Never did I dream of such happiness, when I was an ugly duckling!'

Why the Sea Is Salty

Long long ago there were two brothers. One was rich and the other poor. As Christmas Eve drew near, the poor brother did not have a slice of bread or a morsel of food in the house. So he went to the rich brother and asked him, for pity's sake, to help him a little at Christmas time. But this was not the first time the elder brother had been asked to help, so he was not too pleased.

'If you do as I ask, I'll give you a whole ham,' said the elder brother at last.

The poor brother promised on the spot and thanked him again.

'Here you are then!' cried the rich brother, throwing him the ham. 'Go to the devil!'

'What I have promised I shall fulfil,' declared the poor brother, taking the ham and leaving. 'I'll go to the devil.'

He set off, and walked and walked — the whole day long. When it was getting dark, he came to a place full of glare and light. This must be it, he thought to himself. The devil must live here.

An old man with a long white beard stood there beneath the roof of a shed, chopping firewood for Christmas.

'Good evening!' said the poor brother.

'Good evening! Whither at this late hour?' the old woodcutter asked.

'To hell, to find the devil! Is this the right way?' replied the poor brother.

'Yes, yes . . . it is right here,' said the old man.

'But listen, I'll give you some advice. When you arrive in hell they will want to buy your ham, for ham is a very rare delicacy in hell. But do not sell it until they give you the hand-mill which stands by the door. Only for that should you exchange your ham! When you get back from hell, I'll show you what to do with the mill. It is indeed something priceless!'

The poor man thanked him for his good advice and knocked at the gate of hell. When he was taken in, all was as the old man had said. The devils, big and small, gathered round him like ants, and they tried to outbid each other for the ham.

'I meant to keep it for Christmas, but since you are so anxious to have it, I'll be glad to leave it for you,' said the poor man. 'But if I am to sell it, it must be for that hand-mill, which stands over by the door.'

This, the devils were unwilling to give him, and they did their best to make him change his mind. But the poor man would not give way, saying that he would sell the ham for nothing else, so in the end the devils had to part with the mill.

When the poor man came out of hell into the courtyard, he asked the old woodcutter what he should do with the hand-mill. And when his friend had shown him how to use it, he thanked him, and set off as fast as he could for home; but it was after midnight when he finally arrived.

'Where in the world have you been?' asked his wife. 'I have sat and waited hour after hour, and I have nothing from which to prepare our Christmas supper.'

'Well — I could not come earlier. I had some business to arrange and I had to walk a long way. But now I'll show you something!' declared the poor man.

He put the mill on the table and asked it to grind, first candles, then a fine linen table-cloth, then food and drink, and all that a Christmas table should contain. And as he gave his commands, the mill ground all he asked. The woman could not believe her eyes, and asked where her husband had found such a wonderful object.

'Where I got it is of no account,' he answered. 'The important thing is that it will always grind what we ask. We shall want no more.'

And straight away he commanded his mill to grind food and drink and all kinds of good things to see them through the Christmas holiday. On Boxing Day he invited all their friends to a feast.

His elder brother came too. When the rich man saw how well off he was, he was annoyed and angry, for he did not wish his brother any good. 'Before Christmas Eve he came to beg me, for pity's sake, for something to eat, and now he is holding a feast worthy of a king!' he said to himself.

'Who the devil helped you to such wealth?' he asked.

'The devil!' smiled the younger brother, but he had no wish to tell him exactly how it was. It was only late in the evening, when he had had his fill of drink, that he decided to show his brother the hand-mill. 'This is what has brought about my wealth,' he said proudly, and asked the mill to grind more food and bottles of wine.

As soon as the rich brother saw the hand-mill, he wanted it at any price. In the end, his brother promised it to him for three hundred thalers, on condition that he would keep it till hay-making, thinking that by then he would be able to grind enough to last for years.

So when the hay-cutting started, he gave his brother the wonderful mill. But one thing he did not do: he did not tell him how to work it!

The rich brother arrived home with the mill in the evening. In the morning he sent his wife to the meadow to turn the grass the mowers had cut, promising to see to their dinner. When it was almost dinner-time, he put the mill on the table and ordered it: 'Grind cod and gruel!' The mill began to grind, and it ground cod and gruel enough to fill all the rich brother's dishes, and then went on grinding until the whole floor was covered with cod and gruel. The rich man wished to stop the mill, but he did not know how, and the mill ground merrily on!

The kitchen was now so deep in gruel that it was a wonder the envious brother did not drown. So he opened the door, but it was not long before the whole cottage was full, and he was soon out of the cottage. Away he ran, and the gruel and cod came after him, and soon flooded the whole garden and barnyard.

Meanwhile, his wife in the meadow was thinking about dinner. 'Let us go home to eat!' she said to the mowers. 'You know what poor cooks men are! I shall have to go and help!'

And so they set off for home. They had not gone very far when they saw a stream of gruel and cod pouring down the hill, with the

nothing for it but to pay his younger brother, who ordered the mill to stop. Now he had both money and mill, and before long he had a much better farm than his rich brother. He even covered his roof with gold, and since the farm was right beside the sea, it shone right across the fjord, far out to sea. Whoever sailed past stopped to greet the rich man in his gold farmyard and to look at the magic mill, for its fame spread far and wide, and there was no one who had not heard of it.

One day a shipowner came to look at the wonderful mill in the golden farmyard. He asked what the mill could grind, and particularly whether it could grind salt. 'Of course it can!' declared its owner.

As soon as the shipowner heard this, he wanted to buy the mill at any price, saying to himself that if he had the mill he would not have to travel far across the sea for salt and carry it so far. The mill would grind it for him.

The poor brother, who was now a very rich man, at first would not hear of parting with the mill; but the shipowner begged and beseeched him so that in the end he sold it. But not cheaply; he took many million thalers for it.

As soon as the shipowner had taken the mill on his back he set off, fearing that the previous owner would change his mind. And thus he did not even think of asking how to stop the mill, as he hurried as fast as he could back to his boat.

Then he set off for the open sea, and when he was far from the shore, set the mill down and ordered it: 'Grind me salt!' And the mill began at once to grind, and it ground and ground, till there was salt everywhere. The shipowner wanted to stop the mill, but how could he when he did not know what to say to it? The mill ground on and on, and the pile of salt grew and grew, until the ship could hold no more and sank.

And so, to this day, the mill goes on grinding salt at the bottom of the sea; and that is why sea-water is always salty!

unhappy owner of the mill running before it.

'If only you had a hundred stomachs!' he called out. 'But take care not to drown in the gruel!' And he ran on past them as if the hounds were after him. He made his way to the cottage where his younger brother lived and begged him for pity's sake to take the mill back again as quickly as he could, before the gruel flooded the whole village.

'Why not!' said the younger brother. 'But you must give me another three hundred thalers!'

What could the rich brother do? There was

The Castle on the Golden Pillars

There was once an old man and his wife who lived in an old cottage a long, long way inside the forest. They had two children, a boy and a girl. But otherwise they were very poor, and the only things they owned were a cow and a cat.

The cottager and his wife were forever squabbling, and it was almost certain that if one wanted one thing the other wanted the opposite!

It happened one day that the old woman cooked some gruel for supper. When each had received his share, the cottager wanted to scrape out the pan. But, straight away, his wife snapped back at him that the pan was hers and that no one might scrape it out but herself!

They fought over the pan, and neither of them would give in, until they were at it tooth and nail. In the end the woman managed to snatch the pan away from her husband and ran out of the house with it. The old man grabbed a spoon from the table and ran after her.

Over hill and dale they ran, the old woman in front and the old man always a couple of paces behind her. And I am afraid the story does not tell which of them finally scraped out the pan!

Well, a long time passed, and the old man and the old woman did not return. The brother and

sister then decided to share what their parents had left them and go out into the world to seek their fortunes. But the sharing was a very difficult business, since both of them wanted the cow and neither wanted the cat. As they were arguing over this, the cat turned to the sister, rubbed itself against her legs, and mewed, 'Take me! Take me!'

And because the brother did not, in any case, want to give up the cow, the sister stopped arguing with him and accepted the cat. Then they took their leave and set off each his own way.

The brother put the cow on a halter and went with her through green meadows. The sister with the cat went towards the forests, and nobody knows what happened to them until they reached a great and beautiful royal castle. Then the cat said, 'If you do as I tell you good fortune shall be yours!'

The girl trusted the cat's wisdom and promised to do all he asked. Then the cat told her to take off her old clothes and hide in the bushes. He said he would run to the castle and say that there was a princess sitting in the thicket who had been attacked by robbers, and that they had taken absolutely everything from her.

The king of that land was very upset to hear what had happened to a foreign princess so close to his royal castle; so he immediately sent servants to take her some new clothes and to say that he would like to invite her to his castle and make up to her what she had suffered in his land.

Servants dressed the cottager's daughter in fine clothes, hung her with precious stones, and took her to the castle. There she was admired by everyone for her beauty and kindness, but most of all by the king's son himself. He deemed life was not worth living if he should have to part with this beautiful creature!

Only the queen had her doubts, and began to ask where Her Highness, the Princess, had come from, and where her palace was. The girl answered, as the cat had told her, 'My castle lies far, far away from here and is called Catton.'

But that was not enough for the old queen. She got the idea into her head that she must find out if the strange girl was really a princess.

So in the evening she prepared her a bed with silken pillows and, in the middle, under the sheet, she placed a bean.

'If she is a real princess she is sure to notice,' she thought to herself.

But the cat had seen all. When the girl was taken to the chamber in the evening, he told her of what the queen had done.

The next morning, the queen came to ask the girl how she had slept. She replied as the cat had told her, 'Ah well, I slept, of course, for I was very tired. But it was as if I were lying on some rock or other, so uneven was the bed. In

secretly came into her room, made her bed with silk pillows, and beneath these she placed a few peas.

'If she is a princess,' she said to herself, 'she is sure to notice.'

But the cat had seen all. When the girl was taken to the chamber again, he told her of the snare the queen had set her. And so it happened that when the queen came the next morning to ask how the foreign princess had slept that night, the girl replied as the cat had taught her, 'Ah well, of course, I slept, for I was very tired. But it was like sleeping on a pile of stones, so

my castle of Catton I have a far better bed!'

The queen thought this must be a most royal princess if a small bean had caused her such discomfort. But still she wanted to test her, to see if all was really as she said.

The next evening, therefore, she again

lumpy were the pillows. In my castle at Catton I have a better bed!'

It seemed to the old queen that the girl had passed the test with flying colours. But again she began to be troubled with doubt until, at last, she said to herself that she would once more test whether the foreign princess was as royal as she said. The third evening, therefore, she again made the cottager's daughter a bed of silk pillows, and beneath the bottom one she laid a blade of grass.

'If she is a real princess,' she thought to herself, 'she is sure to notice.'

But again the cat was on watch, and he told his mistress what the queen had prepared for her.

And so in the morning when the queen came to ask how the foreign princess had slept, the girl replied as the cat had taught her, 'Ah well, of course, I slept, because I was very tired. But I felt as if I had some sort of wooden beam beneath my head, so uneven was my bed. At

princess did all day, and if she did not in some way reveal who she really was!

The next day, the queen sent the girl a beautiful robe of embroidered silk with a long, long train — the kind that is worn by only the finest ladies. The cottager's daughter was very pleased with the gift and had no thought of any ill intent. But the cat quickly came to her and whispered that she should be careful, for the queen was testing her again.

After a while, the queen came and invited the girl to walk with her. They went into the garden, and all the ladies of the court were afraid lest they should soil their trains, for it had rained the night before. Only the foreign princess walked contentedly about and gave no thought to the

home, in my castle of Catton, I have a far better bed!'

The queen saw that the strange girl was clever and that she would never find out how things really stood. So she said to herself that she would keep an eye open to see what the

fact that the train of her new robe was soaking wet and covered with mud.

Finally the queen could contain herself no longer, and said, 'Dear princess, do have a care for your train!'

But the cottager's daughter replied haughtily,

'Why, is there no other robe but this in the castle? How many of them I have at home in my castle of Catton!'

And so the old queen could not but think that this princess was accustomed to wearing only embroidered silk clothes, and decided that she really must be a king's daughter. She no longer tried to prevent the prince from courting the foreign princess, who clearly liked the prince and showed she was ready to be his wife.

One day, the girl and the prince were sitting by the window talking. Quite by chance the girl looked from the window and saw her parents running from the forest, first the old woman with the pan, then, a couple of paces behind her, the old man, waving the wooden spoon. It seemed to the girl so funny that she could not contain herself and laughed out loud.

The prince asked what she was laughing at, and the girl answered as the cat had quickly whispered in her ear, 'I must always laugh when I think that your royal castle stands on stone pillars, but my castle at Catton is on pillars of gold.'

The prince was surprised at this, and said, 'I can see that you are ever thinking of your beautiful Catton, where everything is better and more beautiful than here. No matter how far it might be, I wish to set off immediately to see it for myself.'

The cottager's daughter wished the ground would swallow her up, so taken aback was she by the prince's words, for she herself knew only too well that she did not even own an ordinary cottage, let alone a castle! But what she had said, she had said, and it could not be helped. So she hid her feelings and replied that she would consider which was the best day to set off on the long journey.

Scarcely had she returned to her chamber when she began to cry bitterly, being miserable and afraid. What would happen to her when everyone found out how she had deceived them! At that moment the cat appeared, rubbed himself against her legs and asked what was wrong.

The girl replied, 'What can I do when the prince insists on going with me to Catton? What a price I shall now pay for having listened to you!'

89

But the cat comforted her and told her not to be afraid, that he would arrange everything better than she could imagine. He told her to set off without delay, the sooner the better for both her and the prince.

The girl had many times seen the wisdom of the cat and so, in the end, she again listened to his advice, though this time with a heavy heart. She could not believe that the affair could turn out well.

Early in the morning, the prince ordered the coachmen to prepare coaches and all that was required for such a long journey. There was a great fuss and flurry everywhere, until finally they set off. The prince and his bride rode in a golden carriage at the head, followed by knights on horseback and a throng of servants, and right at the front the cat ran along to show them the way.

They travelled thus for a long time, until the cat met some shepherds driving a great flock of fat sheep. He ran up to them, greeted them, and said, 'Good day, shepherds! In a while, a prince in a golden carriage will pass by and ask whose these fine sheep are. You must answer that they belong to the young princess from Catton, sitting beside him. If you do so you shall be well rewarded, and if not, I shall return and tear you all to pieces.'

When the shepherds heard this, they were quite frightened and promised to do all the cat had asked. It was not long before the prince and his procession arrived. As soon as he saw the beautiful flock he ordered the carriage to stop, and he asked the shepherds whose the animals were.

'They belong to the Princess of Catton, who is sitting beside you in your coach,' answered the shepherds, just as the cat had told them.

The prince was surprised at this and thought to himself how rich the princess, his bride, must be. The cottager's daughter sighed with relief and began once more to hope that all would turn out well, as the cat had promised. And she said to herself that she had indeed done well out of her inheritance.

So they continued on their way, with the cat going on ahead as he seemed to prefer. After some time, he saw a meadow and some people making hay. The cat ran up to them and greeted

them, 'Good day, folk! In a while a prince will pass by in a golden carriage and ask to whom this beautiful meadow belongs. You must answer that it belongs to the young princess from Catton, sitting next to him. If you do so, you will be well rewarded, but if not, I shall return and tear you all to pieces.'

When the people heard this they were afraid and promised to do all the cat had asked.

It was not long before the prince and his train were there. When he saw the fertile meadow and the crowd of people working in it, he halted the party so that he could ask about it.

'It belongs to the Princess of Catton, who is sitting beside you in your coach!' he was told.

The prince was even more surprised, and thought to himself that his bride must be a very rich princess to own such a great meadow.

Then they drove on, the cat keeping well ahead of them. Soon he came to a cornfield. It stretched far and wide, as far as the eye could see, and was full of workers taking in the harvest.

The cat greeted the harvesters, 'Good day, dear folk, may your work go well. In a little while a prince in a golden carriage will pass by and ask to whom this fertile field belongs. You must reply that it belongs to the young princess of Catton, sitting beside him. If you do so you will be well rewarded, but if not I shall return and tear you all to pieces.'

When the harvesters heard this they were afraid, and promised to do all the cat had asked.

In a while, the prince came to the field with

his train, and he stopped and asked the harvesters about the fertile fields.

'They belong to the Princess of Catton, sitting in the coach beside you,' answered the harvesters, as the cat had told them.

The prince was most pleased with this reply, though the cottager's daughter did not know what to think of all this.

They went a little further, but it soon grew dark, and the prince ordered them to stop for the night. Only the cat did not sleep, but ran on until he reached a beautiful castle, with massive battlements and many towers. The castle stood on golden pillars and belonged to a terrible ogre, who ruled the whole kingdom.

Fortunately the ogre was not at home. The cat ran through the gate and shut it after him. Then he changed himself into a loaf of bread, just big enough to fit inside the enormous keyhole, and waited for the ogre to return.

Early in the morning before daybreak, the terrible ogre arrived, and he was so big and heavy that the ground shook beneath him. He wished to open the gate quickly, but he could not get the key in the keyhole because of the great loaf of bread which was in it.

The ogre grew angry and shouted, 'Out of my way! Let me in!'

But the cat replied, 'Wait just a little while until I tell you what has happened to me: first they beat me, and I wonder they did not beat me to death.'

'Out of my way! Let me in!' The ogre began to shout again, but the cat replied as before, 'Wait just a little while, till I tell you what has happened to me: first they beat me, and I wonder they did not beat me to death. Then they ground me, and I wonder they did not grind me to death!'

'Out of my way! Let me in!' cried the angry ogre. But the cat began once more, 'Just wait a little while, till I tell you what has happened to me: first they beat me, and I wonder they didn't beat me to death. Then they ground me, and I wonder they did not grind me to death. Then they mixed me in a kneading trough, and I wonder they did not mix me to death!'

The giant was beside himself with rage, and shouted angrily until the whole castle began to shake, 'Out of my way! Let me in!'

But the cat took no notice and replied as ever, 'Just wait a little while, until I tell you what has happened to me: first they beat me, and I wonder they did not beat me to death; then they ground me, and I wonder they did not grind me to death. Then they mixed me in a kneading trough, and I wonder they did not mix me to death. In the end they baked me in the oven, and I wonder they did not bake me to death!'

At this the ogre became afraid and began to plead, 'Out of my way, let me in!'

But, it was no use. The loaf of bread sat in the keyhole as before, until suddenly the cat called out, 'Do you see that beautiful maiden up there?'

The ogre turned round, but at that moment the sun came out, and as the ogre looked at it, he exploded and flew away in little pieces.

Then the loaf of bread rolled out of the keyhole to the ground, and changed back into the cat, and he quickly made ready to receive guests. This was soon done, and he went out in front of the gates, just in time to welcome the prince and the beautiful cottager's daughter with their courtiers.

All were amazed by the beauty of the place, and nothing was lacking, there being food and drink for all to suit their taste. The chambers were full of gold and silver and precious stones and treasures which made the prince gasp!

After the visit, the cottager's daughter returned with the prince to his castle, and they were married with great ceremony. And all those who had been on the journey and seen all the riches vowed that the princess was quite, quite right when she had said: 'Everything at home in my castle of Catton is a hundred times better.'

Afterwards the prince and his wife lived happily for many, many years, but I never heard what happened to the cat. I am sure he had a good time of it, though I was no longer there to see for myself!

The Stork Calif

I.

Calif Chasid of Baghdad was sitting on his couch one beautiful afternoon. He had just had a nap, for it was a hot day, and now he was happy and content. He was smoking a long rosewood pipe, and sipping coffee, offered to him by a slave, and whenever something pleased him, he would stroke his beard with pleasure. In short, you could see that the calif had everything he wanted. At this hour of day, you could best speak to him, for then he was always very mild and kind. That was why his grand vizier, Mansor, always visited him then.

On this particular afternoon, the vizier came, but he looked unusually deep in thought. The calif removed the pipe a little from his mouth, watched the vizier for a while, and then said, 'Why do you look so thoughtful, grand vizier?'

The grand vizier laid his arms across his breast, bowed to his master, and answered, 'Master, I did not know I looked thoughtful, but outside your palace is a storekeeper who has such fine things that I regret I have no money to spare to purchase them.'

The calif, who had long wanted to do something to please his grand vizier, sent a slave to bring the storekeeper up to him. The slave was soon back with the storekeeper, a small, fat man, with a dark brown face and tattered clothes. He was carrying a box containing many different things, pearls and rings, richly inlaid pistols, cups and combs. The calif and his vizier looked at everything, and in the end the calif bought himself and Mansor a beautiful pistol each, and a comb for the vizier's wife. As the storekeeper was closing his box, the calif noticed a small drawer in it, and asked what goods he had there. The storekeeper drew out the drawer and showed them a box of black powder and a piece of paper containing strange writing on it, which

neither the calif nor Mansor were able to understand.

'I received these two things from a certain merchant, who found them in a street in Mecca,' said the storekeeper. 'I do not know what they are, you may have them for a small sum, for I do not know what to do with them.'

The calif, who liked old manuscripts for his library, even if he could not read them, bought the paper and the box and sent the storekeeper away. But he thought he would like to know what the scroll contained, and he asked the vizier if he did not know someone who could decipher it.

'Most gracious lord and master,' replied the latter, 'near the great mosque there lives a man called Selim the Learned, who understands all tongues. Have him sent for, he may be able to solve the mystery of this strange writing.'

The learned Selim was soon brought.

'Selim,' the calif said to him, 'you are said to be very learned. Have a look at this writing to see if you can read it. If you succeed, you will receive from me a new suit of clothes, and if you cannot you will receive twelve lashes and twenty-five on the soles of your feet, for in that case they call you Selim the Learned for nothing!'

Selim bowed and said, 'Thy will be done, my lord!'

He studied the writing for a long time; then suddenly he cried, 'It is Latin, my lord, or let me be hanged!'

'Tell us what is written there,' the calif ordered, 'if it is really Latin.'

Selim began translating, 'You who find this, praise Allah for his mercy! Whoever sniffs the powder in this box and says the word *Mutabor* can change into any animal he wishes and will understand the language of animals. If he wishes to return to human form he must bow

three times to the East and again say that word. He who is transformed must not laugh, or the magic word will disappear from his memory and he will remain an animal!'

When Selim the Learned translated this to the calif he was extremely pleased. He made the learned man swear to say nothing of the secret, gave him a fine suit of clothes, and let him go. But he said to the vizier, 'That is what I call a good buy, Mansor! How I am looking forward to being an animal! Come here early in the morning. Then we shall go together into the fields, sniff a little of the powder from the box, and secretly listen to what is said in the air and the water, the forest and the field!'

II

The next day, as soon as Calif Chasid had breakfasted and dressed, his grand vizier appeared, ready to go for a walk with him as he had ordered. The calif put the box with the magic powder into his girdle, and, ordering his entourage to stay behind, went off alone with the grand vizier. First they went through the calif's great gardens, but they could find no animal on which to practise their magic. In the end, the vizier suggested they should go down to the fishpond. They would be certain to find animals there — especially storks. These birds had always attracted his attention and admiration.

The calif agreed to the vizier's proposal and together they made for the fishpond. As soon as they arrived, they saw a stork walking gravely up and down in search of frogs, and occasionally chattering to himself. At the same time they saw another stork in the air.

'I'll wager my beard, my most gracious lord,' said the grand vizier, 'that those two are having

a fine talk together. Why don't we become storks?'

'A splendid idea!' exclaimed the calif. 'But we must first read the translation again to find out how to become human again. Yes, that's it! Three times bow to the East and say *Mutabor,* and then we shall be ourselves again. But we must not laugh, or we are lost!'

As he was speaking, the calif saw that the second stork was hovering above their heads before landing. Quickly he took the box from his girdle, sniffed at the powder, offered it to the grand vizier, who also took a sniff. Then they both called out *Mutabor!*

They changed almost at once. Their sturdy legs became long and slender. Their arms became wings; their necks grew up from their shoulders till they were a yard long, their beards disappeared, and their bodies were covered with soft feathers.

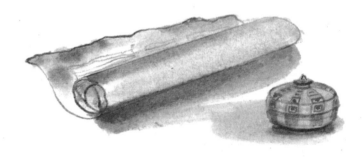

'What a nice beak you have, grand vizier!' said the calif when he had recovered from his wonder. 'By all that's holy, I have never seen anything like it!'

'I most humbly thank you,' replied the vizier, with a bow, 'but if I might be so bold, I may say that Your Highness is almost more handsome as a stork than as a calif. But let us try, if you agree, to listen, and find out if we really understand the language of the storks!'

Meanwhile, the second stork was now preening itself, and the two false storks went over to listen to his conversation with his friend.

'Good morning, Long Legs, out and about so early?'

'Indeed, I am, dear Claptrap! I've just landed for a little breakfast. Would you care for a piece of lizard or a frog's leg?'

'Thank you kindly, but I don't feel at all like it today. I have come to the meadow for quite another reason. Today I am to dance before my father's guests and I wish to practise here, where there's peace and quiet.'

And the young stork strolled off into the field with strange, prancing movements. The calif and Mansor watched her in wonder. But when she began posing on one leg and clapping her wings, they could contain themselves no longer — uncontrollable laughter burst from their beaks, and it was a long time before they were able to stop. The calif came to his senses first. 'A joke worth more than gold!' he cried. 'What a pity the stupid birds were frightened off by our laughter!'

Only then did it occur to the grand vizier that they had been warned never to laugh whilst in their stork shapes. He told the calif of his fears. 'Thunder on Mecca and Medina! It would be a very poor joke if we were to remain storks! Do you remember that stupid word? I can't think of it!'

'We must bow three times to the East and say the word "Mu — Mu — Mu — ..."'

They turned to face the East, and bowed until their beaks almost touched the ground. But, alas! They had quite forgotten the magic word, and though the calif bowed repeatedly, and his vizier called hopefully 'Mu — Mu —,' all memory of the word had vanished from their minds, and poor Chasid and his vizier were still storks, and so they remained!

III

The two bewitched men wandered sadly through the fields; they had no idea what to do. They could not get out of their stork skins, nor could they return to the town to reveal who they were, for who would believe a stork when he said he was the calif? And even if their story was believed — would the inhabitants of Baghdad want a stork for their calif?

So they wandered around for several days, eating what wild fruits they could find, though they could scarcely manage to eat them with their long beaks. They did not feel at all like eating lizards and frogs, being afraid that such stork delicacies would make them ill! The only pleasant thing about their state was being able to fly, so they often flew over the roofs of Baghdad to see what was happening.

Whenever they did so, they noticed great unrest and sadness in the streets. Then, towards

the end of their first week as storks, when they were sitting on the calif's palace, they saw a fine procession in the street; there was a sound of drums and pipes as a princely man in a scarlet and gold embroidered cloak appeared on a handsome horse, attended by fine servants. Half the inhabitants of Baghdad were following him. They were shouting, 'Long live Mizra, ruler of Baghdad!'

The two storks on the roof of the palace looked at each other and Calif Chasid said, 'Now do you see why I remain a stork, grand vizier? This Mizra is the son of my arch enemy, the powerful wizard Kashnur, who once swore vengeance on me. But I have not yet given up hope. Come with me, faithful companion in distress. Let us make a pilgrimage to the Prophet's tomb — perhaps the spell will be broken in that holy place.'

They took off from the roof of the palace and flew to Medina.

But their wings did not bear them too well, for the two storks were not skilled in flying.

'Oh, my lord,' sighed the grand vizier after some hours, 'if you please, I cannot fly much farther. You fly too fast for me. And as it is already evening, it would be wise to find refuge for the night.'

Chasid listened to his servant's plea, and since he could see a ruin down below in the valley, where they might find shelter, they flew down. Their home for the night must have once been a castle. Stately pillars reached out from the ruins, and the crumbling rooms suggested that it had been a fine house. Chasid and his companion walked the corridors looking for a dry place to shelter. Suddenly, Mansor stopped.

'Lord and master,' he whispered quietly, 'how foolish of a grand vizier and how much more of a stork to be afraid of ghosts! But I have an unpleasant feeling that something sighed and groaned just beside me here!'

The calif also stopped and quite clearly heard a low weeping, which he thought sounded very human. Filled with curiosity, he made as if to go towards the plaintive sound, but the grand vizier caught him by the wing with his beak and implored him not to enter any new, unknown danger. The calif, who had a bold heart, stork or no stork, pulled himself away, losing a few feathers, and hurried into the dark corridor. Soon he came to a door which was only half shut, and heard from within deep sighs and a low hooting. He pushed the door open with his beak, but stopped on the threshold in surprise. In a ruined chamber, lit only by a small window covered with bars, he saw, on the floor, a large owl.

Huge tears flowed from its round eyes, and it was moaning hoarsely through its crooked beak. When it saw the calif and the vizier, who had meanwhile crept up to them, the owl let out a loud hoot of joy. It wiped its tears gracefully with a blotchy brown wing and, to the great wonder of the two storks, called out in clear human speech, 'Welcome, storks! You are a good omen that I shall soon be set free!'

When the calif had recovered from the shock of hearing an owl speak, he bowed his long neck, took up a graceful pose on his slender legs, and said, 'Owl of the night! I might suppose from your words that I find in you a companion in distress. But, alas, your hopes of salvation through our help are in vain. When you hear our tale you yourself will see how helpless we are.'

The owl asked him to tell their story, and the calif began the tale which we already know.

IV

When the calif had finished his story, the owl thanked him and said, 'Now hear my story and you will see that I am as unfortunate as you. My father is a king in India, I am his hapless only daughter, and I am called Lusa. The same wizard Kashnur, who cast his spell over you, is the cause of my misfortune too. He came one day to my father to ask that I might marry his

son Mizra. But my father, who has a short temper, had him thrown out of the palace. The wretch was able to take on another guise. And one day, when I wished to take refreshment in my garden, he came dressed as a slave, and offered me a drink which changed me into this ugly form. I fainted in horror. He brought me here, and threatened me with these terrible words: "Here you shall stay, ugly and repulsive even to animals, until your death, or until someone willingly seeks your hand just as you are. This is my revenge on you and your proud father!"'

The princess sighed and continued, 'That was many months ago. And here I live, alone and sad within these walls, like a hermit, ugly and miserable. I cannot even see the beauties of nature, for I am blind in the daytime, and at night the pale light of the moon, shining on the walls, draws down a veil which hides every-thing from my eyes!'

The owl-princess finished her tale and again wiped her eyes with her wings. The telling of her own suffering had brought forth fresh tears!

As the princess was speaking, the calif had fallen into deep thought. 'Unless I am mistaken,' he said at last, 'there is a mysterious connection between our misfortunes; but where am I to find the key to the mystery?'

The owl-princess replied, 'My lord, I feel the same! For in my youth, a wise woman prophesied that a stork would bring me great good fortune.'

The calif was filled with wonder and asked how they could save her and save themselves.

'The wizard, who is the cause of our unhappiness,' she said, 'comes every month to these ruins. Not far from this chamber there is a hall. There, he feasts with many companions. I have often listened secretly. They tell each other of their shameful deeds; perhaps they may mention the magic word you have forgotten.'

'Dearest princess,' cried the calif, 'tell me when he will come and if you will conduct us to this hall?'

The princess was silent for a moment. Then she replied, 'Do not be angry with me, but I can only fulfil your wishes on one condition.'

'Speak, speak!' cried Chasid. 'Whatever you wish, I am ready to fulfil any condition.'

'I should like my freedom when you gain yours. But it can only be if one of you offers me marriage.'

The storks were somewhat taken aback by this suggestion, and the calif asked his faithful servant to step outside with him.

'Grand vizier,' he said when they were alone, 'it is a poor bargain; will you marry her?'

'How can I?' cried the grand vizier. 'My wife would scratch my eyes out when I came home! In any case I am old and you are still young and unmarried. No, it is up to you to accept the hand of a young and beautiful princess.'

'That is exactly the point,' sighed the stork-calif, and he bowed his head sadly. 'How do we know that she is young and beautiful? She is really a pig in a poke!'

They argued for some time. But when the calif saw that his vizier would rather stay a stork than marry an owl, he decided finally to fulfil the condition himself. The owl-princess was very pleased, and told them that the wizards were to come that very night.

The storks then followed her to the hall. They walked for a long time through a dark corridor until they saw a bright light through the crumbling wall. And soon they were able to see the whole hall through a chink in the wall. It was surrounded by pillars and splendidly decorated. In the middle of the hall was a round table laden with choice foods, and around this table were couches on which eight men reclined.

The storks saw that one of them was the storekeeper who had sold them the magic powder, and then they heard him begin to tell of his latest deeds. With great relish, he told the story of the calif and his vizier.

'What word did you give them?' asked one of the wizards.

'A very difficult, Latin one; it was Mutabor,' came the reply.

V

When the storks heard the magic word, they were almost beside themselves with joy. They ran so quickly to the gate of the ruin that the owl could scarcely keep up with them. Once there, the calif said, with emotion, 'Saviour of

my life and that of my friend, take me as your husband! It is a way of showing my gratitude for what you have done for us!'

And he turned to the East. Three times, both storks bowed their long necks towards the sun, which was just rising beyond the mountains, calling out 'Mutabor!'

In a trice they were humans again, and so great was their joy that master and servant fell into each other's arms, laughing and crying at the same time. But who can describe their wonder when they looked around!

Before them stood a beautiful, grandly dressed lady. With a smile she gave the calif her hand, 'Do you no longer recognize your owl?' she asked. And the calif was so taken with her beauty and grace that there and then he declared his love for her.

The three set off for Baghdad. In his robes the calif found not only the box with the magic powder but also his bag of money. Thus he was able to buy what they needed for their journey. The calif's arrival in Baghdad caused great amazement. The people had thought him dead. Now they were overjoyed to see their beloved ruler once more.

But the calif's subjects were now enraged with Mizra. They stormed the palace and captured the old wizard and his son.

The calif banished Mizra to the ruins where the princess had been held captive. Mizra's son was given the choice of death or sniffing the magic powder. He chose the powder. A good sniff and he was changed into a stork! The calif had him shut up in an iron cage and exhibited in his garden!

Calif Chasid lived happily and long with his beautiful wife. His merriest hours were always in the afternoon when the grand vizier visited him. They often spoke of their stork adventure, and the calif, when he was in a good mood, would pretend he was a stork again. He would walk gravely up and down the room on stiff legs, flapping his arms. This always greatly amused the calif's wife and children. But if the calif went on too long with his clapping and bowing, the vizier would threaten, with a smile, to tell his wife all that had gone on in the ruins of the old castle, and how he had once said that the owl-princess was a pig in a poke!

Old Sultan

There was a farmer who had a faithful dog called Sultan. Sultan grew old, and lost all his teeth, so that he could no longer hold anything firmly in his jaws.

One day the farmer was standing in front of the cottage with his wife, when he said, 'Tomorrow I shall shoot old Sultan, he's no use any more.'

His wife, who was sorry for the faithful creature, replied, 'Since he has served us so long, we might keep him now out of kindness.'

'Go on with you,' said the farmer, who was not to be persuaded, 'you are a silly woman. Sultan has not a single tooth in his head, and no thief is afraid of him. So it's time for him to go. And what if he has served us? Didn't he eat well on that account?'

The poor dog, who was sunning himself not far away, heard everything. And he was sad that tomorrow was to be his last day on earth. He had one good friend, and that was the wolf, and that evening he slipped off into the forest to see him, and bemoaned the fate which awaited him.

'Listen, old son,' said the wolf, 'don't lose heart. I'll help you out of this mess. I have an idea. Tomorrow morning early, your master and his wife will go haymaking, and they'll take the baby with them, since there'll be no one at home. When they're working, they always leave the baby behind a bush in the shade. Lie down beside him as if you wanted to guard him. Then I'll come out of the forest and carry the baby off. You jump up quickly and run after me, as if to get him back again. I'll let the child go, and you take him back to his parents. They'll think you've saved him, and they'll be so grateful, they're sure to do you no harm. On the contrary, they'll think so highly of you that they'll give you everything you need!'

The dog liked the idea. And, as it had been planned, so it was done. The father called out when he saw the wolf making off across the fields with his child. And when old Sultan brought the baby back again, he was overjoyed; he stroked the dog and said, 'I shan't touch a hair of your head; as long as you live you shall have a full bowl at our house.'

And he told his wife, 'Go home right away and cook old Sultan some gruel; he doesn't have to chew that. And bring the pillow from my own bed. He shall have it to sleep on.'

From then on Sultan was better off than he could ever have wished. Soon afterwards the wolf came to see him, pleased that everything had gone so well.

'But now, old son, you will turn a blind eye if

I steal the odd fat sheep from your master, won't you? It's hard for a fellow to make his living these days.'

'It's no use,' replied Sultan. 'I remain faithful to my master, and I couldn't allow it.'

The wolf didn't take the dog seriously. In the night he came and tried to carry off a sheep. But the farmer, whom Sultan had warned of the wolf's intention, lay in wait for him and fetched him a sharp blow across the back with his flail. The wolf was forced to run away, but he called to the dog, 'Just you wait, pal, you'll pay for this!'

In the morning the wolf sent the wild boar to challenge the dog to a duel in the forest. The only second old Sultan could find was a three-legged cat. And so they set off into the forest, the cat limping along on its three legs and thrusting its tail in the air with pain. The wolf and his second were waiting. But when they saw the pair of them approaching, they mistook the cat's tail for a sabre, which they supposed the wolf's opponent was to fight with. And the way the poor creature was limping along on three legs, looked to them as if he was picking up stones to throw at them.

The wolf and the boar took fright. The boar hid among the bushes, and the wolf climbed into a tree. The cat and the dog arrived at the appointed place, and were surprised to see no one. But the boar hadn't hidden himself properly, and his ears stuck out of the leaves. As the cat looked around, sharp-eyed, the boar drew his ears out of sight. The cat thought it was a mouse, leapt into the bushes, and snapped his jaws shut. The boar leapt out with a wild squeak, and scampered off, screeching, 'There's the one you want, up in the tree!'

The cat and the dog looked up and saw the wolf, who was so ashamed of his cowardice that he thought it wise to make it up with old Sultan and be his friend again!

Cleverkin
and the Giant

There was once a king in the Land of Roundaround, and among his servants he had a page-boy whom he loved above all things. The king was for ever granting him special favours and showering him with gifts.

This page-boy was called Cleverkin, and he was uncommonly sharp and well-mannered, performing every task the king gave him with great skill. All the other courtiers and servants envied him, and wished him harm, for while Cleverkin was always receiving rich rewards for his services, they were always being punished for their stupidity. And, to make matters worse, the king was always praising Cleverkin, and reproaching his other servants. No wonder they turned against him, and spent their free time plotting how they could make Cleverkin lose the king's favour.

One day, one of the courtiers scattered peas around the throne so that Cleverkin would fall and smash the glass sceptre which he always handed to the king! Another nailed melon skins to his soles, so that he would slip and spill the soup on the king's tunic. A third filled a tube with gnats and midges and other unpleasant insects, and blew them into the king's wig, which Cleverkin was dressing for him. But all their evil tricks to make the king turn against his page

thick, dark forests. His only companions apart from his wife, Thickfinger, were the lion, Fearcock, the bear, Honeybeard, the wolf, Woollychops, and the terrible dog, Harebane. These were his only servants. In his stable there lived his wonder horse, Fleetfoot.

Near to the Land of Roundaround lived a beautiful queen called Trippity, who had a daughter called Skippity. Now, the King of Roundaround, who would have liked to own all the lands around his kingdom, was most anxious to marry Queen Trippity. But she told him that many other kings had sought her hand, and that she would only marry the king who could travel the fastest. Accordingly, she sent out a proclamation that whoever was the first to come to her the following Monday at half-past nine in the morning, when she went to church, would win her hand in marriage, and the whole of her kingdom! When the King of Roundaround heard her conditions, he called together all his courtiers, and put to them this question, 'How am I to manage to be the first at church on Monday, and win Queen Trippity for my wife?'

And his courtiers replied, 'Sire, you must somehow take possession of Fleetfoot, the giant's horse. If you ride him, no one can catch you. And the very person to get you the horse is your page, Cleverkin, for does he not do everything perfectly?'

The wicked courtiers said this in the hope that the giant, Longbelly, would do away with Cleverkin. But the king had such faith in his page that he sent him off to capture the wonderful horse.

First of all, Cleverkin found out all he could about Longbelly's castle, then he took a handcart, on which he placed a beehive and a sack containing a cock, a hare and a sheep. Next he took a piece of rope and a large box of snuff and he hung on the cart a horsewhip — such as those used by fast messengers — fastened a good pair of spurs to his high boots, and set off on his journey.

Towards evening, he reached the top of the high mountain, passing through the thick forest, and there, before him, was the giant's castle. As night fell, Cleverkin could hear the gigantic snoring of Longbelly and his wife, Thickfinger;

were in vain. Cleverkin was so clever, thoughtful and careful that he discovered them in time, and so he carried out the royal commands perfectly.

When their plotting came to nothing, they decided to try something else, knowing that the king had an enemy he could not get rid of, and of whom he was constantly falling foul. This was a giant called Longbelly, and he lived on top of a huge mountain, in a fine castle amid his lion, Fearcock, his bear, Honeybeard, his wolf, Woollychops, and his dog, Harebane! Only the horse, Fleetfoot, was still wide awake, and was scraping his hooves against the stable-door.

As silent as a mouse, Cleverkin took his long piece of rope and ran it between two trees in front of the castle gates. In the middle, he placed the box of snuff. Then he took the beehive, and fastened it to a tree by the path, and went into the stable and untied Fleetfoot. Cleverkin climbed on his back with the sack containing the cock, the sheep and the hare, dug in his spurs, and clattered out of the castle.

But the wonder horse was able to talk, and cried out in a loud voice, 'Thickfinger, Longbelly, Honeybeard, Fearcock, Woollychops, Harebane — Cleverkin is riding off with Fleetfoot!'

Then he galloped on.

Longbelly and Thickfinger heard his shouts and woke up. They roused the lion, Fearcock, the bear, Honeybeard, the wolf, Woollychops, and the dog, Harebane, and they all rushed out of the castle to catch Cleverkin and the magic horse, Fleetfoot.

But in the dark, Longbelly and Thickfinger tripped over the rope which Cleverkin had stretched in front of the gates, and — CRASH! — they fell, head first into the box of snuff which Cleverkin had prepared for them.

They wiped their eyes and sneezed and sneezed, until Longbelly gasped, 'Bless you, Thickfinger!'

'Bless you!' said Thickfinger. And then Thickfinger said, 'Bless you, Longbelly!'

And 'Bless you!' said Longbelly, rubbing his stinging eyes.

In short, by the time they had rid themselves of the snuff in their eyes, and sneezed it out of their noses, Cleverkin was almost out of the forest!

The bear, Honeybeard, was quite close to them until he reached the beehive. But he couldn't resist the temptation to help himself to the honey and so he stopped. The bees swarmed out and stung him so fiercely that he ran, half-blinded, back to the castle!

When Cleverkin had left the forest behind him, he heard the lion, Fearcock, close behind

him. He took the cock from the sack. It flew up into a tree and began to crow. Then Fearcock grew scared and ran away.

When Cleverkin heard the wolf, Woollychops, close behind him, he let the sheep out of the sack, and the wolf jumped on it, and paid no more heed to chasing Cleverkin!

After a while, Cleverkin turned and saw that the dog, Harebane, was upon him and he let the hare out of the sack. The dog ran after it, forgetting everything else, and so Cleverkin and Fleetfoot soon arrived safely in the city.

The king thanked Cleverkin graciously for the wonder horse. But the envious courtiers were most disappointed that Cleverkin had escaped with his life!

On the Monday morning, the king mounted the wonder horse, and rode to Queen Trippity. The horse galloped so fast that the king was first at the church and had already enjoyed several dances at his wedding with Queen Trippity by the time the kings from the other neighbouring lands appeared! But when the King of Roundaround wanted to set off home with his new wife, his courtiers said to him, 'Your Majesty has the giant's horse, but how fine it would be if you also had his handsome clothes, which are the most exquisite ever seen. Cleverkin is so skilful that, if you order him, he will surely bring them to you!'

The king was at once filled with a great desire to have the giant's magnificent clothes, and Cleverkin was given this new task. As he prepared for his journey, the wicked courtiers were sure that he would not escape the giant a second time.

This time, Cleverkin took with him only several large sacks, and when he came to Longbelly's castle, he climbed a tree and waited until all in the castle had gone to sleep. When there was no longer any sound of movement, he climbed down from the tree, and it was then that he heard Thickfinger call out, 'Husband, my head is far too low; bring me a bundle of straw from outside.'

Cleverkin hid himself in the bundle of straw

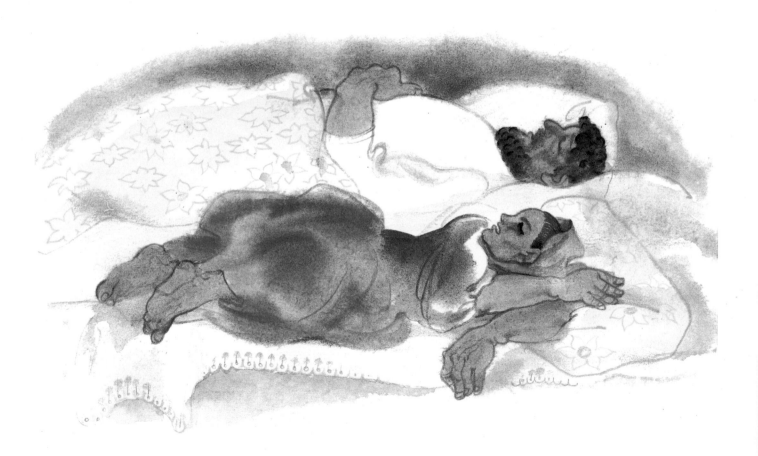

lying in front of the gate, and the giant carried him to his chamber without knowing it! He put the straw under his wife's pillow and lay down again.

As they fell asleep, Cleverkin stuck his arm out of the straw and tugged at Longbelly's hair. Then he tugged at Thickfinger's hair. Husband and wife awoke immediately and each thought the other was guilty of pulling their hair. They began to fight fiercely, and Cleverkin was soon able to climb out of the bundle of straw and hide under the bed.

At last they went back to sleep, tired out with their fighting, and all was quiet. Cleverkin put all the clothes he could find into his sack and tied it to the tail of the sleeping lion, Fearcock. Then he tied the wolf, Woollychops, the bear, Honeybeard, and the dog, Harebane, who were also sleeping there, to the giants' bed, and opened the door wide.

All went as he had planned. But, at the last moment, he decided to take the giants' fine counterpane as well. He pulled at it gently until he had got it off the bed. Then he wrapped it around himself and sat down on the sack of clothes which was tied to the lion's tail. The cold night wind blew in through the door, and chilled Thickfinger's feet, so that she called out, 'Husband, you have pulled away the cover and I am completely uncovered!'

The giant woke up, and said, 'No, no, it is I who am uncovered, Thickfinger; you have taken the blanket from me.'

And again they began to argue and fight. Cleverkin started to laugh at the way they were going on, and the giant and his wife realized that something was amiss. They began to shout, 'Thief, thief! Catch him, Woollychops! Catch him, Fearcock, Honeybeard and Harebane! Thief! Thief! Thief!'

The animals awoke and the lion, Fearcock, leapt forward. But since he was tied to the sack on which Cleverkin was sitting, the lion could not help but pull him along, and Cleverkin was out of the castle as if in a carriage! But he had only to crow several times like a cock — cock-a-doodle-doo, cock-a-doodle-doo! — to scare the lion out of his wits! The lion tried to struggle free as he made a dash for the city gates, for now they were just outside the city!

The rope held him back, and Cleverkin took out his knife and cut the rope. With nothing now to hold him back, the lion crashed, head first, into the huge gates and knocked out his brains!

As for the wolf, Woollychops, the bear, Honeybeard, and the dog, Harebane, which Cleverkin had tied to the giants' bed — they were doing their best to tug the wide bed through the narrow door of the bedchamber. They strained and pulled, and made rushes at the door, which so upset the two giants that in the end they tumbled out of bed. Giant Longbelly was, by now, in such a rage that he took a club and beat them until they were senseless, and of no use to anybody!

Cleverkin, meanwhile, had reached the palace safely. He handed the giants' magnificent clothes to the king, who was greatly pleased —

for no one had ever seen such strangely beautiful robes in their life.

There was a hunting tunic, made out of the feathers taken from birds not seen by ordinary men, and which was known to have magical powers. In the pocket of this coat was

a music-box which played bird songs. There were also fishing clothes sewn from the skins and scales of all the fishes in the seas, and there were Thickfinger's special gardening clothes, decorated with flowers and grasses. But most beautiful of all was the counterpane, made up of bat skins and decorated with stars which sparkled like diamonds.

The king's family was beside itself with wonder. They all embraced Cleverkin warmly, and his enemies almost exploded with rage when they saw that Cleverkin was more popular than ever! But they did not give up their wish to destroy the page-boy. They told the king that the only thing he now needed was the giants' castle!

And the king, who was like a small child and wanted anything that was better than what he had, ordered Cleverkin to win the giants' castle for him, promising he would be richly rewarded.

Cleverkin did not hesitate. He set off for Longbelly's castle for the third time. When he arrived the giant was not at home, and he heard a sound from within like the lowing of a calf. He looked through the window and saw the giantess, Thickfinger, chopping firewood, and clutching a small, very ugly baby giant, who was grinning and making a noise like a calf.

Cleverkin went inside and said, 'Good-day,

my tall, broad, fat woman! What, have you no grooms or maidservants here? You have such a handsome baby, you should give him all your attention! Where is your dear husband?'

'Alas,' said Thickfinger, 'my husband is visiting our relations to invite them to a feast which we are to hold. And I must do all the cooking myself. My husband has killed the wolf, the dog and the bear who used to help us, and the lion is also gone.'

'But how tiring it must be for you,' said Cleverkin. 'I should be glad to help you.'

And at once Thickfinger asked him to chop four pieces of wood with the axe. Cleverkin took the axe and said to the giantess, 'Hold the wood for me, please!'

When the giantess bent over, Cleverkin raised the axe up high, and — CRASH! — cut off the wicked Thickfinger's head, and — SMACK! — chopped off the baby's head too, and the two of them lay dead and motionless.

Then he dug a wide and deep pit in front of the castle and threw in the bodies of Thickfinger and the baby giant, and covered them with branches and leaves. After that, he lit lamps in all the rooms of the castle, and banged on a great copper cauldron with a wooden spoon. Then he took a metal funnel, blew it like a trumpet, and called out through it, 'Long live His Majesty, the King of Roundaround!'

That evening, the giant Longbelly returned home. He saw so many lights in his castle that he grew angry and rushed furiously towards the gate. As soon as he came to the pit covered with branches, he fell into it and was trapped. Cleverkin cut off his head and filled the pit with earth and stones.

Then Cleverkin took the key of the giants' castle and brought it to the King of Roundaround, who set off at once with Queen Trippity and her daughter, Princess Skippity, and the page to look the castle over. It took them a whole fortnight to inspect all the rooms, cellars and attics, chimney flues, fireplaces and stoves, lumber-rooms, larders, smoking-chambers and laundries!

Then the king asked Cleverkin how he might reward him for his faithful service and the page asked for the hand of Princess Skippity. She was happy to oblige and the wedding took place almost at once. Afterwards Cleverkin and Princess Skippity went to live in the giants' castle and you can visit them if you care to, any day in the week!

Prince Bajaja

A young king was forced to part with his wife and go off to the wars. Not long after his departure, the queen gave birth to twin sons. There was tremendous rejoicing throughout the land and messengers were sent at once to take the king the good news.

The boys were healthy, and grew up strong and sturdy. But the boy who was some minutes older was a far livelier child than the other, and as they grew older nothing changed in this respect. The elder was always in the courtyard, running, jumping, and riding his pony, which was the same age as himself. His brother would rather play on a soft carpet, at the feet of his mother, going out only when she took him into the garden! The queen soon grew less fond of her first born son, and made a pet of her younger boy.

The brothers were seven years old when the king returned from the wars. He held mother and sons to his breast with unspeakable joy.

'Which is the elder, and which the younger?' the father asked the queen.

Thinking that her husband asked so that he might know which was to be his heir, the queen passed off her favourite as the elder. Now, the king loved his children equally, but when they approached manhood, he proclaimed the younger brother heir to the throne because he did not know the truth of the matter. This so disappointed the true son and heir that he grew weary of his life at home, and longed to go out into the world. One day he was speaking of his pain and disappointment to his pony, and telling him he would rather leave home, when, to his surprise, the pony replied in a human voice, 'If you are not content at home, then go out into the world. But do not take a single step without your father's consent. And I advise you to take no one with you, and to ride no other mount but myself. It will be to your advantage.'

The prince was so astonished to hear his pony speak with a human voice, that it was some time before he asked how it came about. The pony answered him, 'Ask not! I will be your protector as long as you are willing to listen to me.'

The prince promised the pony to follow his counsel, and went to the castle to ask his father if he might go out into the world. At first, when he made his request, his father would not hear of it — though his mother agreed at once. But the prince was resolute, and in the end he

persuaded his father to agree. Servants, horses and a baggage train were made ready for the prince's journey. But he refused them all, and told his father, 'Why should I need so much baggage, so many horses, and servants, father? I will take just a little money, and ride away on my own pony. I wish to go out into the world alone.'

Again he had to plead with his father before he won his consent. But at last the pony stood saddled by the gates, and in the castle above the prince took leave of his parents and his brother. They all wept bitterly, and even his mother regretted that her son was going away. She gave him strict instructions to come home or to send news of himself in a year's time.

Some hours later, the pony had taken him far across the open fields beyond the city. You might think that a pony in his seventeenth year was past his best; but this pony had not grown old for he was no ordinary beast. He had a coat like velvet, legs like saplings, and he was as sprightly as a roe-deer. No wonder horse and rider made good speed, though the prince had

no idea where the pony was taking him. After a long time, a beautiful city came into view, and the pony left the track and trotted across the fields to a cliff, close to a pretty wood. When they arrived, the pony kicked the rock face, which opened up, and let them inside.

'Here you must leave me in this comfortable stable,' said the pony, 'and go to yonder city. When you meet the king, you must pretend to be dumb and wear a patch over one eye. The king will take you into his service, but take care not to give yourself away. If you need anything, no matter what it might be, come to the cliff, knock three times, and the rock will open up.'

The prince thought to himself, 'My pony is so wise, he must know what is best for me.' And he left the stable, and went to the royal city. Once there, he made signs that he should be taken to the king. The king, seeing that he was dumb, took pity on his tender years, and accepted him into his service. The youth, he could see, would be of great service to him. And so it turned out. Nothing escaped the dumb servant. He made himself useful in a thousand different ways. If the king needed a scribe, there was none more skilled than he. And the courtiers liked him, too. But because he never spoke, saying only 'bajaja' when addressed, this became his name.

The king had three daughters, each more beautiful than the next. The eldest was called Ruby, the second Amber, and the youngest Sapphire. In their company, Bajaja was always happy, and he was often free to spend the whole day with them if he wished. After all, he was dumb, with a face as brown as a berry, and a patch over one eye. How could the king imagine that any of the princesses would fall in love with him! But the princesses were fond of him, and insisted he went everywhere with them. He wove garlands for them, brought them wild flowers, spun golden threads, drew birds and all manner of flowers for them to embroider, and served them willingly. But most willingly of all he served the youngest, Sapphire, and all the things he did for her were done with the utmost care, so that her sisters would tease her about it. Sapphire was sweetness itself, and bore their taunts without anger.

Bajaja had not been long at court when, one morning, he entered the hall where the king was breakfasting, and saw him sitting there, mournful and silent. He made signs to ask what the matter was. The king looked at him sadly, and said, 'Dear boy, why do you ask? You do not know what misfortune threatens us, nor what a bitter three days awaits me?'

Bajaja shook his head and looked greatly concerned.

The king went on, 'Then I shall tell you, though you can do nothing. Years ago, three dragons settled here, one nine-headed, the second eighteen-headed, and the third twenty-seven-headed! Such misfortune came to

my city at that time that many died of grief, and my heart all but broke. The people hid themselves away, fearful for their lives. Soon there were no cattle left, for all had to be given to the monsters to keep them from the city. But they devoured many of my subjects, nonetheless. Since I could no longer witness such terrible happenings, I had some magicians brought to court to help me rid my land of the monsters. But, alas, they told me I must pledge them my three daughters, when they were in the flower of their youth. I thought that if I could persuade the monsters to leave, I would be safe in promising them my daughters. The queen died of grief at the very idea of her children being devoured, but my daughters knew nothing of my promise until now. The dragons went away, and we have not heard of them all these years. But last night a shepherd came running to the city, beside himself with fear, crying that the dragons had returned to the same rock where they used to dwell. Hapless father that I am, I must tomorrow sacrifice the first of my children for my country's sake; the day after the second; and on the third day, my youngest. Then shall I be beggar indeed!'

Thus the unhappy king bemoaned his fate and tore his hair. Greatly upset, Bajaja went to the princesses, but they were a sorry sight. Dressed in black, faces like marble, all three of them sat close together, weeping inconsolably over their cruel fate.

Bajaja began to comfort them, making signs that he believed a deliverer would come. But

the poor princesses only continued to weep.
Indeed, throughout the whole city came the
sound of weeping and moaning, for everyone
loved the royal family.

Bajaja hurried away, secretly, from the city.
He crossed the fields to the cliff where his pony
was stabled. When he knocked three times, the
cliff-face opened and he went inside. He stroked
the pony's shiny mane, kissed his white blaze,
and said, 'Dear pony, I have come for your
advice, and, if you can help me, I shall be happy
forever!'

And he began to tell the pony all that had
passed in the castle.

'This I know already,' replied the pony. 'And
that is why I brought you here, so that you
might help the princesses. Come back early
tomorrow morning, and I will tell you what to
do!'

Bajaja ran back to the castle, full of hope. He
remained all day in the princesses' rooms, and
thought up all manner of things to relieve their
sorrow, but with little success.

The next morning it was not yet light when
he reached the cliff. The pony greeted him, and
said, 'Now, raise the stone beneath my stall, and
take out what you find there!'

Bajaja obeyed with a will, and, from the hole
which the stone revealed, he drew out a large

chest. The pony told him to open it, and, when he had done so he took out three magnificent suits of clothes, a sword and a jewelled bridle. One suit of clothes was red, embroidered with silver and diamonds, and the breast was of shining steel — with a red and white crest. The second suit was all white, embroidered with gold, and the armour and helmet were of gold; the crest was white. The third suit was light blue, richly embroidered with silver, diamonds and pearls; the crest was blue and white. Each suit had a sword in a scabbard, gleaming with precious stones.

'These three suits are yours. You must wear the red one first,' said the pony.

Bajaja dressed himself, buckled on the sword, and threw the bridle over the pony's head.

'Do not be afraid. And do not dismount. Rely on your trusty sword!' said the pony, as they left the stable.

Meanwhile, at the castle, there was much sobbing as the king's subjects lined up to accompany the unfortunate Princess Ruby to her fate. When they were not far from the dragons' rock, the princess fell to the ground in a faint.

At that moment, a horse galloped into view, bearing a knight with a red and white crest. When he reached the rock, he shouted to the crowd to take the princess with them, and leave him to face the dreaded dragon.

You can imagine the relief with which they obeyed. But the princess, who had by now recovered her senses, did not want to leave, for she longed to know the fate of the brave knight who had ridden to her rescue.

Scarcely had the people retreated to a safe distance when the rock shuddered and opened, and the nine-headed dragon appeared. Bajaja, astride his pony, advanced and drew his sword. With a single stroke, he cut off three heads of the monster. The dragon quivered, spat fire, and threw itself from side to side, spraying poison all about it. But the prince, undaunted, continued to fight — until he had cut off all the dragon's nine heads.

When the dragon had breathed its last, the prince turned about and rode off towards the cliff. Princess Ruby longed to know the name of the valiant knight. But she was forced to return to the castle without finding out anything about him.

The king's joy cannot be described when he saw his daughter alive. And his two other daughters began to hope that they, too, might be delivered.

Bajaja appeared later that day, and made signs as if to say that the other two princesses

would be saved — though Princess Amber remained pale and depressed, for she knew that she must face the dragon the very next day.

When Princess Amber was led forth in the morning, she prayed that the brave knight would come to her rescue.

And so it was to be — though, this time, the knight was clad all in white. Before long he had engaged the eighteen-headed dragon in combat, and the battle was long and furious. But at length, his task was done. The dragon lay dead, and the knight rode away as he had done on the previous day. The princess returned to the castle, disappointed that she could not show her gratitude to her knight.

'Sisters,' said Sapphire, when they were together. 'When my turn comes tomorrow, I shall kneel before him, if he saves me, and beseech him to return to the castle with me!'

As she spoke, Sapphire saw Bajaja smile, and she asked him the reason why he did so. But their servant only made signs that he, too, looked forward to seeing such a brave knight!

The next day, the lovely Princess Sapphire was led out to the rock. And this time the king himself went with her. The poor girl's heart nearly failed her when she thought that, should her deliverer fail to come, she would be given to the dragon. But at that moment, a joyous cry went up as the knight appeared. Just as it had been with the first two dragons, so it was with the third — though it was a wonder that both he and his pony did not collapse with weariness.

Then the king and Sapphire came forward, and begged the knight to go with them to the castle. He seemed very reluctant to do this, and Sapphire knelt before him and, grasping his sleeve, beseeched him so earnestly, so sweetly, to accompany them that the knight almost agreed. His pony, however, carried him off, but the knight was seen no more.

Sapphire returned home with her father, sad that she could not reward her deliverer. And her sisters and those in the castle deeply regretted that they would not meet the valiant knight.

The dreaded dragons were destroyed. But it was not long before a new tribulation came upon the king. One day, he received a declaration of war from a neighbouring king. This caused him great concern, for he knew that this neighbour was much stronger. He wrote at once to summon the barons and lords to the royal court for a council of war, and soon there was a vast array of noblemen in attendance at the castle. The king told them of the challenge from his royal neighbour and asked for their help, offering his daughters to the bravest leaders, as a reward for their services. For such a prize, who would have hesitated?

The lords certainly did not! They promised to return with their armies on an appointed day. Now all was made ready for war, and the king himself promised to lead his army into battle.

On the appointed day, the nobles gathered, and a great feast was held; then the king took leave of his weeping daughters, bidding Bajaja watch over them and his affairs, and, to the sound of trumpets and pipes, they took to the field.

Bajaja obeyed the king's orders and watched over his household, but he did not forget to create all manner of diversions for the princesses, so that they should not be too sad.

One morning, however, he announced that he did not feel well and, ignoring the physicians who wished to help him, said he would go himself to find a herb which would cure him more quickly than all their medicines. The princesses let him go. But Bajaja did not go looking for a herb. He knew that the only cure for his illness lay in the bright eyes of the beautiful Princess Sapphire.

He returned to the stable to ask advice from his pony. Should he help the king in the war, or remain in the castle? The pony told him to put on the white armour, buckle on his sword and ride him into battle, and Bajaja kissed him in gratitude.

As the war progressed, the king's army grew weaker, unable to resist the great strength of the enemy. One final battle would decide the issue. The king sent messengers to his daughters with orders as to what they should do if the battle were lost. On the morning of the final great battle, the trumpets were sounded, the soldiers drew their swords and rushed into the fray, and the noise of the fighting was heard for miles around.

Suddenly, there appeared amidst the foe
a stranger in white garments, with a golden
helmet and white crest. He sat on a small horse,
and held in his hand a huge sword, with which
he smote the enemy so fiercely that they began
to think some evil spirit was attacking them.
Thus encouraged, the king's army rushed to the
hero's side, and soon the enemy was in retreat.
When the white knight slew their leader, they
lost heart and fled the battlefield.

The white knight was slightly wounded in the
leg, so that blood stained his white garments,
and when the king saw this, he leapt from his
horse, tore strips from his cloak, and himself
bound the wound, begging the knight to go to
his tent. But though the knight thanked him, he
finally spurred on his horse and was gone. The
king almost wept with grief that the brave
knight should ride away from him a fourth time
— when he owed him so much. But he soon
forgot his grief when he rode home, laden with
the spoils of war. And soon all manner of
celebrations and merry-making were put in
hand at the castle.

'Well, my steward,' the king said, when he saw
Bajaja again, 'how have you kept our house
while I have been away?'

Bajaja indicated that he had done so well, but
the princesses began to laugh, and Sapphire
said, 'Father, I must accuse your steward of
disobedience. When he became ill, our physician
wished to give him a potion, but he said that he
would go himself and find a healing herb. He

returned only recently, quite lame, and weaker
than before.'

The king turned to Bajaja, but the latter only
smiled, and left the room, trying to disguise his
limp.

When the princesses heard that the brave
knight had again come to the rescue, they were
loath to marry the noble leaders, thinking that
the knight might at last come and claim one of
them. But they did not even know if he were
handsome, for they had never seen his face,
though each of them pictured him looking like
an angel behind his helmet.

The king was at a loss as to how to reward
his nobles, for surely the knight had first claim
on his daughters! At last, he thought of
a solution which would find favour with them.

'Dear friends!' he said to his barons, 'I have
made certain promises to you regarding my
three daughters. But you have all served me
faithfully, though none more so than the white
knight. Still — I have decided that if you will
stand in a line, each of my daughters will throw

a golden apple from the balcony. Whosoever the apple rolls to, shall be that princess's husband. Do you agree to this?'

All agreed, and the king told the princesses his plan. They too agreed, so as not to shame their father. They dressed themselves splendidly; each took a golden apple in her hand, and went onto the balcony, beneath which the lords and barons were standing in line. Among the crowd of onlookers, close to the barons, stood Bajaja.

First, Princess Ruby threw her apple; it rolled and rolled, right to the feet of the dumb Bajaja. But Bajaja stepped quickly aside, and it rolled on, to stop at a certain handsome baron, who picked it up joyfully and stepped forward. Then Amber threw her apple; again it rolled towards Bajaja's feet, but again he stepped aside so skilfully that it seemed to roll straight to another well-favoured lord, who picked it up and gazed longingly towards the balcony at his lovely bride-to-be.

Sapphire threw her apple, last of all. This time Bajaja stood his ground when it came to him. He picked it up with great joy, ran to the balcony, knelt before the princess, and kissed her hand. But she drew away from him, and fled to her rooms, weeping bitterly that she should have to marry a dumb servant.

The king was angry, the nobles grumbled, but there was no going back. A feast followed, and after it there was a jousting contest, at which one of the princesses was to hand out the prizes. During the banquet, Sapphire sat as if stunned and did not say a word; her bridegroom, Bajaja, was nowhere to be seen, and the king thought perhaps he had run off in anger. All were sorry for the poor girl, and, wishing to raise her spirits, asked her to present the prizes at the games which followed.

Finally, Sapphire agreed. The nobles were already around the rail, the jousters were already tilting at each other and scoring their victories, when the herald announced that a knight on a pony was outside, and asking to be admitted to the tournament. The king signalled his assent. And into the lists rode a knight in blue and silver, a blue and white crest on his helmet. The three princesses cried out when they recognized their deliverer.

The knight bowed to the ladies, and began to joust with the barons; he defeated one after the other, and was left the victor; then Sapphire stepped down to him, carrying the victor's golden sash. The knight dismounted and fell on his knees before her, and she hung the sash, which she herself had embroidered, around his neck. Her hands were shaking and her cheeks

were afire as she heard the knight whisper, 'Beautiful bride, today I shall again deliver you!'

The king and his two daughters came down to bid the knight tarry, saying that now they could reward him for all he had done. But he quickly kissed Sapphire's hand, and was gone in a trice. She thought of the words he had whispered to her, and she blushed again, choosing to sit alone in her room rather than join the guests in feasting and dancing in the Great Hall, below.

The moon rose, and the pony carried his master from the cliff for the last time. When they came to the castle, Bajaja leapt down and kissed the pony's nose, whereafter it vanished! Our knight was loath to lose such a faithful friend, but a sweeter companion was to take his place.

Sapphire sat lost in thought, and certain that the knight would not come. As she dreamed of him, her maid opened the door, and said that Bajaja wished to speak to her. She did not answer. Then the knight of her dreams appeared and took her hand.

'Are you angry with your bridegroom that you hide yourself from him?' the knight asked tenderly.

'Why do you ask? You are not my bridegroom,' whispered Sapphire. 'I must marry Bajaja!'

The knight lifted his golden helmet, saying, 'I am both Bajaja and your deliverer! As your servant — did I not weave garlands for you, and serve you in countless ways? Then came the time when I saved you and your sisters from the dreaded dragons, and helped your father to win the war. I am your true bridegroom.'

You may be sure that Sapphire did not question the knight — for he stifled her words by gently kissing her and telling her of his love and devotion!

Some time later, the doors of the great banqueting hall burst open, and in walked Princess Sapphire with the white knight, whom she presented to her father.

'He is my true bridegroom!' she cried. 'He is both Bajaja and our brave deliverer!'

When the king heard the whole story, he was overjoyed, and ordered that the feasting should begin all over again, and the three beautiful princesses danced with their bridegrooms until dawn was breaking.

After the wedding, Bajaja took Sapphire to visit his parents. His brother had died, and they were sad and lonely. But when they saw him and his royal bride, they were filled with happiness again, for they had long given him up for dead.

The next day, his father proclaimed him the rightful king, and he lived the rest of his life in great happiness, growing to love his gentle Sapphire more and more!

The Twelve Months

There was once a mother who had two daughters: one was her own, the other a stepdaughter. She loved her own daughter dearly, but hated her stepdaughter, simply because Marie was more beautiful than Holena.

Now, Marie did not know how beautiful she was; so she had no idea why her stepmother frowned whenever she looked at her. She thought to herself that she must have somehow failed to please her!

Holena spent all her time dressing up, lounging about the parlour, slouching up and down the yard, or strutting along the street. Marie spent her time cleaning the whole house, dusting, cooking, washing, sewing, spinning, weaving. She mowed the grass, milked the cow, and did all there was to do, but her stepmother only cursed and scolded her. It was all for nothing that she tried to please her. Day by day,

things grew worse and worse, and Marie grew lovelier all the time, whilst Holena grew uglier.

The mother began to think to herself: 'Why should I keep such a pretty stepdaughter at home? When the young men come courting, they will all fall in love with Marie, and will not want Holena.' She spoke of this to Holena, and they came up with a scheme which was really very wicked.

One day — it was just after the New Year, and bitterly cold — Holena said that she must have some violets.

'Marie, go into the forest and pick me a bunch of violets; I want to put them in my belt, so that I may smell them.'

'Gracious me, dear sister, what are you thinking of? Whoever heard of violets growing under the snow?' exclaimed poor Marie.

'You slut, you scallywag, how dare you

123

answer back when I tell you to do something,' Holena shouted at her. 'Be off with you, and if you do not bring violets from the forest, I will kill you!' she threatened.

Then the stepmother pushed Marie out of the house, slammed the door shut, and shot the bolt.

Weeping, the poor girl set off into the forest. The snow was piled high all around, and no human footprint was to be seen. Marie wandered for a long time, quite lost. She was hungry, and shivered with cold. She wept and wept. When she saw a light in the distance, she went towards its glow and came to the top of a hill. A great fire was burning there, and around it stood twelve boulders, on each of which sat a man. Three had white beards, three were younger, three still younger, the remaining three were the youngest of all. They sat quietly, without speaking, gazing fixedly into the fire. The twelve men were the twelve Months!

Great January sat on the largest and tallest boulder. His hair and beard were as white as snow, and in his hand he held a club.

Marie was startled, and stood stock still. Then she took courage, came closer, and said, 'Good people, allow me to warm myself, for I am shivering with cold.'

Great January nodded his head, and asked her, 'Why have you come, child; what are you looking for?'

'I am looking for violets,' answered Marie.

'This is no time to find violets: the snow is here,' said Great January.

'Indeed I know; but my sister Holena and my stepmother told me to bring violets from the forest. If I do not bring them they will kill me. I beg of you, good people, tell me where I can pick them.'

At that Great January rose, went across to the youngest Month, placed the club in his hand, and said, 'Brother March, sit in my place!'

The Month of March sat on the tallest boulder, and waved the club over the fire. The fire burst into flame, the snow began to melt, the trees to bud, the grass grew green beneath the beech trees, and flower-buds pushed up through the grass. In the bushes, hidden beneath the leaves, violets began to flower. And before Marie knew what was happening, the ground was covered with a blue carpet.

'Pick them quickly, Marie, quickly!' ordered the young March.

Marie picked them with a will, and soon had a large bunch. Then she thanked the Months kindly, and hurried home.

Holena was amazed, and the stepmother was amazed, to see her coming with violets, and when they opened the door, the scent of the flowers filled the house.

'Where did you pick them?' asked Holena angrily.

'High in the forest, among the bushes, and there are plenty of them,' answered Marie softly.

Holena tore the bouquet from her hand, shoved it into her belt, and bent to sniff at it, but she did not thank her sister for the gift.

The next day Holena sat by the stove, and she had a fancy for some strawberries.

'Marie, go and bring me strawberries from the forest!'

'Gracious me, dear sister, what are you thinking of! Who ever heard of strawberries growing under the snow!' said Marie.

'You slut, you scallywag, what right have you to answer back when I tell you to do something? Go at once, and if you do not bring me strawberries, I will kill you!' threatened Holena.

Then the stepmother pushed her out of the door, banged it shut, and shot the bolt.

Weeping, the girl went off into the forest. The snow was piled all around, and there was no human footprint to be seen. She lost her way, and was lost for a long time. She was hungry and shivered with cold. Then, once again she saw a light in the distance. She went towards its glow, and again came to the fire. The twelve men — the twelve Months — were there, seated around the fire. Great January, white-haired and bearded, sat at the head with the club in his hand.

'Good people, allow me to warm myself, I am frozen through,' Marie begged them.

Great January nodded, and asked her, 'Why have you come again, child; what are you looking for?'

'I have come to look for strawberries,' said the girl.

'But strawberries do not grow in winter under the snow,' said Great January.

'Indeed I know,' said the sad Marie, 'but my sister, Holena, and my stepmother told me to pick strawberries for them; if I do not bring them they will kill me. I beg of you, good

people, tell me where I might find them.'

Great January stood up, went to the Month sitting opposite him, gave him the club, and said, 'Brother July, sit in my place!'

The Month of July sat on the tallest boulder and waved the club over the fire. Flames shot up three times as high as before. The snow quickly melted, the trees burst into leaf, the birds twittered and sang all around, everything was in flower: it was summer! Tiny white stars appeared beneath the bushes, and changed, before Marie's eyes, into strawberries, which quickly ripened. There were so many that it was as if the ground had been spattered with blood.

'Gather them quickly, Marie, quickly!' ordered July.

Marie gathered the strawberries gladly, and almost filled her apron. She thanked the Months kindly and hurried home.

Holena was amazed and the stepmother was amazed, when they saw her coming with her apron full of fruit. When she entered — the whole house was filled with the scent of strawberries.

'Where did you pick them?' asked Holena angrily.

And Marie said softly, 'They grow high up in the hills, and there are plenty of them.'

Holena took the strawberries and ate her fill; the stepmother, too, ate all she could, but they did not say to Marie: 'take one.'

Holena grew even more demanding.

'Marie, go into the forest and bring me red apples!' she ordered one day.

'Gracious me, dear sister, what are you thinking of! Who ever heard of apples ripening in winter?'

'You slut, you scallywag, how dare you answer back? Go into the forest, and if you do not bring me red apples, I will kill you!' threatened Holena.

Then the stepmother pushed Marie out of the door, banged it, and shot the bolt.

Weeping, the girl made off into the forest. The snow lay all around, with never a human footprint to be seen. She wandered, lost, for many hours. She was hungry, and shivering with cold. Once again she saw the light in the distance, and made towards its glow. The twelve men — the twelve Months — were sitting, as usual, around the fire, as if fixed to the spot, and Great January, white and bearded, sat at the head with the club in his hand.

'Good people, let me warm myself at your fire; I am frozen to the bone,' Marie pleaded.

Great January nodded his head, and asked, 'And why have you come again, child?'

'I have come for red apples,' answered the girl.

'It is winter, and red apples do not ripen in winter,' said Great January.

'Indeed I know,' answered Marie sadly. 'But Holena and my stepmother threatened to kill me if I did not bring them red apples from the forest. I beg of you, good people, help me one more time.'

And Great January stood up, went to one of the older Months, gave him the club and said, 'Brother October, sit in my place!'

The Month of October sat on the tallest boulder, and waved the club over the fire. The flames leapt up, and the snow disappeared. But the leaves on the trees did not spread, only grew yellow and brown and began to fall. It was autumn. Marie saw no spring flowers this time, nor was she looking for them. She gazed only at

the trees. And behold, there was an apple tree, and high on its branches were red apples!

'Shake them down, Marie, quickly!' called October.

Marie shook the tree, and an apple fell; she shook it again, and another red apple dropped to the ground.

'Gather them up, Marie, gather them quickly and hurry home!' called October.

Holena was amazed, the stepmother was amazed, when Marie returned home. They opened the door, and she gave them the two apples.

'Where did you pick them?' asked Holena.

'They grow high in the forest, and there are more of them there!' said Marie.

As soon as Holena heard that there were plenty of apples left, she snapped at her sister, 'You slut, you scallywag, why did you not bring more! Or have you eaten them on the way?'

'No, dear sister, I did not eat a single one. When I shook the tree the first time, one apple fell; when I shook it a second time, a second fell, and they did not let me shake any more. They shouted at me to go home,' said Marie.

'The devil take you!' Holena scolded her, and made as if to strike her. And the stepmother took a stick to her so that she ran into the kitchen and hid behind the stove.

The ungrateful Holena gave up scolding her, and began to eat one of the apples, giving her mother the other. They had never before eaten such sweet apples, and they longed to have more.

'Mother, give me my fur, I shall go into the forest myself! The slut will only eat them if we send her again. But I shall find the place, no matter where it is, and shake down all the apples. If there are so many, even the devil himself won't stop me!'

Thus spoke Holena, and in vain did her mother try to dissuade her. She put on her fur, wound a scarf around her head, wrapped herself up, and set off into the forest. Her mother watched her go from the doorway, wringing her hands at her daughter's folly.

Holena went into the forest. The snow was piled up all around, and not a trace of a human footprint was to be seen. She got lost and wandered for a long time, but greed for the apples drove her on and on. Suddenly she saw a light in the distance. She went towards it, and came to the fire around which the twelve men — twelve Months — were sitting. But she neither bowed to them nor asked their leave to join them. She just held her hands out towards the fire as though it had been lit just for her.

'Why have you come; what are you looking for?' growled Great January.

'Who are you to ask, you old fool! It is none of your business whence and where I go!' Holena snapped back, and she went off into the forest, as though the apples were waiting there for her.

Great January furrowed his brow and waved his club above his head. In a flash the skies clouded over, the fire went out, thick snow began to fall, and a cold wind got up. Holena could not see a step in front of her, and tumbled into ever deeper drifts. Her limbs froze, her knees gave way beneath her; and she sank into deep snow.

The mother waited for Holena, peering out of the window, and frequently going outside the door to look for her. Hour after hour went by, but there was no sign of her.

'Does she refuse to leave the apples, or what? I must go and see!' said the woman to herself, and she put on her fur, wrapped herself in a blanket, and hurried off after her daughter.

The snow fell thicker and thicker, the wind blew ever colder, the drifts rose up like walls. The woman waded through them, calling her daughter, but not a sound was to be heard. She wandered she knew not where, and she began to cry out. Her limbs grew stiff, her knees gave way beneath her, and she fell into the snow.

At home Marie cooked lunch, fed and milked the cow, but neither Holena nor her stepmother came.

'Why are they so long?' Marie asked herself anxiously, as she sat down to her spinning wheel.

She sat far into the night, her spindle long since full; but there was neither sight nor sound of either Holena or her stepmother.

'Alas, what has become of them?' cried the kind-hearted girl, looking anxiously out of the window.

There was not a soul to be seen, only the twinkling of the stars in the dark sky. It was so cold that the ground sparkled, and the thatches crackled with the frost. Sadly, she shut the window. The next morning she had breakfast ready for them, then lunch, but neither Holena nor her stepmother returned. Both had perished in the forest!

Now, Marie had the cottage, the cow, the garden, the fields and the meadows around the house all to herself. And when spring came, she found a husband to share them — a handsome young fellow who loved her dearly — and they lived together happily for many a long year.

Stupid Vardiello

In a certain village there lived a widow who had a son named Vardiello. Though he was the most stupid fellow in the whole village, she loved him dearly, and took care of him as if he were the most beautiful and the cleverest creature in the world.

The widow had a broody hen and was hoping that it would hatch a fine brood of chickens, from which she would make a good profit. And when one day she went off to town on some business, she said to her son, 'Come here, mother's little pet, keep an eye on the broody hen, and if she leaves the nest to peck around, drive her back onto it, or the eggs will get cold,

and you will have neither eggs nor chickens.'

'Leave it to me,' answered Vardiello, 'I am not stupid.'

'And, son,' his mother added, 'here, in the cupboard, is a bowl of poison. Whatever you do, do not take the bowl and drink from it, for it would be the end of you.'

'I wouldn't think of it,' replied Vardiello, 'I shall not drink any poison. But it is well you told me of it, for I should certainly have drunk from the bowl to quench my thirst.'

As soon as his mother had gone, Vardiello, to keep himself busy, went into the garden to dig a pit and cover it with branches and earth so that his friends would fall into it! When he was well into his work, he noticed that the broody hen had left the nest and was going into the parlour. Right away, he began to shout, 'Shoo, shoo, get back, get away from there!'

But the broody hen did not go back, and Vardiello, seeing that the hen was as stubborn as a mule, for he had shouted 'shoo, shoo' until he was breathless, began to stamp his feet. When that too did no good, he threw his cap at her, but also to no avail, so in the end he threw the noodle roller at her, hit her, and injured her so gravely that she was soon lying on her back, her feet in the air!

Now he had done it! And Vardiello pondered how to put the damage right again. So, making a virtue of necessity, he sat on the nest himself to prevent the eggs from getting cold, but when he sat on them he smashed them to pulp. When he saw that he had again made a mess of things, he thought of beating his head against the wall. But since all worry passes in time, and since his stomach was rumbling, he decided to roast the hen and assuage his hunger instead. So he took the hen, plucked it, stuck it on the spit, made a big fire, and began to roast it.

When it was almost done, he laid a white napkin on an old trunk, and, so that all might be ready in time, took a jug and went into the cellar to draw some wine from the cask. But when he was in the middle of this, he heard a noise, a din, a clatter, as though horses were galloping through the house. Quite startled, he turned and saw that a cat, which had grabbed the hen, spit and all, was being chased by a second cat, which was making a terrible mewing in an effort to get its share.

Vardiello leapt at the cat like an angry lion, to prevent further damage, and in his haste forgot to put the bung back in the cask. After chasing both cats hither and thither for quite some time he managed to get the hen back. In the meantime all the wine from the cask had run out on the floor. When he went back to the cellar and saw what had happened, he was petrified!

Common sense told him to put right the damage. His mother must not see such a flood in the cellar, and he grabbed a full sack of flour and tipped it over the spilt wine.

But when he counted up on his fingers all the things he had to account for, he decided that he had made a real fool of himself! He would certainly have to answer to his mother for the damage. Well, she would not find him alive!

So he took the bowl of pickled nuts, which his mother had said were poison, out of the cupboard, and did not put it down until he had emptied it. Then he climbed up on the stove.

Meanwhile his mother returned home. After knocking for a long time, and getting no reply, she kicked the door open and went into the parlour. Then she began calling loudly to her son. When he did not reply, she decided that some misfortune must have befallen him, and called out still louder, 'Vardiello, Vardiello, are you deaf, that you do not hear me? Are your legs tied that you do not come running? Where are you, you street-urchin? Where have you got to, you scoundrel? I should have thrown you in the well when you were born.'

Vardiello heard her calling, and finally answered in a plaintive voice, 'Here I am, mother, on the stove! You will never see me again!'

'Why not?' called out the unhappy mother.

'Because I have poisoned myself,' her son answered.

'Alas, and why did you do it? And who gave you poison?'

Vardiello told her in detail all the damage he had managed to do, and that he had drunk all the poison from the bowl in the cupboard, because he did not want to stay in the world, since he was a prey to such cruel misfortune!

His mother heaved a sigh of relief. But what was she to do in order to talk her son out of such melancholy thoughts? And since she loved him fondly, she gave him some more preserved fruit to drive from his head the fear of the pickled nuts, for she knew they were not poisonous at all, but actually good for the stomach. Then she consoled him with kind words, and showered him with a thousand compliments, until he took notice and came down from the stove. In order to restore him completely, she gave him a roll of fine linen to take and sell, and said he must not deal with talkative customers.

'Very well, I shall do as you say,' said Vardiello. 'You will be satisfied with me this time.'

Vardiello took the linen, and set off to the town with it. He walked about the streets and squares with his wares, crying, 'Linen, linen for sale!' But if anyone came up to ask what the linen was like, he said at once, 'We shall strike no bargain.' And if a woman asked how much the linen was, he called her a chatterbox, and said she talked so much.

Finally, in front of a house which was empty

because it was haunted, he saw an alabaster statue. He stopped in front of it and looked at it for a while. When he saw no one enter or leave the house, he addressed the statue, 'Tell me, my friend, does anyone live in this house?'

And since the statue said nothing, he considered him a man of few words, and at once made him an offer, 'Do you wish to buy this linen? You can have it cheap.'

But the statue remained silent, and Vardiello said, 'Upon my soul, you are the very one I am looking for. Take the linen: have a good look at it, and give me what you think it is worth. I shall come for the money tomorrow.'

Then he laid the linen beside the statue and went home. The first passer-by who passed the house and saw the roll of linen lying by the statue picked it up and took it home.

When Vardiello returned to his mother without the linen and told her what he had done with it, the poor woman thought her heart would break with grief. She began to scold him, 'When will you come to your senses? Don't you see what you have done? But this is, above all, my fault, for I have been too kind to you. I should have beaten you from the first. However, I shall not put up with it much longer. One of these days I shall give you a sound beating for your stupidity!'

But Vardiello kept saying, 'Oh, no, mother, everything will be all right, mother, you'll see! You will get a fine pile of gold pieces for your linen. Do you really think I am so stupid? You'll see tomorrow.'

As soon as dawn broke, Vardiello hurried off into town, went to the house where the statue stood, and addressed it, 'Good day, sir. You have, by now, had a good look at the linen, and you will pay me what you owe!'

But the statue said nothing. And when he repeated his demand, and there was still no answer, Vardiello grabbed a stone and struck it with all his strength, so that it broke open. This was a lucky act, for when the plaster fell apart, he found, inside the statue, a pot brimming with gold pieces. Smiling, Vardiello stuffed his pockets with the gold and dashed off home.

He rushed inside, crying, 'Mother, mother, look at these gold pieces! See how many there are!'

His mother was delighted with their unexpected wealth, but it occurred to her at once that, in his stupidity, Vardiello would blurt out the whole story to all and sundry. She decided to take steps to prevent this, so she told him to sit by the front door and watch for the milkman, saying she wanted to buy milk with one of the gold pieces.

The worthy Vardiello sat down at once in the doorway, and his mother poured dried figs and raisins on him for more than half an hour from an upper window.

Vardiello began to gather them up. Then he called out to his mother, 'Mother, mother, bring tubs — fetch the dough trough — get some baskets — if these dried figs and raisins rain down from heaven much longer, we shall both have great riches!'

And when he had eaten his fill of figs and raisins, till it was a wonder his stomach did not burst, he went into the parlour and lay down on a bench to have a sleep. He slept more soundly than he had for a long time.

The next day he saw two beggars in the street fighting over a gold piece they had found on the ground. Vardiello went up to them, and said, 'What fools you are to fight over a single poor gold piece! Why, one piece of gold means nothing to me, for I found a pot full of them in the town.'

The beggars spread the tale through the whole town, and when, after some days, the judge came to hear of it, he had Vardiello brought to him, and began to go into the whole matter of where, when and how he had found the gold about which he had told the beggars.

'I found them in front of a certain house, in the body of a dumb man, who was standing there, and that was the day it rained dried figs and raisins!' answered Vardiello.

When the judge heard this strange and surprising reply, he realized he was speaking to a fool and an idiot and, waving his hand, he said, 'Be off home with you, you fool, or I shall have you shut up in the madhouse!'

Thus the son's stupidity saved their new fortune, but it was really his mother's wit which fooled the judge!

The Golden Apple Tree and the Nine Peahens

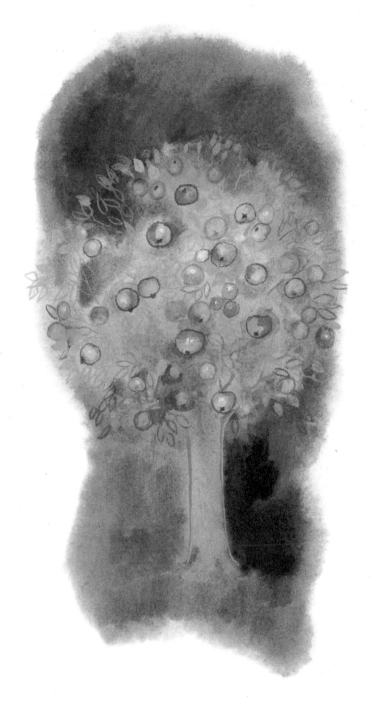

There was once a czar who had three sons. Now, in front of his palace there grew a golden apple tree, which blossomed and bore fruit in the space of a single night. But a thief always picked the fruit, and they could not find out who did it.

One day the czar said to his sons, 'Who is the thief who steals our fruit?'

At this, the eldest son said, 'Tonight I shall watch over the apple tree and discover who picks the fruit.'

When night fell, he went to the apple tree and lay down beneath it. But when the apples were beginning to ripen he fell asleep. The next morning he awoke to find they had all been picked! So he went to his father and told him truthfully what had happened.

Then the second son offered to guard the tree, but it was the same with him as with his elder brother. He fell asleep under the tree, and when he awoke in the morning, the apples were gone.

Now it was the turn of the youngest son to stand guard over the tree. He kept awake, and when the apples were beginning to ripen he saw nine golden peahens fly into view. Eight of them sat on the apple tree, but the ninth came down and sat beside the young prince. As she did so, she changed into a girl more beautiful than any he had ever seen! The two embraced and talked until after midnight. Then the girl rose, and thanked the prince for the apples. He begged her to leave him at least one. So she left him two: one for himself, and the other to take to his father. Then she changed back into a peahen, and flew off with the others.

When dawn broke, the prince returned to the palace with both apples.

His father was very pleased, and praised his youngest son. And when evening drew near, the prince went again to the apple tree to guard the apples. All happened as on the previous night, and the next morning he brought his father another two golden apples.

This went on for several nights. Then his brothers grew envious of him because they had been unable to guard the apples, while he had been successful. Whilst they grumbled against their brother, a wicked old hag appeared in the palace, and promised to find out for them how it was that their brother had been able to guard

the apples. When evening drew near, the old woman crept up to the apple tree, and hid herself, so that the prince did not see her when he came as usual to guard the golden apples.

Around midnight, the nine peahens arrived. Eight of them sat in the apple tree, and the ninth flew down to the prince and changed into a girl. The hag took hold of the girl's plait, and cut it off. She sprang to her feet at once, changed into a peahen and flew off. The other peahens flew out of the tree after her and were gone.

Then the prince, now miserably alone, suddenly spied the old hag. He grabbed hold of her and took her prisoner, and the next day had her put to death.

But the peahens came to the apple tree no more, and the young prince pined and wept. Finally, he resolved to go into the world to search for his peahen, and never to return home until he had found her. He told his father of his intention, and his father tried to dissuade him, saying that he should put such thoughts out of his head, and that he would find him a suitable girl for his bride in his own country. But all persuasion was in vain: the young man prepared for his journey, and set off, with one servant, to look for his peahen.

He wandered the world for a long time, until he happened upon a certain lake. Beside the lake he found a large and splendid palace, in which there lived an old czarina, and one girl, her daughter.

He asked the old woman, 'For pity's sake, old woman, do you know anything of nine golden peahens?'

And the old woman answered, 'Indeed,
I should know! Each day, at noon, they fly to
yonder lake to bathe. But forget the peahens —
here, you have my daughter, a beautiful girl,
with great riches. They shall be yours if you
marry her!'

But the prince wished only to find the
peahens, and did not want to hear about the old
woman's daughter. When morning came, he
rose and rode off to the lake to wait for the
peahens.

However, the old woman had bribed his
servant, giving him a pair of bellows, and saying
to him, 'Take these bellows. When you reach the
lake, blow secretly on the back of his neck, and
he will go to sleep, and will not be able to speak
with the peahens.'

The faithless servant did this. When they got
to the lake, he blew on the back of his master's
neck when he was not looking, and the youth
fell into a deep sleep, still on his horse!

Scarcely had he fallen asleep when the nine
peahens appeared. Eight of them flew to the
water, and the ninth to the prince on his horse.
She embraced him and tried to wake him,
'Awake, my life, awake, my heart, awake, my
soul!' she whispered.

But he heard nothing, sleeping as if he were
dead. When the peahens had finished bathing,
they flew off together. Then the prince awoke,
and asked his servant, 'What has happened?
Have they been here?'

The servant told him that the peahens had

come, and how eight of them had flown to the lake, and the ninth had come up to him on his horse, embraced him and tried to wake him. When the poor young man heard this, he was bitterly disappointed.

The next morning he set off again with his servant, and rode up and down the lake-side on his horse. But again, when he was not looking, the servant blew his neck with the bellows, and he fell into a deep sleep.

Scarcely had he fallen asleep when the nine peahens arrived. Eight of them flew to the lake, and the ninth came up to him on his horse, and again embraced him, and tried to wake him, 'Awake, my life, awake, my heart, awake, my soul!' she whispered. But all to no avail — he slept as if dead!

Then the peahen said to the servant, 'Tell your master that he may expect us again tomorrow. After that he will not see us again!'

When the birds had flown away, the prince awoke, and asked his servant, 'Have they been here?'

And the servant replied, 'They have, and they said that you might expect them again tomorrow, but for the last time.'

When the poor fellow heard this, he did not know what to do; in his pain and grief he began to tear his hair!

When dawn broke the third day, he rode to the lake again. This time he galloped up and down to make sure he kept awake. But his faithless servant still managed to use the bellows on the back of his neck! And he slumped forward on his horse and fell asleep.

As he slept, the nine peahens arrived; eight of them flew to the lake, and the ninth came up to him on his horse. At once she began to embrace him, and tried to wake him, 'Awake, my life, awake, my heart, awake, my soul!' she whispered.

But to no avail — he slept as if he were dead. Then the peahen said to the servant, 'When your master awakes, tell him that he must strike down that which is on top, and then he shall find me.'

Then all the peahens flew off. When they were gone, the prince woke up, and asked his servant, 'Have they been here?'

The servant replied, 'They have, and the one who came to you on your horse said to tell you that you are to strike down that which is on top, and that then you will find her!'

When the young man heard this, he drew his

sword and cut off the servant's head! Then he set off on his journey again.

He travelled far and long, until he came to a forest. There he spent the night with a hermit, and he asked him if he could tell him anything of nine golden peahens.

The hermit said to him, 'You are in luck, my son. Fate has led you here, to the right place. They are not more than half-a-day's journey from here on foot. Just continue straight on, and you will come to a great gate. When you pass through this gate, turn to the right, and you will reach their city, where you will find their palace.'

When dawn broke the next morning, the prince arose, prepared himself for his journey, thanked the hermit, and went the way he had been told. He arrived at the great gate, went through it, turned to the right, and around midday, saw a city, all shining white.

When he entered the city, he asked for the palace of the golden peahens. When he arrived at the palace gates, the guards stopped him, and asked who he was and whence he came. He told them his name, and the guards brought the czarina. She was the golden girl of his dreams, and the prince almost fainted for joy! In a few days they were married, and the prince stayed in the peahen palace.

Some time later, the czarina had to go out by herself. As she was leaving the palace, she gave her husband the key to twelve vaults, and told him, 'You may go into all the vaults except the twelfth, and that one you must not on any account enter, or even open: if you do, you will pay with your life!'

And she left.

The prince remained in the palace alone, and began to ask himself, 'What could there be in the twelfth vault?' Then he began to open one vault after another. When he came to the twelfth, he did not at first dare to open it. Then he began to wonder more and more what might be inside it and, in the end, he opened it!

In the middle of the vault, he saw a large cask without a bung, and bound with iron hoops. From within the cask, there came a voice, 'For pity's sake, brother, I beg you, I am dying of thirst — give me a cup of water!'

The prince took a cup of water, and poured it

into the cask. But scarcely had he done so, when one of the hoops burst. Then the voice from within the cask came again, 'For pity's sake, brother, I beg you, I am dying of thirst, give me another cup of water!'

The prince again poured a cup of water into the cask, and another hoop burst. A third time the voice came from within the cask, 'For pity's

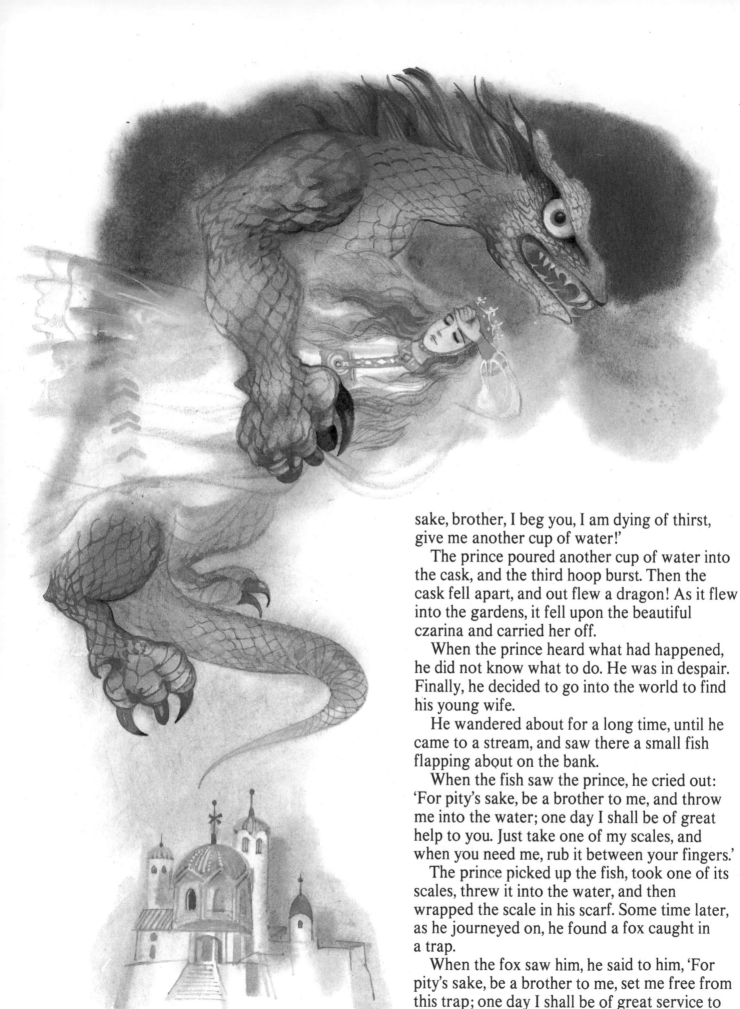

sake, brother, I beg you, I am dying of thirst, give me another cup of water!'

The prince poured another cup of water into the cask, and the third hoop burst. Then the cask fell apart, and out flew a dragon! As it flew into the gardens, it fell upon the beautiful czarina and carried her off.

When the prince heard what had happened, he did not know what to do. He was in despair. Finally, he decided to go into the world to find his young wife.

He wandered about for a long time, until he came to a stream, and saw there a small fish flapping about on the bank.

When the fish saw the prince, he cried out: 'For pity's sake, be a brother to me, and throw me into the water; one day I shall be of great help to you. Just take one of my scales, and when you need me, rub it between your fingers.'

The prince picked up the fish, took one of its scales, threw it into the water, and then wrapped the scale in his scarf. Some time later, as he journeyed on, he found a fox caught in a trap.

When the fox saw him, he said to him, 'For pity's sake, be a brother to me, set me free from this trap; one day I shall be of great service to you. Just take one of my hairs, and when you need me, rub it between your fingers.'

So he took one of the fox's hairs, and then released him.

And as he was walking through a forest, he found a wolf which was also caught in a trap.

When the wolf saw him, he said to him, 'For pity's sake, be a brother to me, and set me free, and I shall help you in distress; just take one of my hairs, and when you have need of me, rub it between your fingers.'

So he took one of the wolf's hairs and let him go.

And after he had walked on for a long time, he met a man, and asked him, 'Brother, I beg of

you, have you ever heard of a castle where the dragon czar might be?'

The man showed him the way, and told him to watch out for himself!

The prince thanked him, went on, and finally came to the dragon city. He entered the dragon's castle and found his wife there. Overjoyed at seeing each other again, they began thinking how they would manage their escape. Finally, the young wife led her husband to the dragon's stables, where they found a horse, climbed on its back and galloped off.

They had only just left the courtyard when the dragon came riding home. On learning that the czarina had fled with her husband, the dragon spoke to his horse, saying, 'What now? Shall we eat and drink first, or set off after them at once?'

And the horse answered, 'Eat and drink, and do not be anxious. We shall catch them!'

The dragon then entered his castle and ate his fill. After the meal, he mounted his horse and galloped away in pursuit of the couple. His horse was so swift that he caught up with them quite soon, and he took the czarina prisoner again.

'This time I forgive you,' he said to the prince, 'because you gave me water in the vault. But if you value your life, do not attempt to rescue the czarina ever again!'

The prince was terrified of the dragon, but the very next day saw him again at the dragon's castle. He found the czarina alone, and weeping bitterly. Now that they were together again, they began plotting an escape.

'When the dragon comes home,' the prince said, 'ask him where he got his fast horse. Then tell me, and I will find another such as his so that we may ride away from him!'

When the dragon came home, the czarina spoke softly to him, and waited upon him. At

last, she said, 'By all the stars, you have a swift horse! Where did you come by him?'

The dragon replied, 'Where I got him, horses are not come by easily. In a certain forest, there is an old woman who has twelve horses in her stables, each of them finer than the next. But in one corner of the stable there is a good-for-nothing looking horse. This only seems so, for he is the swiftest of all the horses and brother to my horse. Whoever has him can ride to the very heavens. But the man who wants one of the old woman's horses must serve her for three days. She has a mare and a foal, and he must guard them for three nights; if he succeeds in this, he will have the horse of his choice. But if he fails to guard the mare and foal, he loses his head.'

The next day, when the dragon had gone, the prince came, and the czarina told him all she had learnt from the dragon. He went off at once to the forest where the old woman lived, and as soon as he arrived at her door, he said, 'Greetings, old woman!'

And she answered, 'Greetings, son. What brings you here?'

'I should like to serve you.'

And the old woman replied, 'Very well. If you can guard my mare and foal for three days, I will give you the horse of your choice. But if you fail, I will have your head!' And she took him to a courtyard, surrounded by stakes, on each of which was a human head, except for one, which kept shouting, 'Old woman, give me a head!'

The old woman bade the prince look carefully, saying, 'Here you see all those who tried to serve me but could not guard the mare!'

The young man was undaunted. And when evening came, he sat on the mare, and rode out with her, the foal running along at her side. He remained on her back until midnight, when he began to nod off. Soon he fell asleep. When he woke up, he was sitting astride a log with the rein in his hands. Filled with horror, he jumped down, and went to look for the mare. He searched in vain until he came to a stream. This reminded him of the fish he had thrown into the water, and he took its scale out of his scarf, rubbed it between his fingers, and suddenly heard the fish calling from the water, 'What is it, my brother?'

The prince answered, 'The old woman's mare

has escaped me, and I do not know where she is.'

And the fish said, 'She is here among us, she changed herself and her foal into fishes. Strike the water with the rein, and say "Whoa, old woman's mare!"'

The prince struck the water with the rein and said, 'Whoa, old woman's mare!' And there was the mare again, coming to the bank with her foal! He put the rein on her and rode her home, the foal trotting alongside.

When they got home, the old woman gave him some food, but she took the mare to the stables and beat her with a poker.

'You should have gone among the fishes, you fool!'

And the mare replied, 'I was among the fishes, but they are his friends, and they gave me away!'

To which the old woman replied, 'Then go among the foxes.'

When evening came, the prince sat upon the mare again and rode out on her, the foal running alongside. He sat on her until around midnight, when he dropped off to sleep. When he awoke from his dreams, he was again astride a log, holding the rein in his hand.

Filled with horror, he leapt down and went off to search for the mare. 'Perhaps the fox will help me,' he suddenly thought, and took the fox's hair out of his scarf, rubbed it, and at once the fox stood in front of him.

'What is it, my brother?'

And the prince said, 'The old woman's mare has escaped me, and I do not know where she is.'

And the fox said, 'She is here among us. She changed herself into a vixen, and her foal into a cub. Strike the rein on the ground and say "Whoa, old woman's mare!"'

The prince struck the rein on the ground and said, 'Whoa, old woman's mare!' And, straight away, there stood the mare together with her foal. Then he put the rein on her, and

rode her home, the foal running alongside.

When they got home, the old woman brought him some food, but she took the mare into the stables and began to beat her with a poker, and said, 'You should have gone among the foxes, you fool!'

And the mare replied, 'I was among the foxes, but they are his friends, and they gave me away!'

So the old woman said, 'Then go among the wolves!'

When evening came, the prince sat on the mare and rode off, the foal running along beside them. He sat there on the mare, until, around midnight, he dropped off to sleep, and when he awoke from his dreams, he was once more astride a log, holding the rein. Terrified, he jumped down at once and set out to find the mare; but then he thought of the wolf's promise, and he pulled the wolf's hair from his scarf, rubbed it, and there in front of him stood the wolf.

'What is it, my brother?'

And he said to the wolf, 'The old woman's mare has run away from me, and I do not know where to find her.'

The wolf said, 'She is here among us. She changed herself into a she-wolf, and the foal into a cub. Strike the rein on the ground and say "Whoa, old woman's mare!"'

He did this, and the she-wolf became a mare again, and stood before him with the foal. The prince put the rein on her and rode her home, the foal running alongside.

When they got home, the old woman gave him some food, but she took the mare into the stables, beat her with a poker, and said to her, 'You should have gone among the wolves, you fool!'

And the mare replied, 'I was among the wolves, but they are his friends, and they betrayed me!'

The old woman went to the prince, who said to her, 'Well, old woman, I have served you well: now give me what we agreed.'

And the old woman answered, 'As we agreed, so it shall be! Here you see twelve horses. Take whichever you want.'

The prince said to the old woman, 'Why should I choose a fine horse? Give me the one

in the corner — that good-for-nothing one —
for I am not fit to have a fine one.'

The old woman tried to make him change his
mind, 'Why should you take such
a good-for-nothing horse, when I have so many
fine ones?'

But the prince would have his way, and said,
'Give me the one I want, as it was agreed!'

So the old woman had to give him the
good-for-nothing horse. Then he took his leave
of her, and walked off, leading the horse by
the rein. He took it into the forest, and groomed
it, until the horse shone as if it had a coat of
gold. Then he mounted his new horse and
spurred it on, and it flew like a bird, until the
two of them were standing in front of the
dragon's palace.

As soon as the prince was inside, he said to
the czarina, 'Prepare yourself for our journey!'

And she made herself ready with all speed.
Then they both sat on the horse, and off they
went. After a while the dragon returned, and
saw that the czarina was gone.

So he said to his horse, 'What now? Shall we
eat and drink, or shall we go after them?'

And the horse replied, 'Eat or not, drink or
not, go after them or not, you will not catch
them!'

When the dragon heard this, he mounted at
once and went after them.

When the two fugitives saw the dragon
following them, they grew fearful and began to
urge their horse to go faster. But the horse
replied, 'Do not be afraid. Why should we
hurry?'

Suddenly the dragon was at their heels, and
his horse called to theirs, 'For pity's sake,
brother, wait for me, or it will be the end of me!'

And his brother replied, 'Why be a fool and
carry that cruel master of yours on your back?
Rear up, throw him against a rock, and then we
shall go off together! Are we not brothers?'

When the dragon's mount heard this, he
reared up violently, and threw his master
against a rock. The dragon was dashed to
pieces, and the horse went at once to join his
brother. Then the czarina sat upon the second
horse, and off they rode together to her
czardom, where they lived and reigned happily
until their death!

The Prince
Who Wanted
to
Live Forever

Once upon a time, beyond seven mountains, seven seas, in the ninety-ninth pleat of an old woman's skirt, lived a white flea, and in that flea's stomach, right in the middle, was a splendid royal city. In the city there lived an old king who had one son, a fine young man; and the king had high hopes of him. He sent him to school that he might learn all things there were to learn, and sent him abroad to learn foreign manners and to see and get to know foreign customs.

The prince remained there until his father summoned him home. During the years he had travelled the world, the young man had changed a great deal, becoming gloomy, pensive and brooding. The king was greatly grieved at this, and wondered what might be the cause of this change. He spoke to no one of it, but only racked his brains, until it occurred to him that the prince might be in love, that this might be the cause of his melancholy.

Once, when they were sitting together in the royal dining hall, he took his son by the hand, led him to an adjoining room, filled with portraits of beautiful young ladies, and said to him, 'I see that you are ever out of temper, dear son. Perhaps it would be good for you to marry. In this room you see the portraits of many imperial, royal and aristocratic daughters; choose one of them and I shall bring you the one who touches your heart to be your wife, that you may be merry again.'

'Oh, my lord, dear father,' the prince said to him, 'it is not love that vexes me, and I do not want to marry. What grieves me is the thought that every man, even the king himself, must one day die. Therefore, I should like to find a kingdom where death holds no sway; indeed I have decided to go and find such a kingdom, even if I were to roam the whole world, until my legs dropped off.'

The old king tried to dissuade his son, explaining to him that the whole idea was impossible, that he himself had ruled his kingdom happily and to the satisfaction of all his subjects for fifty years. He even offered to step down and let his son be king — just to make him merry and to keep him at home. But the son was adamant; the next morning he took a sword, girded himself with it, and set off on his journey.

He walked for several days, until he came to the edge of his father's kingdom. He was walking along the road when he saw, far off, a tall and spreading tree, above which an eagle appeared to hover. When he came near, he saw that it really was a huge eagle, which was striking the highest branches of the tree till sparks flew up. As the prince gazed in wonder, the eagle flew down from the tree, turned a somersault in the air, and in a flash turned into a man, a king, who asked the wondering prince, 'Why are you so astonished, son?'

'I find it strange that you peck the top of that great tree,' replied the prince.

But the eagle king said to him, 'Then know you that I am cursed, and neither I nor my family can die until I destroy this tree to its very roots. But I have had enough for today, and I shall go home. You, honest traveller, are welcome in my humble home tonight.'

This suited the prince well, so they went together to the king's palace. And behold, the eagle king's beautiful daughter greeted him, and at once ordered the table to be laid and supper to be brought. While they were sitting at table talking, the eagle king asked why the prince was roaming the world. The prince explained to him that his journey would not end until he had found the kingdom where death had no power.

'Then you see, my son, that you have come to the right place,' the king said to him, 'for you have heard that death has no power over myself and my family, until I peck that great tree down to the roots. And that will take at least six hundred years. So take my daughter for a wife and live with us. You will live well!'

'That would be fine indeed, my lord, but I should have to die in six hundred years, and I wish to go where death has no power over me at all,' replied the prince.

The princess, too, wished him to delay his travels, now that she had got to know him, but he could not be persuaded. So she gave him a small box as a remembrance, on the base of which her portrait was painted, and said, 'If you will not stay, take this box in memory of me; when you are tired of travelling, open it and look at my picture, and you will gain strength; you can, if you wish, fly in the air, and if the wind is very strong, you will be able to stay on the ground and move along as fast as thought, as fast as the wind.'

The prince accepted the box, thanked the princess kindly, and took his leave of the eagle castle.

He walked along the road for some time, until he began to feel very tired. Then he remembered the little box; he opened it, looked at the beautiful princess's likeness, and thought to himself: 'If only I could fly in the air with the speed of the wind!' Almost at once, he found himself flying above the clouds. He flew a long way, until suddenly, as he soared over a high mountain, he saw a bald-headed old man with a spade and a shovel, filling a basket with earth and taking it from the mountain peak to the valley below. He was very surprised at this, but the bald-headed old man stopped his work and called out, 'Why are you so surprised, my son?'

'Well, I wonder why you carry earth in a basket into the valley!' exclaimed the prince as he landed beside him.

'Alas, my dear boy,' answered the old man, 'I am cursed, and neither I nor any member of my family may die until I have carried down the whole mountain and levelled it to the ground! But come, evening is upon us, that is enough for today!' And he turned a somersault in the air and changed into a bald-headed king.

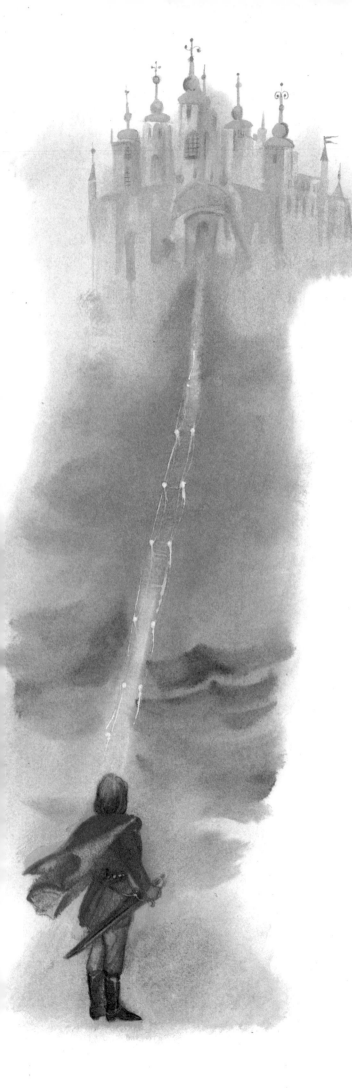

He, too, invited the prince to his home for the
night, and they went off together to his palace;
and the prince was amazed, for the bald king
had a daughter a hundred times more beautiful
than the eagle king's! She welcomed them
pleasantly and gave them a good supper. At
supper the bald king asked the prince where he
was going, and the prince told him that his
wandering would not come to an end until he
had found the land where death had no sway.

'Then you have come to the right place,' said
the bald king. 'As I have told you, I am
sentenced to carry away the whole of that
mountain, and no one in my family may die until
I do so. And that may take eight hundred years;
marry my daughter, for I can see that you get on
well together, and you may live happily for
eight hundred years.'

'But I want to go where death will never have
power over me,' said the prince.

He wished the king and his daughter pleasant
dreams and went to sleep. In the morning they
all rose early, and the princess again began to
plead with him to stay with them. But he would
not hear of it. And so that he might not leave
without some remembrance, she gave him
a golden ring which had the power to help its
wearer to get where he wanted to be, if he just
twisted it on his finger.

The prince took the ring, thanked the
princess kindly, and set off again on his journey.
He walked for a while along the road until he
remembered the princess's gift. Then he twisted
the ring and wished he were at the very end of
the world. He closed his eyes, and a moment

149

later, when he opened them, he was in the most beautiful of royal cities. As he was walking through the streets of the city, he saw crowds of finely dressed and handsome people; he tried to speak to them in twenty-seven languages — for he knew so many — but no one answered him. Then he grew deeply melancholy: what was he to do here if no one understood him?

And as he walked on, gazing sadly in front of him, he saw a man dressed like the people in his own land; he spoke to him in his own language, and the man replied likewise.

The prince asked him what city it was, and the stranger explained that it was the capital city of the kingdom of King Blusky. King Blusky himself had already died, but his beautiful daughter was now queen, and ruled over seven lands, since the rest of the royal family had died. The prince was pleased to hear this, and he asked the man to show him the way to the castle.

'Willingly,' said the man, and led him to the castle, where he took leave of him.

When the prince entered the castle, he saw that the princess was sitting on a balcony doing embroidery. He went to her and greeted her. She rose and thanked him for his greeting, took him to her chambers and entertained him royally. And when he told her why he had come out into the world, and that he wanted to live for ever, she asked him to stay and rule with her. But the prince said that he did not intend to stay in any place other than the kingdom where

death had no sway. At that, the princess took the young man's hand and led him to a small room, the floor of which was set with needles, so thickly that even the finest needle would not have found a place there!

'Do you see how many needles are here?' she asked him. 'I and my whole family will live until I have used up every one of these needles, and blunted them with sewing. And that will take at least a thousand years! If you stay with me, we can live together and rule for a thousand years!'

'That is all very well,' said the prince, 'but in a thousand years we should have to die, and I am seeking the land where death has no power over me at all.'

The princess tried in vain to dissuade him, but, in the end, he said he meant to continue his journey. Then the princess moved close to him and said, 'Then if nothing will persuade you to stay here with me, take this little golden wand as a souvenir; it has the power to turn into whatever you wish it to be.'

The prince thanked her for the present, put the wand in his pocket, said good-bye, and set off again.

He had scarcely left the city when he came to a great river, on whose far bank the heavenly globe touched the Earth; it was the very end of the Earth, and he could go no farther. So he set off upstream along the river. He had gone some way when he suddenly saw a beautiful castle in the air above the river; but, try as he might, he could find no path leading to it, either through the air or over water, and he had no way of

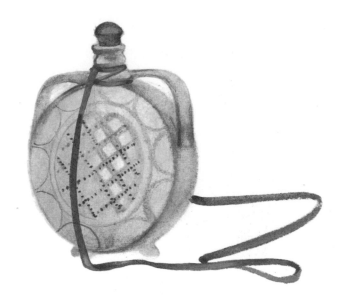

getting to it, though he would dearly have liked
to see inside it! Then he remembered the golden
wand which the princess-of-the-needles had
given him. He took the wand, threw it on the
ground, and wished it were a bridge to the
splendid castle. And, lo and behold! As soon as
he spoke his wish, the wand became a golden
bridge. The prince did not hesitate, but crossed
the bridge and hurried into the castle.

When he passed through the gates, he saw
the castle was guarded by some kind of
unimaginably strange prehistoric monsters, the
like of which he had never seen. He took fright,
and ordered his sword, Swiftblade, out of its
sheath, and the sword jumped out and cut off
several of the monsters' heads. But each time it
did so, a new head appeared. The prince was
greatly astonished, and ordered his sword back
into its sheath. But the queen saw all from the
window, and sent a page down to say that her
strange guards were not to harm the prince, and
to bring him up to her. So it was done. The page
ran quickly to the gates and escorted the prince
into the castle.

Presently, he stood before the queen, who
said to him pleasantly, 'I see that you are no

ordinary man. Tell me who you are and why
you come here.'

The prince told her about his father, and how
he had set off on his journey because he longed
for the land where death had no power.

'Then you have come to the right place,' said
the queen, 'I am the Queen of Life and
Immortality, here you are safe from death.'

She offered him a place at her table, and the
prince had the opportunity to test her generous
hospitality. Then he lived there in the beautiful
castle for exactly a thousand years, though the
time passed so quickly that it seemed like
a mere six months.

After the thousand years, the prince dreamt
one night that he spoke to his father and
mother, and he was filled with such a longing to
see them that he arose the next morning and
announced that he wished to go home to see his
parents once more.

The queen was greatly astonished, and said,
'What are you thinking of? Your parents died
more than eight hundred years ago; for many
hundreds of years they have been dust and
ashes!'

But she could not make him change his mind,

so she said, 'If I cannot persuade you, come with me, and I shall prepare you for your journey.'

And she hung around his neck one golden and one silver flask. Then she took him to a small, secret chamber.

'Fill the silver flask with the liquid you find in this tub. Whoever you sprinkle with that liquid will die immediately, even if he has a thousand lives!'

Then she took him to another small chamber, in which there stood a similar tub. She raised the lid, filled the golden flask with liquid, and said, 'Listen carefully to what I say, prince! This liquid is from the Rock of Eternity, and it has the power to bring back to life the dead, even if they died a thousand thousand years ago. You need only to obtain the smallest bone from the body and to sprinkle it with this water of life — the dead will rise and be alive and healthy.'

The prince thanked the Queen of Immortality kindly, took his leave of her and the others at the castle, and set off on his journey.

He soon came to the town where the princess-of-the-needles lived. He would scarcely have recognized it, so much had it changed. In the castle, too, a silence reigned as if no one was there. When he entered the royal chambers, he found the princess sitting over her embroidery. He crept up to her and greeted her pleasantly, but she did not move. He went into the chamber where the needles had been, but there was not a single one, for the princess had broken the last needle as she sewed, and died. He quickly sprinkled her with the liquid from the golden flask, and she came to life at once, raised her head, and said to him, 'Ah, dear friend, it is well that you have wakened me, I seem to have been asleep a long time.'

'And if I had not raised you from the dead, you would have slept to the end of the world,' he said.

Only then did she realize that she had died and that the prince had brought her back to life. She thanked him with all her heart and promised to return the good deed. Then the prince took his leave of her and set off towards the kingdom of King Baldhead!

He saw from afar that the mountain had gone. And when he drew nearer, he saw that the poor king had carried all the earth into the valley. He had put his basket down, placed his spade and shovel beside him, and died!

Once again, the prince took out the golden flask, sprinkled King Baldhead with the water of life, and the king came to life as the princess had done. King Baldhead also promised that he would return the favour.

The prince took his leave of him, and set off for the kingdom of the eagle king. There he saw that the eagle king had pecked away the huge tree and its branches down to the roots, and that there was not a trace of it. And the king lay dead, his feathers spread out and his beak thrust into the ground, and flies swarmed all around him.

The prince sprinkled the eagle king with the water of life from his golden flask; the king came to life, looked around and said, 'Ah, how long I have slept! Thank you for waking me, dear young friend!'

'You would have slept till judgement day if I had not brought you to life!'

Only then did the eagle king realize that he had been dead. He recalled the prince clearly, thanked him for his kindness in coming back to him, and promised to reward him.

The prince took his leave of him, and went on. Soon he came to the city which was the seat of his royal father. From afar he saw that the royal castle had fallen to the ground, and that where the city had stood there was a great sulphur lake, which burned with a blue flame.

Then the prince gave up all hope of finding his father or his mother. He turned around and walked away sadly. At the far end of the city, he suddenly heard above him a voice, 'Do not go away, prince, you are in the right place, for I have been seeking you a thousand years!'

The prince looked around and, what should he see! Death itself — may his name be cursed forever — was calling him. He quickly twisted his ring and found himself with the eagle king, then with King Baldhead, and then with the princess-of-the-needles. He asked them to send their armies against Death, saying that he would go to the kingdom of the Queen of Immortality. But Death was at his heels the whole time!

When he found himself at the castle of the Queen of Immortality, and had one foot inside the walls, Death took hold of the other and

cried, 'Now I have you. You will never escape!'

The Queen of Immortality saw this from her window, called out and reproached Death for daring to come to her kingdom, telling him that he had no power there!

'That is true,' said Death, 'but the prince still has one foot in my kingdom, and it belongs to me.'

'But there is no doubt that half of the prince belongs to me,' said the Queen of Immortality. 'And what would be the use of dividing him between us — half a prince is no use either to you or to me. I tell you what, come to me — I will make an exception and let you in — and we shall draw lots for him.'

Death agreed, and entered the queen's castle. The Queen of Immortality suggested that the prince be sent to the seventh heaven, to where the morning star rises. If he fell back within her walls, he should be hers; if he fell without, Death should have him.

'Very well,' said Death, and the queen asked the prince to come in to the courtyard. She placed her foot firmly against the prince's heels and flung him up among the stars so that he was lost from sight in a flash. But in the effort she made, the queen swayed a little, and she was afraid that the prince would fall just outside the castle walls, into the arms of Death.

Then, all at once, she saw a tiny wasp trying to fly into the courtyard. Its efforts were so feeble that it looked as if it would land outside the walls, and the queen's heart sank with dismay. But, at the right moment, a southerly wind lent the wasp its assistance — the wasp continued its efforts and, quick as a flash, the queen rushed forward and caught it in her hand, and carried it into the castle!

When the wasp assumed the prince's form again, the queen kissed him and held him in her arms until the young man was fully recovered. Then she ordered her servants to light all the brooms they could find, and drive Death from her castle with their burning broom-heads.

Well, you will not be surprised to hear that the prince and the queen live happily to this day, and reign in glory.

Whoever does not believe this is so, let him go to the end of the world — as far as the airy castle of the Queen of Life and Immortality. When he finds her castle above the river, he will see that my story is true!

Three Gilded Pomegranates

Once upon a time there was a king who had a son. One day, as the son was sitting by the window, he saw an old woman carrying a jug to the well to get some water. Who knows why he did it, but he picked up a stone, threw it towards the well, hit the jug and broke it. The old woman, seeing where the stone had come from, raised her eyes towards the castle, and saw the king's son, who was laughing at what he had done.

The old woman said, 'Until you find three gilded pomegranates, my dear, you will not marry.'

And she returned home sadly, with neither jug nor water.

When the king's son heard the curse, he became very thoughtful, and he began to wonder what the three gilded pomegranates could be like. Day after day, they filled his thoughts, until he was seized with a great desire to go into the world and search for them. At last he went to his father and said, 'Father, have made for me three iron suits to wear. I am going on a long journey!'

In vain, the king tried to change his son's mind; it was to no avail! When he saw that he could not be persuaded, he had the clothes made. The prince took them, mounted his horse, and rode away.

For a whole year he travelled, until he reached a wilderness where no human beings lived. He wandered the length and breadth of the land, wore out two suits, and threw them away. He did not know what to do next, but decided to go a little farther, and if he found nothing, to return to his own kingdom.

He had gone only a little way, when he saw ahead of him a hovel. He went towards it as fast as he could, and was soon close to it. The hermit-woman, who lived there, came out, and said to him, 'What are you doing here, dear boy? Why, not even the smallest little songbird ever comes here, let alone a poor human being!'

'Sister,' said the prince, 'I am seeking three gilded pomegranates. Do you know where I might look for them?'

'I do not know, my boy, I have never heard of such things! But perhaps my sister, who lives a little way on, may know. If you have the courage to go farther, ask her!'

The prince did not wait to be told a second time, but set off at once, and went on and on, until he came to a second hovel, from which an even older and more wrinkled hermit-woman appeared, and said to him, 'What are you doing here, poor fellow? Not even the smallest songbird comes this way!'

'Sister,' said the prince, 'I am seeking three gilded pomegranates, and my desire for them has brought me all this way. Do you not know where they might be found?'

At these words, the old woman burst into tears, and said, 'Ah! I had a son who had also heard of these accursed pomegranates. He searched for them a long time. Then, one day, he returned to me in a sorry state. He had destroyed himself on their account! If I had known then how to obtain them without danger, I should not have lost my son!'

When the prince heard this, he begged her to tell him how to find the pomegranates. The old woman told him where to go and what to do. Then she made him swear on his youth that, if he succeeded, he would call on her on his way home and show her the gilded pomegranates for which her son had died.

When he had promised to return, the prince thanked her for her good advice, and disappeared like a ghost into the wilderness. After travelling for more than a week, he came upon a dragon whose upper jaw reached to the skies, the lower to the ground, and he greeted it, 'Good-day, brother!'

The dragon answered, 'Good luck to you, my boy!'

As he went on, he came to a well, covered with slime and full of mud. He cleaned it, and took out the stale water, so that fresh water might run in. Then he went on, until he came to a closed gate, smothered in dust and cobwebs. He removed the cobwebs, wiped off the dust, opened the gate wide, and went on. Next, he saw a baker-woman wiping out her hot oven with her bare hands. When he saw this, he greeted her, took off a piece of his clothing, and said to her, 'Here you are, my good woman, use this to wipe your oven.'

The baker-woman took it and thanked him.

Beyond the oven, the prince came to a garden as lovely as paradise, and for a while he walked in it. Suddenly, he saw the three gilded pomegranates hanging from the branch of a tree. He summoned up his courage, took out a knife, cut off the branch on which they were hanging, and rushed off as fast as his legs could carry him.

Before he had gone ten paces, the whole garden began to shout, calling for help to the baker-woman, to the gate, to the well and to the dragon.

'What a noise!' said the baker-woman. 'In all the time I have been condemned to live here, no one has ever thought of coming to save me from scorching myself in the oven each day! I will not help you!'

'I am of exactly the same opinion,' answered the gate. 'Why, from the time I was made, no one has been to clean me and open me, nor even to move me a little.'

'I am sorry, I will not help you,' said the well, 'for in all the time I have stood here, no human hand has touched me to clean out my dirty water and leave me smelling fresh and clean until now.'

'It is true,' replied the dragon. 'Ever since I was condemned to keep my jaws open and gaze at the stars, no one has even greeted me, let alone called me brother!'

The prince, who had done everything just as the old woman told him, returned to her, showed her the gilded fruit, and gave her something for her pains, before setting off for his father's kingdom.

No one can say what came over him, but on the way, the prince could restrain himself no

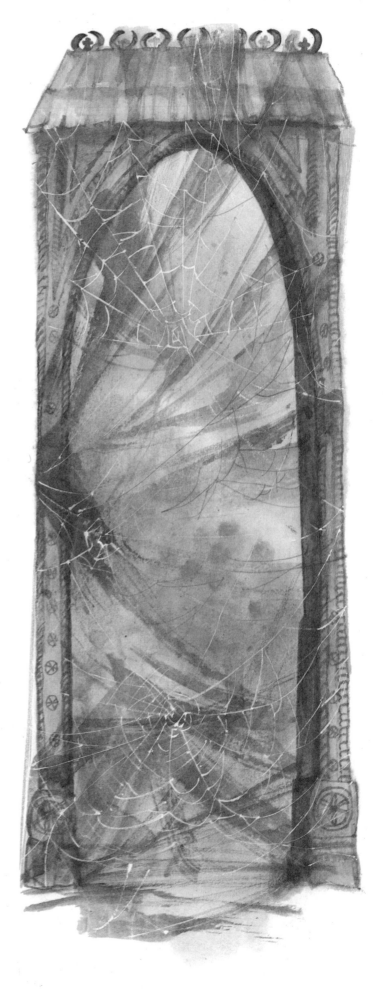

longer! He took out one of the pomegranates to taste it and find out how good it was! But, at that very moment, a girl as beautiful as a fairy stepped out of the pomegranate, and began to cry out piteously, 'Water, water, or I shall die!'

The prince looked around him for water, but in vain; there was none to be seen, and the girl fell down dead. He was himself on the point of collapsing. But he struggled on.

On and on he went until, unable to resist tasting a second pomegranate, he took out his knife and cut one open. At once, a girl like a fairy stepped out of the fruit. And she, like the first girl, died because he had no water for her. Upset and unhappy, he returned to his father's kingdom with the last pomegranate. As he drew near to the castle, he came to a beautiful meadow. Now he felt that nothing could happen, and he sat down to rest for a while. He could not rid himself of the thought of the pomegranates and the strange, beautiful girls who had died. As he was thinking about them, he was filled with a desire to taste the last pomegranate, and he decided to cut it open. But since he was afraid that what had happened before would repeat itself, he walked until he found a well, so that he could fill his cap with water. Then, in the shade of a large tree, he cut open the remaining pomegranate. At once, out stepped a girl as beautiful as the sun, with golden hair.

'Water, water!' she cried.

He gave her a drink, sprinkled her with water, and so saved her life. The prince gazed at her, marvelling at her beauty and grace!

Then he took her by the hand and asked her to be his wife, and she agreed. He did not like to ask her to walk with him as far as his castle. She was so small that he could have eaten her for dessert, and so slender that he could pass a ring over her!

He told her to climb a tree by the well, and said that she should wait for him until he returned from his castle with royal carriages and riders.

The beautiful girl told the tree to bend down, which it did, and she sat in it; then the tree lifted her up. The prince opened his mouth wide with wonder at this marvel! Then he made for home as though someone had said, 'Be off with you!' He ran so fast that he kicked up a cloud of dust behind him!

Shortly after the prince had departed, a young gipsy-girl came to the well for water, and when she saw the face that was reflected in the water, she thought it was hers, hurled the jug to the ground, and ran to her mother, crying, 'I shall go for water no more! Beauties such as I do not go for water!'

'Bring the water at once! What silliness is this?' said her mother, threatening her with the broom handle.

The girl went, but again returned without water, and said the same as before.

Finally, it occurred to her mother that there must be some other explanation, and she stuck a needle with magic power in the girl's hair, which would tell her what to do if she met anyone. Then she sent her back to the well.

When the gipsy-girl came to the well, she looked up and realized where the angelic face in the well had come from.

'Help me up, please!' said the gipsy-girl, gazing imploringly at the beautiful fairy.

The fairy-girl told the tree to bend down and draw the gipsy-girl towards her, so that she could comfort her, and the tree righted itself again.

As they spoke together, the gipsy-girl

159

flattered the fairy, and begged her to sleep
a little, and to lay her head on her lap, so that
she might caress her hair.

The fairy agreed, and laid her head on the
gipsy's lap. When she had fallen asleep, the
gipsy-girl thrust the poisoned needle into her
head, and the fairy turned into a golden bird,
and began to fly about from branch to branch.

The gipsy-girl cried spitefully, 'How stupid
you are to fly away from me! I thought you
were asleep; but no matter, you will not get far!'

Some time later, the prince came with
soldiers, riders, and the royal carriages, to fetch
his fairy-girl.

When the gipsy saw him, she exclaimed,
'Prince, why have you kept me waiting so long?
See how the sun has burnt my face, and the
wind tangled my hair!'

The prince was puzzled. He could not believe
that this was the fairy he had left behind. But
when she persisted that she was truly the girl he
had loved, he began to believe her, and he took
her with him, in one of the carriages, back to the
castle.

Who knows why, but his heart seemed to tell
him this was not his fairy-girl; she was so
changed — and he did not know what to say to
his father, who was expecting to see a very
different kind of girl!

When he reached the royal court, the king
came out to meet them. Now, instead of
a beautiful fairy with a face like the sun and
golden hair, he was confronted with a gipsy-girl,
as black as an old cooking pot, and he stood
transfixed. And though his son assured him that
the sun had scorched her face and the wind
tangled her hair, the king still could not believe

it. However, he set aside a wing of the castle for them, but postponed the wedding as long as he could.

The very next day, a small bird began coming to the royal gardens. It sang so touchingly that it moved everyone's heart. Then, one day, it called out at the top of its little voice,

'Gardener! Is the king asleep?'

'He is,' answered the gardener.

'Then let him sleep as sweet, as sweet can be, and let nothing trouble him,' said the bird. 'And the black stranger — is she also asleep?'

'She is!'

'Then let her sleep deeply and ill, and let nothing ever give her joy again!'

And no matter which tree the bird sat upon to sing, it began to wither.

The gardener told the king all, saying that the royal trees were dying because the bird sat upon them to sing. The king fell into deep thought at this.

After a few days, nearly all the trees in the garden had withered away. Only one was left, and the king ordered snares to be set on each of its branches.

The next day at dawn, servants brought the king the golden bird, which had been caught in one of the snares, and the king ordered a golden cage to be made. The bird was put in it, and the cage hung by the window so that he might watch it all the time.

When the gipsy-girl heard about the bird, her heart sank. She pretended to be ill, and bribed the doctors to tell the king that she would not get well until he had the golden bird killed and given to her to eat.

The king grew angry and would have none of

it. But when his son, too, asked him, he gave him the bird. It grieved him deeply to do this, and he hated the gipsy even more.

They took the bird and killed it, cooked it, and brought it to the gipsy. She said that she was well again, almost at once. And the wedding plans were put in hand. But a tall and beautiful fir tree grew up from the blood of the dead bird. It grew beside the gipsy's window, and the wonderful thing about it was that it grew so tall and beautiful in a single night! The king told the gardeners to take good care of the tree. But when the gipsy-girl heard this, she was afraid, and pondered how she might be rid of the tree. The wicked creature realized that she had not yet overcome the fairy's power.

Again she pretended to be ill, and again bribed the doctors, who told the king that the girl would not be well again until the fir tree had been chopped down, and a bath prepared for her from its sap.

The king simmered with rage when he saw that his son's betrothed was bringing unhappiness to his house, for since the time she had come, he could take pleasure in nothing. He had the fir tree felled, for the sake of peace and quiet, but he decided that the next time he would not give way if something dear to him was at stake.

When the fir tree, which all admired, was being felled, an old beggar-woman was among the watching crowd. As she left, she took a splinter from the fir tree and carried it home. Then she noticed that a needle was stuck in the splinter, and she drew it out. Since the splinter was quite long and broad, she made of it a cover for a pot which she particularly liked.

The next day, as usual, she went begging. But when she came home, she was amazed to find her hut swept and cleaned till it was a delight to see.

The old woman did not understand this miracle, or who might have come and worked for her. The same thing happened several days running. In the end, she decided to hide, and watch who cleaned and tidied her hut. The next day, she only pretended to leave. Instead, she hid and looked secretly through a crack in the door, and she saw a girl, whiter than snow and with golden hair, leap from the pot cover.

'Who are you, my girl?' she asked, showing herself. 'Why do you serve me so?'

'An unfortunate girl,' came the answer. 'But if you let me stay here, I will reward you well!'

It was agreed, and the girl stayed with her. And the old woman told herself that such a beauty, such a lovely and hard-working girl could not be found even at the king's court!

The old woman went begging every day. But one day, the girl told her to buy linen and red and green embroidery silks in the market, and the woman bought them with the money she had gained from begging. The girl embroidered her sad story on two fine scarves, and she told the old woman to take them to the king, and to place the green embroidered scarf on the king's knee, and the red one on that of his son.

The old woman did as she was told and went to the castle. The soldiers would not let her in, and she began to shout so loudly that the king heard her and ordered her to be admitted. Once in the royal chambers, she did just as the girl had told her, and went outside to await the result.

When the king and his son saw the embroidery on the scarves, they understood everything. The king then ordered the gipsy-girl into his presence and said, 'Since you are to be queen, you must learn to judge women when the judges themselves are at a loss. Today, a woman came to us with a grievance, saying that she had a cock for mating, and that she wandered far and wide to find a suitable hen for him. When she did so, her neighbour not only killed the hen, but also stole the cock and gave it to her own hen. Now the woman demands justice. What is your opinion?'

'I think,' said the gipsy-girl, after a moment's silence, 'that the woman who killed the hen and stole the cock should be punished with death, and that the cock should be returned to its owner, together with the neighbour's hen and the eggs it has laid.'

'You have judged righteously,' said the king. 'I am that woman with the cock, and you are the one who stole him. Prepare yourself for the punishment you yourself have chosen.'

The gipsy-girl began to lament, to beg, to cry out in woe, but to no avail. She was handed over to the soldiers, who punished her severely for all the evil she had done.

Then the king and his son went to the old woman's hut to conduct the real princess to the castle. As soon as this was done, the royal wedding was arranged. It was celebrated for three days and three nights throughout the kingdom. And all were filled with joy that the golden-haired girl the prince had sought so long had been found alive and unharmed.

The Fern Flower

From olden times, grandmothers by the fireside on dark evenings, when the wood blazes and crackles merrily, have told this tale.

On Midsummer's Eve, the shortest night of the whole year, a fern comes into flower. This fern flower brings great good fortune to whoever picks and keeps it. But the sad thing about it is that this mystical night comes only once a year and that it is so short. Furthermore, only one fern in the forest flowers, and only in some hidden corner, so that a person must be especially fortunate to find it!

Those who know about such marvels go on to say that the path to the miraculous flower is very difficult and dangerous, full of ghostly spectres, who protect the flower, and that it takes exceptional courage to find it and carry it off.

Then they go on to warn how the fern flower is difficult to recognize, seeming so ugly and insignificant, and that only when it is picked does it change into a gleaming calyx of wondrous beauty!

It is so difficult to find and take this flower, and so very few have seen it that when the story of the fern flower is told, something new is often added in the telling!

But everyone knows that on Midsummer's Eve the fern flower blossoms only for a short while — until the moment the cocks crow — and that he who plucks the flower may have all he wishes. No matter how wonderful the things he wants, his wishes are granted at once.

And everyone knows, too, that only someone young may obtain the flower, and that he must have clean hands. If a man is old, and has committed many sins in his life-time, the midsummer fern flower will turn to dust in his fingers!

These are the tales people tell, and each of

them contains a grain of truth, though it is difficult to extract it.

But one thing is certain: the fern flower blossoms only once a year — on Midsummer's Eve.

There once lived a young man called Janek, and the people of his village called him Curious Janek, for he was interested in all things. He wanted to know about everything, and he listened to everyone. He was also very determined. All this was in Janek's nature. Whatever was easy to obtain, within an arm's length, meant nothing to him, and he had no desire for it; but whatever he had to risk his neck for — that was what he liked to go after most!

It happened that one evening, when he was sitting around the fire with his friends and carving a dog's head on a stick, a certain very wise and clever woman, who knew the world and understood all things, suddenly began to tell, slowly and quietly, the story of the fern flower.

Curious Janek listened intently, ears pricked, till the stick fell from his hands, and he nearly cut his fingers.

The old woman told of the fern flower as though she had seen it with her own eyes, though you would never have guessed from her poor and ragged clothes that she had had any good fortune at all in her life, at least not more than a thimbleful! When she had finished, Janek said to himself, 'Come what may, I must have that flower! And have it I shall, for if someone wants something enough, and says to himself that it shall be so, in the end he has his way and gains all!'

Janek repeated this wisdom to himself so often that in the end he believed it!

Not far from the village where Janek's cottage stood, with its garden and field, was a wood, below which Midsummer's Eve was celebrated with the burning of a bonfire. So Janek said to himself, 'While they are all hopping around the fire, I shall go into the forest and find the fern flower. If I do not succeed this year, I will go again next year, and then the next. In short, I will keep going there until the flower is mine!'

He had to wait several months until

Midsummer's Eve came round, and the whole time he thought of nothing but the wondrous fern flower. Time seemed to stand still for him.

At last the long-awaited day arrived, and then the long-awaited night was upon him. All the young people of the village ran off to light a fire, jump around it and make merry, as was the ancient custom. Curious Janek washed himself thoroughly, put on a white smock, a red sash and a cap with a peacock's feather, and, when the moment came and twilight fell, he ran pell-mell to the forest.

The forest was dark, silent, covered by a black night, with sparkling stars which shone only for themselves, since they cast no light on the ground. Janek knew the way to the depths of the forest well, but it seemed strange to him that now, in the darkness, when he set off into the deep forest, he could not find the familiar path, or recognize the trees. All seemed different. The tree-trunks were huge, and lay on the ground. There were so many logs that he could neither climb over them nor go around them; dense bushes appeared, which were not usually there, and everywhere he went there were many nettles to sting and irritate his skin. Darkness lay all around, black clouds appeared over his head, and in the midst of the clouds eyes would flash, staring at Janek as if they wanted to swallow him up! Sometimes they were yellow, sometimes green, red or white; they would flash and disappear. There were many such eyes, shining to the right, to the left, above and below; but Janek was not afraid of them. He knew they were only trying to frighten him, and he repeated to himself the old truth, often heard in his village — fear has big eyes!

On and on he went, but what a tiring walk it was!

A huge log suddenly appeared in the path, and Janek tripped and fell over it. He climbed

up on it, summoning all his strength, but when he was on top of it, he saw that the log was so small that he could have stepped over it easily!

A little farther, a pine tree barred his way. Janek could not see the top of it, but the base was as thick as a tower. He walked round it and saw that it was in fact only a slender sapling that could easily have served as a stick!

Now he realized that everything around him was no more than an illusion meant to trick his senses!

There appeared in front of him impenetrable thickets, and Janek threw himself at them. He forced his way through, broke them and stamped on them, until he was safely on the other side.

On and on he went, until he came to a quagmire. To walk round it was unthinkable. He tried to step on to it, but his feet sank into it. Suddenly, from out of nowhere, small islets appeared on it, and Janek began to leap from one to another. As soon as he stepped on one it would sink, but Janek moved so fast that he managed to reach the other side. He glanced back and saw that the islets looked like human heads made of mud and that they were laughing at him! He went on, and though he could no longer see the way, he found it easier now, though he was so confused that he did not even know where his village lay.

Then he saw it! There, in front of him, was a tall fern and, on one of its lower leaves, a tiny flower shining like a jewel. It had five golden petals, and in the centre, a smiling eye, which turned like a mill-wheel.

Janek's heart began to thump, and he was already reaching for the golden flower, when, suddenly, somewhere in the distance, a cock crowed. The flower opened its shining eye wide, blinked it, and disappeared. All around him he heard the sound of laughter, but Janek did not know whether it was the rustle of leaves or the croaking of frogs, for his head began to swim, his legs turned to jelly, and he fell to the ground.

After that he knew nothing until he woke up at home in bed, and heard his worried mother telling him how she had searched the forest all night for him, until she had finally found him, half dead, just before daybreak, and taken him home.

Only now did Curious Janek remember all that had passed, but he said nothing of it. He just thought to himself that all was not yet lost, for there would be another Midsummer's Eve, and then he would see . . .!

That whole year he thought of nothing but the flower, and when Midsummer's Eve came round again, he washed carefully, put on a white smock, his red sash, new shoes and the cap with the peacock's feather and, after his friends had gone to the bonfire, set off into the forest.

He thought that he would again have to force his way through thickets, but now the forest was not what he expected. There were slender oaks and pines growing in a parched field, strewn with boulders, and he had to jump from one to the next. The trees seemed to grow close together, but he could not stretch out and touch them. They seemed to be running away from him! The giant boulders, covered with moss, slippery and slimy, lay motionless, as if growing out of the ground. In between these grew large and small ferns, as though planted there, but none of them bore a flower. At first they were ankle-high, then knee-high, then waist-high, and then, as Janek went on, he was up to his head in them! It was as if he were drowning in a sea of ferns! The ferns made a noise like waves breaking on the shore, and out of that noise came the sound of crying and laughter. If Janek stepped on a fern it hissed, and when he touched one, it was as though blood flowed from it . . .

Janek seemed to have been walking for

a whole year, so endlessly did he wander. And nowhere was a flower to be seen! He did not turn back, did not lose heart, but went on. Then, lo and behold, he looked, and saw — shining in the distance — the precious fern flower with its five petals, and in its centre, an eye, turning like a mill-wheel! Janek leapt towards it, stretched out his hand to pluck it, and at that very moment, a cock crowed in the distance and, in a flash, the flower was gone!

But this time Janek did not faint, did not sink to the ground! He kept all his senses, and there was anger in his heart, and indignation.

'Third time lucky!' he cried, at last. And, tired out, he lay down on the moss and went to sleep.

He had scarcely closed his eyes when he began to dream. He saw in front of him the flower with its five petals and the eye in the centre, smiling.

'Well, Janek, have you had enough?' the flower asked. 'Or will you pursue me still?'

'What I have said will be!' said Curious Janek. 'All is not over. Just wait — I will have you yet!'

One of the petals grew in length until it looked like a long tongue, and it reminded Janek of naughty children who put out their tongues when they wish to be rude! Then the flower disappeared, and Janek slept soundly until morning. When he awoke, he was lying not far from the village, in a spot he knew well, and he began to wonder if all he had been through was a dream or reality, but he said nothing to anyone, though he could think of little else but how he might obtain the fern flower. Surely, the next time he tried, luck would be on his side.

A year passed, again it was Midsummer's Eve, and again Janek put on a white smock, red sash and new shoes, and took the hat with the peacock's feather. His mother tried to persuade him to stay at home. But Janek waited until nightfall and then set off for the woods.

Janek was surprised to find the forest looking as it had always looked. There was nothing strange about it. The paths and trees were familiar, and he noticed nothing unusual. There was no sign of any ferns, and he walked along quickly, for the way was familiar. Soon he was deep in the forest, and had reached the place where ferns always grew. He knew the place well, and found it easily, but, there was no sign of the fern flower. It was as though the ground had swallowed it up. Snails crawled over the leaves, caterpillars slept under them, and Janek noticed that some of the leaves were even withered.

He was about to give up his search when he spied the fern flower at his feet. It had five golden petals, and in the centre a gleaming eye. Holding his breath, Janek reached out and took the flower, to make sure it would not disappear. He felt a burning glow as the flower grew before his eyes. It glowed and shone until Janek had to close his eyes before the flood of light. He pressed the flower to his heart, and a voice

said, 'Now you have me! That is your good luck! But remember — whoever has the fern flower will have all he wishes, but he can never share his good fortune with anyone . . .'

Janek was so full of joy and excitement that he hardly noticed what the voice said, 'What does it matter,' he thought to himself, 'as long as I have all I want in the world.'

He began to sing triumphantly, as he set off home with jaunty steps. The path shone in front of him, the trees moved out of his way, the bushes parted for him, and the flowers bowed their heads to the ground before him. Head held high, he walked on and on, thinking of all he would ask for. First, he longed for a palace, and for many servants. Then he dreamt of being ruler of a vast country. No sooner did he have these thoughts, than he found himself on the edge of a forest, which he did not recognize.

He looked down at himself, and could not believe his eyes. He was dressed in a suit of handsome clothes, his shoes had golden buckles on them, and his belt was set with jewels, while his shirt was of the finest linen!

And there before him stood a coach with six white horses in gilded harness and servants in braided uniforms. A footman bowed low and helped him into the coach, and then the horses galloped away.

Janek did not for a moment doubt that they were driving to a palace, and indeed it was so! Presently, the coach drew up in the courtyard of a grand palace, where servants were already waiting. But he saw no one he knew; all the faces were strange, and some looked fearful.

But Janek could only think that his wishes had come true. He was almost overcome with awe at the power he had. Now he had everything he could possibly want.

'And I will make the most of it!' he told himself, when he had taken stock of everything.

And when, at last, weariness overtook him, he lay down on a magnificent couch covered with a silk counterpane. He did not know for how long he slept, but when he woke up he was conscious of feeling very hungry. Immediately, a table was laid, and the odd thing was that whatever delicacy he thought he would like to eat — there it was on the plate in front of him.

Janek ate and drank for a long time, until he was so stuffed with food that he lost his appetite altogether!

Then he went out into the garden.

The garden was richly planted with trees which, though full of blossom, had all manner of fruits hanging from their branches. On one side, the garden reached to the sea, on the other to a beautiful forest. Janek walked up and down, open-mouthed with wonder, but there was only one thing he could not understand. Why was his own countryside, the forest from which he had emerged, or his village, nowhere to be seen? He was not yet homesick, but he would dearly have liked to know what had become of the familiar landmarks.

All about Janek was a strange new world, splendid, but nonetheless unknown. He began to feel uncomfortable. But when he called out, servants came running, eager to carry out his slightest wish, and Janek soon forgot his native village, his cottage and his parents.

The next day, he went to inspect his treasure-house, which was crammed full of gold, silver and diamonds enough to buy all his heart might desire.

And Janek thought to himself, 'Goodness, if only I could send just a few of these riches to my mother and father, my brothers and sisters, so that they might buy more land and some cattle. How fine that would be.'

But Janek knew full well that if he shared his fortune with anyone, he would lose it all.

'Gracious me, why should I worry about others?' he asked himself after a moment. 'Why should I have to help them? They have brains,

and strength. Let them go and seek the fern flower; let them find their own way of making their fortunes.'

So the days passed, and Janek thought only of new diversions and pleasures for himself.

He built new palaces, had the gardens altered, ordered the white horses be changed for chestnuts, the greys for duns. He had treasures brought to him from the end of the world, and obtained delicacies from across the seas. But then, at last, he grew weary of everything. The rich foods sickened him and he began to eat raw

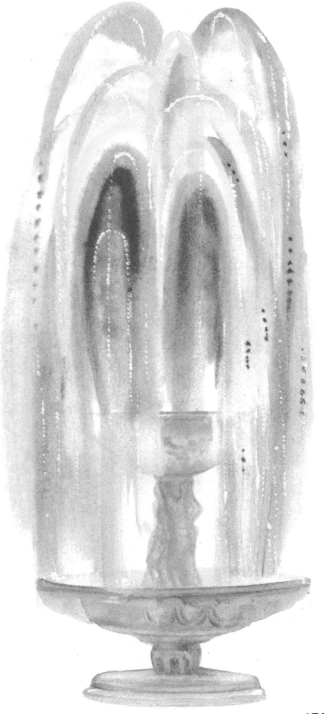

turnip, potatoes, beef. But, finally, he tired even of these plain foods, having lost his appetite completely.

But worse than never being hungry was never having any proper work to do. It was unfitting for him to take up an axe, a rake or a spade, and he grew bored, behaved wickedly, and when he had nothing else to do, began to torment his servants. This entertained him for a while, but, in the end, even that irked him.

Soon one whole year passed, and Janek had all he could want, but sometimes his good fortune seemed to him such a stupid thing that he even grew tired of life itself.

Most of all, he pined for his village, his cottage, and his parents. If only he could have seen them, just for a while, to find out what they were doing. He loved his mother very much, and whenever he remembered her now, his heart was wrung with grief.

One day, Janek felt such a longing for his home that he sat in his coach and wished he were in his own village, in front of his parents' cottage. No sooner had he wished this, than the horses broke into a gallop, flew like the wind, and were presently drawing up before the familiar farmyard. Tears filled Janek's eyes. All was there as he had left it, but everything was older and shabbier, and, after the splendour he had grown accustomed to, it seemed to him very wretched.

The old well, the tree-stump on which he used to chop wood, the cottage door, the roof overgrown with moss, the ladder leaning against it — all were there as if he had seen yesterday. But what of his parents?

From the cottage hobbled an old, bent woman in a dirty apron. She gazed fearfully at the coach as Janek climbed down and went towards his old home. Then he saw the old dog, Burek, skinnier than ever, his hair now standing menacingly on end. He barked fiercely at Janek, not knowing him.

Janek went up to the cottage, where his mother stood in the doorway. She looked at the stranger searchingly, but she too, failed to recognize her son.

Janek's heart thumped with excitement.

172

'Mother!' he cried. 'It's me, your Janek.'

When the woman heard the voice she shuddered, and through dim, tear-filled eyes she peered at Janek standing there as if glued to the spot. At last, she shook her head.

'Janek! You mock me, noble sir! Our son is dead. If he were alive, he would long ago have got in touch with his parents. And if he were a rich noble like you, he would not leave us to die of hunger.'

The old woman nodded her head and added, 'The idea of it! Janek had a good heart, and would never seek a fortune he could not share with us!'

Deep in his heart, Janek felt shame. He dropped his eyes. His pockets were full of gold pieces, but no sooner did he think of giving them to his mother, than he was overcome with the fear of losing all his fortune!

So he stood silent and abashed, and his mother went on staring at him. Behind her the whole family appeared, and when he saw his old father, Janek's heart almost broke. But then he thought of his fine coach, his horses, his servants, and best of all, his grand palace, and his heart again hardened! The warning of the fern flower could not be ignored! He turned away from his mother without speaking, and was seen off the premises by Burek's fierce barking. Words cannot tell, nor pen describe what went on inside Janek as he was taken back to his palace. Now his mother's words sounded in his ears like a curse!

When he returned, he ordered music to be played, saying there must be dancing and merry-making. But the parties, the feasting and the music did nothing to banish the gloom which filled Janek's waking hours.

Another year went by, and though he still had all he could wish for, there was a bitter taste in Janek's mouth, and his heart was heavy.

Again he drove to his native village.

He saw that everything was as it had been; the well, the stump for wood-chopping, the roof, the ladder, the door, and old Burek with his hair standing on end — but he did not see his mother in the doorway. Presently, his youngest brother, Matthew, came out of the cottage.

'Where is mother?' Janek asked.

'She is lying ill,' answered Matthew sadly.

'And father?'
'In the churchyard!'
Even though Burek flew at him barking

furiously, Janek went into the cottage. On a bed, in the corner of a shabby room, lay his mother, groaning with pain. Janek went up to her. She looked at him, but did not know him. She could no longer speak and Janek, too, was silent. His heart ached. A hand went into his pocket to give her gold, but then his fist closed, and he was again overcome by the shameful fear of losing all his good fortune. He began to comfort himself with the thought that his old mother no longer needed anything in this world. She would not suffer much longer, while he had his whole life before him!

He ran to his coach and was soon back in his palace. Once there, he shut himself in his room and wept. His conscience would not leave him in peace! He ordered the musicians to play and the courtiers to dance. He rode, shot, ate, drank, wandered in the garden, but all to no avail.

Within a year he had changed beyond recognition. He was thin and withered, had grown as sallow as wax, and was bitterly unhappy with his wealth and good fortune.

Finally, after a sleepless night, he filled his pockets with gold, and gave orders to be driven to his native cottage. He had decided that, even if he lost all, he must save his mother and his brothers and sisters from their terrible poverty.

The horses pulled up in front of the cottage. All was there as before: the old well, the stump, the roof overgrown with moss, the ladder — but there was not a living soul on the threshhold. Janek ran up to the door. It was locked. He looked through the window into the parlour — it was empty.

Then a beggar, standing a little way off by the fence, called to Janek, 'What are you looking for, noble sir? The cottage is empty; all inside died of hunger, want and sickness!'

Rich Janek stood in front of his cottage as if suddenly turned to stone. He was speechless with grief.

'They have died through my fault,' he said at last, quietly. 'Then let me die too!'

And no sooner had he said this than the ground opened, and the unhappy rich man disappeared into the bowls of the earth!

The fern flower, too, was lost for ever. It disappeared, as if it had been drowned in the sea, and no man ever set eyes on it again.

The Tale of the Fisherman and the Fish

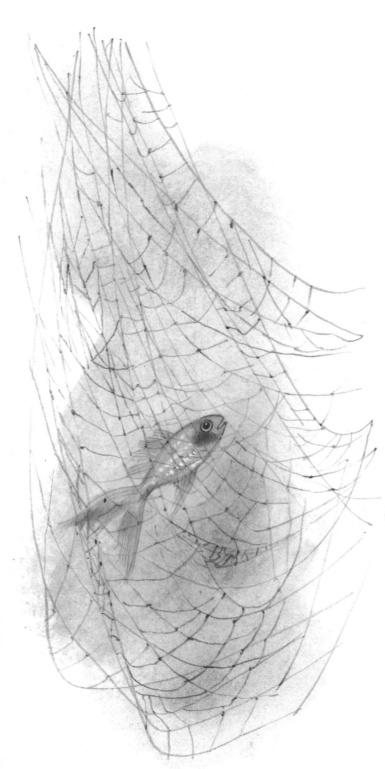

Once upon a time an old man and an old woman lived by the shore of the blue sea. They had lived in their stone cottage for three-and-thirty years. The old man caught fish in his nets, and the old woman spun thread.

One day the old man cast his nets into the sea and they came back full of mud. Again he cast them into the sea, and they came back filled with a ball of seaweed. When he cast them a third time, they came back containing a single fish. This was no ordinary fish — it was a golden fish!

The golden fish began to speak and, in a human voice, begged the old man for mercy.

'Let me go back into the sea, old man, and you will have a fine reward. I will grant you anything you ask for!'

The old man was surprised and startled. He had been fishing for thirty-three years, but had never before heard a fish speak. He let the golden fish go back into the sea, saying, 'God be with you, golden fish. I have no need of any reward. Swim away in the blue sea — rejoice and be merry in your freedom!'

The old man went back home to his wife and told her at once of the great marvel: 'Today, I caught a strange fish, no ordinary one, a golden fish. It spoke in a human voice, and wanted to be put back into the blue sea, saying that it would buy its freedom, that it would give me all I asked for. I did not have the courage to ask it for any reward, so I let it go back into the blue sea.'

'You stupid idiot, you fool!' the old woman thundered at her husband. 'You hadn't the courage to take a reward! If you had only asked for a new washtub; just look how my old one is falling to pieces!'

So the old man again rowed out to sea. Gentle waves were breaking. He began to call the golden fish. And the fish came swimming up to him. 'What do you need, old man?'

The old man bowed and answered, 'Take pity on me, gracious fish. My wife scolded me — she gives me no peace in my old age. She says that she needs a new washtub; that our old one is falling apart!'

The golden fish replied, 'Do not grieve, but go home with a light heart, she will have a new washtub!'

The old man returned to his wife and saw that she had a new washtub.

But now the woman scolded him more than ever, 'You stupid idiot, you fool! You were silly enough to ask only for a washtub? Go back to the fish at once, you fool, bow to him, and ask him for a new house!'

So the old man went out to sea again. The sea looked dark and menacing. But when he called the golden fish, it swam to him and asked, 'What do you need, old man?'

The old man bowed and answered, 'Take pity on me, gracious fish! My wife scolds me more than ever — she gives me no peace in my old age; she would have a new house!'

The golden fish replied, 'Do not grieve, go home with a light heart, you will have a new house.'

The old man made his way home. There was no sign of his stone cottage. In front of him stood a house with an upstairs parlour, a brick, whitewashed chimney, and a door made of oak. The old woman sat in the window, scolding and abusing the old fisherman as soon as he appeared.

'You stupid idiot, you slow fellow! You were silly enough to ask for an ordinary house? Go back to the fish at once, you simpleton. I don't want to live in this kind of house. I wish to be a high-born lady, and live away from the village!'

So the old man rowed out to sea — the blue sea — which was getting rough — and began calling the golden fish. The fish swam up, and asked, 'What do you need, old man?'

The old man bowed and answered, 'Take pity on me, gracious fish! My wife has grown even more foolish — she gives me no peace in my old age. She no longer wants to be a simple villager, but would like to be a high-born lady!'

The golden fish replied, 'Do not grieve, but go home with a light heart.'

The old man went home to his wife, and what

did he see! A tall mansion, and on its marble steps stood the old woman, dressed in a costly fur jacket, and an embroidered brocade hood. There were strings of pearls wrapped around her neck and ring upon ring on her fingers; white boots of real scarlet leather were on her feet. In front of her stood a respectful servant, and the old dame was beating him and pulling his hair!

The fisherman spoke to his wife, saying, 'Greetings, your illustrious ladyship. I hope you are now satisfied.'

But his wife began to scream at him, and then she sent him off to work in the stables.

One Sunday passed, and another, and the old woman grew more foolish than ever. Again she sent the old man to the golden fish, 'Go back, bow to the fish, and tell him I no longer wish to be a high-born lady. I want to be a mighty czarina!'

The old man was startled at this, and he tried to make her forget the whole idea.

'Woman, have you no sense at all? You do not know how to behave in royal company, you cannot speak graciously! Why, you will be the laughing-stock of the whole czardom!'

But his wife began to fret and fume, and she struck her husband across the cheek, 'How dare you argue with me! You are a peasant, and I am a high-born lady! Go down to the sea at once. If you do not, I will have you taken there by force!'

So the old man went down to the sea — the blue sea — which had grown black and threatening — and he began to call the golden fish. The fish came swimming up, and said, 'What do you need, old man?'

The old man bowed, and replied, 'Take pity on me, gracious fish! My wife is raging again. She no longer wants to be a high-born lady, but would be a mighty czarina!'

The golden fish replied, 'Do not grieve, go home with a light heart; your wife will be czarina if she so desires.'

The old man went back to his wife, and what did he see! His wife held sway in a palace. She was czarina! All were under her command, bowing and scraping! As she sat at table nibbling gingerbread hearts, an armed guard, with halberds on their shoulders, stood to attention. When the old man saw this, he, too, bowed almost to the ground in his wife's presence.

'Greetings,' he said, 'mighty Czarina! Now you must surely be satisfied!'

The old woman did not even look at him, but showed that she wished him removed from the throne room. And the old fisherman was thrown out. At the palace gates the soldiers took hold of him roughly and pretended they would chop him to pieces!

'Serves you right, you old fool! At least you see now the truth of the old saying: The shoemaker should stick to his last!'

One Sunday passed, then another, and the old woman grew more foolish. She sent her footmen to fetch the old man to her. They found him, and brought him to her.

She ordered, 'Go back, old man, bow to that fish of yours, and tell him I no longer want to be a mighty czarina. I want to be ruler of the seas, and live in the ocean. And your golden fish will serve me, and run errands for me!'

The old man did not dare protest; he did not dare to say a word! Instead, he went to the blue sea. He saw a black storm over the sea. Angry waves had risen. They rolled and roared and crashed. He began to call the golden fish. The fish swam up and asked, 'What do you need, old man?'

The old man bowed, and replied, 'Take pity on me, gracious fish; what can I do with the terrible woman! She no longer wants to be a mighty czarina, she wants to be ruler of the seas, to live in the ocean, and she wants you to serve her — to run errands for her!'

The fish said nothing. It flapped its tail on the surface and then disappeared into the deep sea.

The old man waited a long time for an answer, but none came.

So he went home to the old woman — and what did he see? Why — the stone cottage and his wife sitting on the step — with the broken washtub beside her!

The Flying Argosy

There once lived a man and his wife, who had three sons, two of them sensible and the third foolish. The mother loved the two sensible ones, and dressed them cleanly; but she always neglected the third. He was poorly dressed, and went about in a black smock. One day they heard that the czar had made a pronouncement, 'Whoever builds a flying argosy, will have my daughter for his wife!'

The older brothers decided to try their luck, and asked their aged parents for their blessing. The mother gave them good provisions for their journey, food and a bottle of wine. The stupid son, too, asked to be allowed to go. His mother tried to persuade him not to: 'Why are you in such a hurry to go — the wolves will eat you!'

But the stupid son droned on and on, 'I shall go, I shall go!'

When the mother saw that it was no good arguing with him, she gave him some black griddle cakes and a bottle of water, and led him out of the house.

The stupid fellow walked until he met an old man. They greeted each other, and the old man asked, 'Where are you going?'

'Well — it is like this — the czar has promised his daughter to whoever makes a flying ship.'

'And you can make such a ship?'

'No, I cannot; how could I do such a thing?'

'Then why are you going?'

'God knows.'

'Very well,' said the old man. 'If that is how it is, sit down here, rest a while, and we shall eat what you have in your bag.'

'I have something there, but I am ashamed to show it.'

'It does not matter; just take it out — whatever you have we shall eat.'

The stupid fellow untied his bag, and could not believe his eyes; instead of black griddle cakes, there were white breadrolls and all kinds of dainty and tasty food. He offered some to the old man.

'You see,' said the old man, 'how God cares for simple folk; although your own mother does not love you, you are not kept short. Well then — let us drink a little wine also!'

And so it was: instead of water the bottle contained wine! When they had eaten their fill and drunk the wine, the old man said, 'Listen carefully. Go into the forest, go up to the first tree you see, cross yourself three times, and strike the tree with an axe; then lie on your back on the ground and wait until you are roused from your sleep. You will see in front of you a ship. Sit in it and fly where you wish, and take with you whoever you meet on the way.'

The stupid fellow thanked the old man, took his leave of him, and went to the forest. When he came to the first tree, he did all he had been told. He crossed himself three times, struck the tree with an axe, fell on his back on the ground, and went to sleep. Some time later someone began to wake him. He woke up, and saw — a finished ship. He did not hesitate, but sat in the

ship, and flew up in the air. He flew and flew,
then — behold, down below him on the path,
a man lay with his ear to the bare ground.

'Greetings, fellow!' he called.

'Good-day,' came the answer.

'What are you doing?'

'I am listening to what is going on in the
world.'

'Sit in the ship with me!'

And the man sat in the ship, and they flew on.
They flew and flew, then they saw a man
hopping on one leg, with the other tied to his
ear.

'Good-day, fellow. Why are you hopping on
one leg?'

'If I were to untie the other, I should jump
across the whole world in one leap.'

'Sit with us!'

The hopping man sat in the ship with them,
and they flew on. They flew and flew, then saw
a man standing with a rifle and aiming at
something or other.

'Greetings, fellow! What are you aiming at?
There is not even the smallest songbird to be
seen!'

'Oh, why should I shoot anything so close!
Why, I mean to shoot an animal or a bird
a thousand leagues from here — that's how well
I can shoot!'

'Sit with us!'

And he too sat with them, and they flew on.
They flew and flew, then saw a man carrying
a sack full of bread on his back.

'Good-day, fellow! Where are you going?'

'I am going to earn the bread for my lunch.'

'Bread for your lunch? How is that? Why,
you have a full sack of bread on your back!'

'That is nothing — it is not enough for a small
snack!'

'Sit with us!'

The glutton sat in the ship, and they flew on.
They flew and flew — then they saw a man
walking around a lake.

'Good-day, fellow! What are you looking
for?'

'I want a drink, and there is no water
anywhere.'

'No water anywhere? Why, you have in front
of you a whole lake; why do you not drink from
it?'

'Oh, all that water is not enough for one draught!'

'Then sit with us!'

He sat down in the ship, and they flew on. They flew and flew — then they saw a man walking through the forest with a bundle of faggots on his back.

'Good-day, fellow! Why are you carrying faggots to the forest?'

'These are no ordinary faggots.'

'What kind are they?'

'If you throw them all about, a whole army will appear here!'

'Sit with us!'

He sat down in the ship, and they flew on. They flew and flew, and suddenly saw a man carrying a bundle of straw.

'Good-day, fellow! Where are you taking the straw?'

'To the village!'

'Have they not enough straw in the village?'

'But this is special straw: however hot the summer is, throw this straw down and there will at once be snow and frost.'

'Sit here with us!'

'Very well!'

They flew and flew, and soon came to the czar's court. The czar was sitting at his lunch. He saw the flying ship, was filled with wonder, and sent his servant to ask who had arrived in such a ship. The servant came to the ship, looked inside it, and told the czar that there were no gentlemen in the ship, only some peasant and his companions. The czar decided it was unfitting to give his daughter to a simple peasant, so he began to wonder how he could rid himself of such a son-in-law. He decided to set him a number of difficult tasks.

He sent the peasant an order to obtain for him — but before his lunch was over — a healing and living water. Now, at the very moment the czar was speaking of this to his servant, the first traveller in the ship, the one who had been listening to what was going on in the world, heard the order and told the master of the flying ship what the czar had said.

'What shall I do now? Why, I could not find such water even if I had a whole year, perhaps never in all my life!' exclaimed the stupid fellow.

'Do not worry,' said the man who hopped on one leg. 'I shall arrange it for you!'

Then the servant appeared and told them of the czar's command.

'Tell him it shall be done!' answered the stupid fellow. His companion untied his leg from his ear, ran to the other end of the world, and took the living and healing water from a wondrous well there.

'I have time enough,' he thought to himself. And he sat down to rest, and went to sleep! The czar's lunch was drawing to a close, but the marvellous runner was nowhere to be seen. There was much ado in the ship, and the first traveller, who could hear all that went on in the world, put his ear to the ground.

'He is asleep!' he answered.

The shooter grabbed his rifle, shot into a tree above the sleeper, and the noise awoke the hopping man. He broke into a run, and in next-to-no-time was back with the water. Thus it was that, before the czar had risen from the table, the order had been carried out!

What was he to do? He must set another task. After a moment's thought, he knew what to ask for!

'If you are so clever,' the czar said, 'show what you can do. You and your companions must eat twelve roast oxen and twelve sacks of baked bread!'

'Why, I could not even eat one loaf of bread at a sitting!' exclaimed the unhappy owner of the flying ship.

'Do not worry,' said the glutton. 'Such a meal will not even be enough for me!'

Servants brought twelve roast oxen and twelve sacks of baked bread. The glutton ate it all by himself, and said, 'Dear me, that was not enough; if only they had given me a little more!'

The czar then ordered the stupid fellow to drink with his companions forty casks of wine — each holding forty firkins.

'Why, I could not even drink a single firkin!' the stupid fellow declared, when he heard the order.

'Do not worry,' said the drinker, 'I shall drink it all myself — and it will not even be enough!'

The forty casks were filled with wine. The drinker came and drank all the wine without pausing. When he had done, he said, 'Dear me, too little, too little! I should like some more!'

Then the czar ordered the stupid fellow to get ready for his wedding. First he was to wash and bathe; but the bathroom was of metal, and the czar ordered it to be heated so fiercely that the stupid fellow would at once pass out from the heat!

It was heated to red hot. The stupid fellow went to wash, but his companion with the straw bundle went with him. He scattered the straw around — and at once it was so cold that, as soon as the stupid fellow had washed, the water began to freeze in the tubs, and he climbed behind the stove and lay there all night.

When they opened the bathroom in the morning, the stupid fellow was alive and well, lying by the stove and singing to himself. When the czar heard this, he was sorely distressed. Now he did not know how to get rid of his unwelcome son-in-law. He thought and thought, and finally ordered him to muster a whole regiment of soldiers. He thought to himself, 'Where would a simple peasant find soldiers? He surely cannot do it!'

As soon as the stupid fellow heard this, he was dismayed, and said, 'Now it really is the end of me. Friends, you have helped me; you have helped me many times in distress, but now there is nothing to be done!'

'Ah,' spoke up the companion with the bundle of faggots, 'you have forgotten me!'

Then the stupid fellow warned the czar's servant that if the czar continued to make excuses, he would conquer his whole empire, and take the princess by force with the army he was about to raise!

In the night, the stupid fellow's companion went into the fields, brought his bundle of faggots, and threw them down on all sides. At once, countless soldiers sprang up — cavalry, infantry, and artillery, all dressed in shining armour, and heavily armed.

In the morning the czar saw the soldiers, and was dismayed. At once he sent the stupid fellow some very fine clothes, and invited him to the palace to marry the princess. When the stupid fellow put on those fine garments, he looked every inch a hero! Then he came to the czar, married the princess, received half the czardom, and became a shrewd and sensible man. The czar and the czarina grew to like him, and the princess loved him with all her heart for the rest of his life.

Grandfather Frost

I'll tell you a fine tale, which old Iriniey told
the children for their entertainment and
instruction:

In a certain house, two sisters, Celia and
Larga, lived with their old nurse. Celia was
a sharp child; she got up by herself, dressed
herself, asked the nurse for nothing, and almost
as soon as she got out of bed, she began to
work. She lit the fire, made dough for the bread,
swept the parlour, gave the cock some grain,
and went to the well for water. In the meantime,
Larga lay snug under her eiderdown. Long after
the church clock had struck noon, there she
would lie, turning from side to side, and when
she grew tired of lying in bed, she got up, and
would call to the nurse, 'Babushka, do you hear
me, Babushka, tie up my shoelaces!'

Then she would whine, 'Babushka, have you
a breadroll for me?'

When she was dressed, she would wander about the house, then sit by the window and count how many flies came and went. When she had finished counting them, she would not know what to do with herself. She would think of going back to bed, but didn't want to. She would think of having something to eat, but did not feel like it. She could have counted the flies on the window again, but even that was no fun any more, so she would sit unhappily, crying a little, and complaining to all and sundry that she had nothing to do, as though it were someone's fault!

Meanwhile, Celia did not stop her work even to rest. She strained the water, and poured it into the jug. She knitted or hemmed dresses, and sometimes even cut out a smock and sewed it. And all the time she sang as she worked. She was never bored, for she had no time to be. She hurried from one task to the next, and before she knew it, it was evening — the day was over!

One day Celia had an accident. She went to

the well for water and let the bucket down, but the rope broke and the bucket fell into the well. What now? Poor Celia burst into tears, and ran to tell the nurse what had happened. The nurse, Praskovia, was an irate and strict old woman, and she said, 'What you have spoilt, you must put right. You dropped the bucket in the well, you must get it out.'

There was nothing else for it. Celia went back to the well and shinned down the rope to the very bottom.

And there a marvel occurred. Scarcely had her feet touched the bottom, when an oven appeared in front of her, and in the oven stood a ruddy-brown, well-baked piroshek. It stood there, winked at her, and sang:

I am a pastry treat,
Filled with sultanas sweet;
Baked in the oven's heat,
Ready for you to eat.

Celia did not hesitate, but grabbed a baker's peel, pulled out the piroshek, and shoved it in her pocket. She went on until she came to an orchard. In that orchard there stood an apple tree covered with golden apples, and the apples rustled the leaves and sang:

Golden apples we,
Hanging on the tree,
And if you wish to take us
You only have to shake us!

Celia jumped up to the tree, shook a branch, and golden apples poured into her apron.

She went on. Then, suddenly, what should she see! Sitting in front of her was Grandfather Frost, all grey, resting on a bench of ice, and swallowing handfuls of snowflakes. When he shook his head, hoar frost fell from his hair, and when he breathed out, thick vapour poured from his mouth.

'Welcome, Celia,' said the old man. 'It is good that you have brought me a piroshek. It is a long time since I ate something warm.'

He sat Celia next to him, and together they ate the piroshek and bit into the golden apples.

'I know well enough why you have come,' said Grandfather Frost, 'you dropped the bucket

into my well, into my shaft. I will give you back your bucket, for why shouldn't I, but in return you must serve me for three days. If you work hard you will not go without a reward. If you are lazy, you will take away a poor payment. But now I must rest; go and prepare my bed, but take heed, do not forget to shake the feathers down well.'

Celia did as she was told. They went into the house. Grandfather Frost's house was made all of ice. The doors, windows, floors, everything was ice, the walls set with snowflakes — the sun shone on them, and everything in the house sparkled like diamonds. On the old man's bed, instead of an eiderdown, was powdery snow. It was cold, but there was no getting round it. Celia began to shake down the snow, so that the old man might sleep, and as she was doing the work her poor hands stiffened, and her fingers whitened like those of us who have to cut holes in frozen rivers and rinse our washing in icy water. The hands freeze, and the wind blows

the washing until it becomes as hard as bone.

'Do not worry,' said Grandfather Frost, 'just rub your fingers with snow; the blood will flow, and they will not chap. You know, I do not have an evil heart — just look how I keep my treasures!'

And the old man lifted the snowy eiderdown and sheet, and Celia saw green grain sprouting beneath the eiderdown. She was sorry for the crisp grain, and said, 'You say you do not have a wicked heart. But why do you keep green grain beneath a snowy eiderdown; why do you not let it go into God's world?'

'I do not let it go, because its time has not yet come; it has not yet enough strength . . . a good farmer sows it in autumn; the seeds sprout, but if the stems grow up, the cold will destroy them, and the grain will not ripen in summer. Therefore, I covered the young grain with my snow eiderdown, and lie on it myself, so that the wind will not blow the snow away. When spring comes, the snow eiderdown will melt, the grain will grow up into ears, and soon grains will swell in the ears, and the farmer will reap them, thresh them, and take them to the mill. The miller will grind the grain into flour, and you, Celia, will make bread from that flour.'

'And can you tell me, old man,' said Celia, 'why you are sitting in a well?'

'I am sitting in a well because spring is on the way,' answered Grandfather Frost. 'It is too hot for me above the ground. You know that it is cold in a well even in summer. Therefore the water in it is cold, even on the hottest days.'

And the good Grandfather Frost stroked Celia's cheek, and lay down to rest on his snow bed.

While he was asleep, Celia cleaned the whole house, then cooked a meal in the kitchen, mended the old man's clothes and darned his linen.

When Grandfather Frost woke up, he was extremely satisfied, and thanked her. Then they had lunch together.

Thus Celia spent three days with Grandfather Frost. The third day, the old man said to her, 'Thank you, you are a clever girl. You have warmed my old heart, and I shall reward you well for that. It is the custom that people receive money for their work. Take your bucket back. I have poured a handful of silver pieces in it for you. And look, I have prepared you a diamond hairpin. Take it as a memento of me.'

Celia thanked him kindly, stuck the diamond hairpin in her plait, picked up the bucket, went back to the well, and climbed up the rope to the world above.

As soon as she got near home, the cock, whom she gave grain to every morning, saw her, flew up on the fence, and crowed joyfully:

Cockadoodledoo!
Celia has come,
Bringing silver home!

When Celia came into the parlour, she told of all that had happened. The nurse was filled with wonder, and said, 'You see, Larga, what rewards you get for good work. You, too, should go to Grandfather Frost, and serve him well, like Celia here, clean for him, cook for him, mend his clothes and darn his linen. You will get a handful of silver pieces, too. We could use them. Easter is coming, and we have hardly any money.'

Larga was not too taken with the idea of going into the old man's service. But the silver pieces were tempting, and she dearly wanted a diamond hairpin!

So at last she went to the well and, like Celia, climbed down the rope, and jumped straight to the bottom. She looked about her until, suddenly, an oven appeared in front of her, and in it stood a ruddy-brown, well-baked piroshek. It stood there, looked at her, and sang:

I am a pastry treat,
Filled with sultanas sweet;
Baked in the oven's heat,
Ready for you to eat.

Larga shouted at it, 'The idea of it! Do you expect me to climb into an oven after you? If you want to, you'll jump out soon enough.'

She went on until she came to the orchard. In the orchard stood the apple tree covered with golden apples, and the apples rustled the leaves and sang:

Golden apples we,
Hanging on the tree,
And if you wish to take us
You only have to shake us!

'To be sure!' said Larga. 'Me, go to all that trouble, put out my hand and shake your heavy branches. I shall wait until the apples fall, then I'll pick as many as I want off the ground!'

And she went on past the apple trees as if they weren't there. She came to Grandfather Frost. Again he was sitting on the icy bench and eating handfuls of snowflakes.

'What do you want, my girl?' he asked.

'I have come to serve you and earn a reward.'

'Well said, my girl,' the old man agreed, 'all work deserves payment. We only have to see what your work is like. Go and shake down my eiderdown, cook some food, mend my clothes and darn my linen!'

Larga went, and on the way she groaned, 'I am not fool enough to slave away with the eiderdown and get my fingers chapped. The old man probably won't notice anyway, and he'll sleep the same whether I shake down his eiderdown or not.'

Grandfather Frost really did not notice anything; at least he pretended not to. He lay down in the bed, went to sleep, and Larga went to the kitchen.

When she got there, she did not know what to do. She enjoyed her food, but she had never taken an interest in how it was prepared; she had never even thought of it! And she was so lazy that it tired her just to watch her sister cooking.

She looked around the kitchen. On the table was everything she needed: vegetables, meat, fish, vinegar, mustard and ferment. Larga thought for a long time what she should do with this, then she began peeling the vegetables, very carelessly. She cut the meat and fish in pieces, and, so as not to make too much work for herself, threw the lot, washed and unwashed, into a pan. She filled it to the brim with vegetables, meat, fish, mustard and vinegar, then poured the ferment over it, and said to herself, 'Why should I take the trouble to cook everything separately? Why, it all gets mixed together in the stomach, anyway!'

The old man woke up and asked for his lunch. Larga thrust the pan in front of him, and didn't even think to lay a tablecloth. Grandfather Frost tried it, and frowned. Grains of sand grated between his teeth.

'What a splendid cook you are!' he smiled. 'Better see how you get on with the rest of the work.'

Larga helped herself from the pan as well, but she spat the food out at once. So the old man, with a groan, set to and cooked something himself, making such a splendid lunch that Larga licked all her fingers as she ate it.

After lunch, the old man again went to rest, and reminded Larga that he needed his clothes mended and his linen darned. Larga's face fell, but there was nothing for it but to go through the clothes and the linen and get on with the mending. There was one small problem. Larga greatly liked to dress up, but she had never in her life asked anyone to show her how clothes were sewn. So she picked up a needle, but since she did not know how to use it, she pricked herself, and, annoyed, put it down again.

Again Grandfather Frost pretended not to notice anything. He invited Larga to supper, and even made up her bed for her.

This, of course, suited Larga well. She said to herself that she would somehow get through the three days, that her sister had waited on the

old man through her own stupidity. Why, he was so kind-hearted, he would surely give her the silver pieces, even if she did no work!

On the third day, Larga came to Grandfather Frost, asking to be allowed home and to be paid for her work.

'And what was your work like? What have you done?' asked Grandfather Frost. 'If we were to settle up fairly, you would have to pay me, for you did not work for me, but I served you!'

'What do you mean?' said Larga, surprised. 'I have lived in your house for a whole three days!'

'My dear,' said Grandfather Frost. 'You should know that living and serving are two different things, and that not all work is alike. Remember it well — you may find it useful. But as you have not a spark of conscience in you, I shall pay you. As you have worked, so you shall be rewarded!'

With these words, Grandfather Frost placed a large piece of silver in one of Larga's hands, and a diamond in the other. Larga was so pleased that she grabbed the presents without even thanking the old man, and dashed off home.

She rushed into the parlour and boasted, 'Look what I have earned! What are Celia's few silver pieces and silly little stone compared to my lump of silver and a diamond as big as a fist . . . I shall be dressed like a queen for the holiday!'

But, before she had finished speaking, the silver lump had melted and changed into a puddle on the floor. And soon the diamond too began to thaw, and the cock leapt up on the fence and started crowing:

Cockadoodledoo! Cockadoodledoo!
Larga, who likes to laze and shirk,
Got ice, not silver, for her work!

And you, children, think for yourselves about that story old Iriniey told you. What is true and what is not! What he told you as a joke. And how much he wanted you to learn from it, when he was winking and nudging the clever ones, and smiling at the lazy ones! And remember well — that good work and good deeds seek no reward, for they are their own rewards!

And do not forget me, do not forget old Iriniey, who has so many tales and stories for you that there is no end to them!

The Tale of the Brave Hare, Matthew Longear

Once upon a time in the forest, there was born a hare who was afraid of everything. Whenever a twig cracked, or a bird flew away, whenever the snowy cap fell from a tree, he was so startled that it is a wonder he did not die of fright!

He was afraid one day, he was afraid the next day; he was afraid for a week, a month, and a whole year! When, at last, he had grown big, he got tired of this constant fear.

'Now I am afraid of nothing!' he shouted to the whole forest. 'Now I am not afraid at all, so there!'

And the old hares gathered round, the young hares came running up, the granny hares hopped along, and all of them listened as Matthew Longear made his boast — listened, and could not believe their ears. It was unheard of for a hare to be afraid of nothing and no one!

'Listen, Matthew, aren't you even afraid of the wolf?'

'I'm not afraid of the wolf, or of the fox, or of the bear. I'm not afraid of anyone at all!'

They all found this very amusing. The young hares burst out laughing, and politely put their front paws over their muzzles. The very, very old granny hares had a laugh, and even the old-men hares had a laugh, for they knew well enough what foxes' claws and wolves' teeth were like.

What a ridiculous hare! What a joke it was! And all were suddenly in a good mood.
They began to turn somersaults, hop and jump and race each other up and down, as if they had gone mad.

'There is nothing more to be said,' shouted Matthew Longear the hare, who was by now

full of courage. 'If I meet a wolf, I shall eat him up!'

What a ridiculous hare! And how stupid!

They all agreed how stupid he was, and all laughed again.

The hares were all thinking about the wolf, and — speak of the devil — suddenly, out of the blue, the wolf was there!

He had walked the length and breadth of the forest, going about his wolf's work, until he got hungry, and it occurred to him, 'How about a nice hare for lunch?' And just at that moment he heard, somewhere nearby, the yelling of hares, and they were speaking of him, of the wolf!

He stopped, moved downwind, and quietly strolled up to them.

When he got near, he heard their laughter, and it seemed that the hare laughing loudest was Matthew Longear! He was all puffed up!

'Just you wait, tubby, I'll make a fine meal of you,' said the wolf to himself. And he looked closely at the hare who boasted that he wasn't even afraid of the wolf.

But the hares knew nothing of the watching wolf, and went on making merry.

In the end, Matthew the Fearless climbed up on a tree-stump, sat down, and began shouting, 'Now, listen to me, you cowardly bunnies, and look at me; I'll show you something: I . . . I . . . I . . .'

Then, it was as though his tongue had frozen. He suddenly saw the wolf gazing at him fixedly.

The others did not see the wolf. But Matthew

Longear could not take his eyes off him! Then the unexpected happened.

The fearless hare jumped like a bouncing ball, but in his fright he somehow managed to land right on the wolf's head. He slid down the wolf's back, turned a somersault in the air, and high-tailed off, in a cloud of dust. He ran and ran, as fast as his legs could carry him. It seemed to him that the wolf was at his heels all the time, and that he would catch him at any moment. In the end, he could run no farther, and, closing his eyes, he rolled, half-dead, under a green bush.

Meanwhile, the wolf was running in the opposite direction. At the moment the hare dropped on his head, he had an idea that someone had shot at him, and he ran off. There were plenty more hares in the forest, and in any case this one had been a little crazy.

It took the other hares some time to come to their senses. Some of them made off into the bushes, some hid behind the tree-stump, and others quickly went to ground.

'But our Matthew really put the wind up that wolf!' they told each other. 'If it hadn't been for him, we should have lost our skins! Where has he got to? Find him, bring him here — our hero!'

They began to look for him. They ran to and fro, but the brave hare, Matthew Longear, was nowhere to be found. Had another wolf eaten him after all?

Finally, they found him, lying in a hole under a bush, half-dead with fear.

'You certainly gave him what for!' the hares cried, with one voice. 'Whoever would have thought it of you? But you really put the fear of death into that old wolf! Thank you, friend. And we thought you were just showing off! Now we know that you are a hero!'

Matthew Longear recovered immediately at this. Behold, the conquering hero! He climbed out of the hole, blinked, and proclaimed proudly, 'You didn't really think I was afraid, did you?'

'No, no, certainly not!' cried all the hares together.

And from that day, Matthew Longear believed that he really was afraid of nothing and no one!

The Young Man
and the Flea

A young man was walking along one day.
After going some way, he sat down beside
a large stone to have a bite to eat. He ate his fill,
lay down in the grass, rested his head on the
stone, and went to sleep. Presently, he began to
dream. It was a strange dream. In it, someone
was singing in a high-pitched voice close to his
ear! He opened his eyes — and there it was
again. So it wasn't a dream! The voice seemed
to come from the stone or under it. The young
man put his ear to the stone — the singing was
coming from inside. Now he could even make
out the words, 'Lucky young man! Free me
from my hard imprisonment. Seven hundred
years I have been trapped by the power of evil
forces, and cannot die. You were born at sunrise
on Easter Day. You are the only one in the
whole world who can help me, if you are
willing.'

The young man was filled with wonder.

'It is not enough to be willing,' he said. 'Where
am I to find the strength to smash this stone?
Tell me of your misfortune, and tell me what
I must do.'

The voice from the stone said, 'Find a rowan
tree which is growing where three courtyards
meet, and cut off a branch a span long and as
thick as your thumb. Then pick a handful of
thyme. Pile these together, the branch and the
thyme. Set fire to them, and smoke the stone
with them; then walk around it nine times
against the sun. But make sure the smoke gets
into all the cracks. Then my prison will open,
and I will be set free. I promise to remain in
your debt; I will be grateful to you all my life,
and make you famous and rich.'

The young man thought a while before he
said, 'One must help one's neighbour in distress.
And I will help you. But I do not yet know
whether you are good or evil. Swear that you
will harm no one when you are free.'

The unknown prisoner inside the stone
promised him, and he set off into the forest to
find the rowan tree and to pick the thyme.

He knew of a place, not far away, where the
boundaries of three courtyards met. And at that
place there grew a rowan tree. But he was
a long time finding the herb, so it was the next

shuddered, and a terrifying noise filled the air. The stone jumped the height of two men into the air. Suddenly, out of it came a manikin, who leapt aside like lightning as the stone crashed to the ground, showering the young man and the manikin with dust and earth.

The manikin recovered himself quickly and began to embrace his deliverer, to kiss his hands and feet, until the young man begged him to stop.

They both sat on the grass, and the manikin told the young man who he was.

'I was a noted magician,' he began, 'and did nothing but good. I treated sick people and animals, saved them from witches and wizards, and they gave me all kinds of presents. But the witches and wizards feared me like fire. More than once these evil spirits attempted to destroy me, but I always discovered their monstrous designs in time. One day the wizards collected much gold, and sent it to the North, to the Black Magician, the most powerful of all their clan. He stole all my magic potions and imprisoned me in that stone. Only someone born at sunrise on the first day of Easter could save me.

Seven hundred years I waited for such a person — a man with an open spirit and a clean heart! You came and freed me from my prison. I will be grateful to you all my life, and serve you all my days. You will become the most fortunate person in the world. And in return you must help me settle accounts with that cruel demon if we find him. Meanwhile, I must hide, so that my enemies will not know I have been delivered. I will change into a flea, and live in the pocket of your trousers. If you need my help or advice, I will jump into your ear and tell you what to do. You need not feed me. I spent seven hundred years inside the stone without food or drink, and now it is enough for me that I am free. That is all I wish to tell you. And now, let us rest — in the morning we shall go to seek our fortune.'

And the manikin, undoubtedly an important magician, composed himself for sleep, while the young man ate a hunk of bread, and then lay down on the grass beside him. When he awoke the sun was already high in the sky. There was no sign of the manikin and he decided that he had been the victim of a strange dream.

day before the young man returned to the stone. When night fell, he began to smoke it. He walked around the stone, and made sure that the smoke went into every crevice and crack. The moment he had walked round it for the ninth time, the ground beneath his feet

He ate some food, and set off on his journey. He had scarcely gone a few paces when he saw three travellers. They looked like artisans, each with a leather bag on his back, and the young man was amazed to hear a whisper in his ear as he approached them.

'Propose to the travellers that they take a rest, and find out where they are going.'

The young man realized that the manikin was no dream, but that he had hidden in the pocket of his trousers and, as he had promised, was telling him what to do.

The young man went up to the travellers, greeted them, and suggested that they should take their rest while they talked together. He asked where they were heading for, and suggested they might all journey together — it would be merrier with four.

The artisans told him that a great misfortune had come about in the capital city. The king's only daughter, while bathing in the river, had drowned. Her body had vanished, despite the fact that the water in the place where she had been bathing was shallow.

There was a tickling behind the young man's ear, and he heard the words, 'Go with them!'

The young man followed the advice and went with the artisans.

They walked a long way, until they came to a dark forest. As they were walking in the forest, they saw beside the ditch a horse's nosebag, very much the worse for wear.

There was a tingling whisper in the young man's ear and he heard the words, 'Pick up the bag; it will be of great service to you.'

'What might I gain from an old nosebag?' the young man thought to himself, but he picked up the bag all the same. He threw it across his shoulder and laughingly said, 'I, poor thing, must spurn no find. It may come about that even this old bag may be useful!'

The travellers replied jokingly, 'Take it, if it appeals to you. It will not weigh you down much!'

Little did they know that they would be

grateful to the young man for taking the old nosebag!

The travellers grew weary with the heat, and decided to rest beneath a spreading tree. They sat down and took their food from their packs. And again there was a whisper in the young man's ear — it was the flea again!

'Tell the bag,' said the voice, 'to give you your fill.'

The young man did not believe the flea, but he thought to himself, 'If he is joking then I, too, may have a jest, and make my new friends merry.'

He took the bag from his shoulder, laid it beside his feet on the grass, tapped it gently with his stick, and said, 'Little bag, little bag, give us something to eat.'

And, lo and behold! In the spot where the bag lay, a table grew up, covered with a white cloth, and on the table were bowls of delicious soup — just asking to be eaten! There were plates of roast pork, sausages, and rich cakes to follow. And, to drink, beer and wine of the finest quality.

The young man and his fellow-travellers needed no persuasion to set to. In all their lives they had never enjoyed such a feast! When they had all drunk and eaten their fill, the table disappeared, and the old bag lay there again on the grass. But now the artisans did not laugh when they looked at it. Each of them wanted to have such a treasure for himself, and they nearly fell out over it. When the young man saw that all was not well, he said to the artisans, 'I was the one who found this bag, and I am the one who will carry it.'

There was no denying the truth of this, and the artisans agreed. But they could not allow this miraculous bag to be treated like a bit of old rubbish. One of the artisans took a needle and thread, sewed a cover out of his bread bag for it, and put the nosebag inside, so that it would feel better.

The travellers rested and went on. After their good lunch the going was easy and very merry. They sang, joked, laughed, and when evening came they lay beneath a bush to sleep. The nosebag again supplied them with food and drink. But now there was a new problem: how were they to protect the bag from robbers?

They discussed this among themselves, and it
was decided that the four of them would put
their heads on the bag, and stretch their legs in
different directions — one to the north, another
to the south, the third to the east, and the fourth
to the west. And, as an extra precaution, the
young man tied the bag to his left hand with
a piece of string, so that he would feel at once if
anyone touched it. It now seemed that they
could sleep peacefully. But time and again one
of them woke up, and groped around to see if
the bag was still with them.

In the morning they arose, ate a carefree
breakfast, and went on. The bag fed them
throughout the whole week it took them to
reach the capital city of the kingdom.

Scarcely had the travellers entered the city
when the young man heard whispering in his
ear. It was the flea telling him that the king's
daughter had been captured by an evil fairy, and
was now in an underwater cave. The flea
promised to help him find the cave. In the
meantime, the young man must go straight to
the king and tell him that he would find the
drowned girl. And if any evil were to befall him,
the king must promise to give half the reward to
his three friends, and to divide the other half
among the poor.

The king did not believe that he would find
his daughter, for a long time had now passed
since she had drowned. But he received the
young man cordially, and promised him that if

he did not return, he would share out the reward as he asked.

The moment the young man left the royal palace the flea advised him, 'Go to the river tonight, and catch three crayfish. They will help you find the wicked fairy!'

The young man did as he was told, went to the river, caught three crayfish, and hid them.

The next day, people crowded the river-bank to watch the young man begin his search for the princess. The king himself came, and he brought the princess's maids with him. They pointed out the spot where their royal mistress had drowned, saying that the accident had happened before their very eyes.

The young man saw that the river was shallow at the fatal place. He could see the bed of the river and he was surprised that such an accident could have happened. It was true that about three hundred paces away, down river, there was a deep pool, but the princess had kept away from it. No doubt some evil force must have been at work!

The young man pondered a while, but the flea whispered in his ear, 'Put one of the crayfish into the river, and watch where it goes to. And keep a tight hold on the nosebag.'

The young man bent over the water and, unnoticed, released one of the crayfish. The crayfish took a dozen paces, turned to the left, and disappeared beneath the bank; the second and the third crayfish followed the first.

The flea whispered, 'Now you know the way. We shall go there too. Stamp your left foot three times and jump from the bank into the river. We will find what we are looking for at once.'

So the young man did as he was told. He stamped his left foot three times and lowered himself into the water. The water began to foam and boil, and the crowds on the bank stiffened with fear, and waited to see what would happen.

As soon as he found himself in the water, the young man noticed a hole beneath the bank. It was so narrow that a man could scarcely crawl through it.

'Crawl in!' whispered the flea.

The young man crawled into the dark hole. And the hole suddenly widened. It was even possible to walk upright as he went along.

'Do not be afraid,' whispered the flea, and the young man went boldly on. It seemed no time at all before he came out into the light, and found himself in a vast green meadow. In this meadow, beyond a fence, there stood a blue stone house.

'Remember well what I tell you, and you will come to no harm,' said the flea. 'The princess is a prisoner of the fairy who lives in that blue house beyond the fence. The gate is guarded by two bears. They will allow no one to enter or leave, and they must be outwitted. When you get to the gates, tell the nosebag to change into a trough of honey. The bears will go for the

honey, and you can then enter. I will tell you what to do next, later.'

The young man went up to the gates and heard a terrifying growling. Then he saw the bears, and they were so enormous that his heart sank. Summoning up all his courage, he put down the nosebag, and ordered it to change into a trough of honey. The trough was so heavy that he couldn't possibly have moved it! As soon as the bears smelt the honey they opened the gates and made for the trough, and they did not even notice him. The young man

The young man shouted, 'Little bag, little bag, come to me quickly!'

And the bag was on his back in a flash.

They reached the cave mouth in safety.

'Do not be afraid,' the young man told the girl. 'It is dark and dank in here, but we shall soon be free. Close your eyes, and do not open them until I carry you to the bank.'

Once out of the cave and into the river the going was easier, and the young man took the princess in his arms and carried her to the bank. The crowds had gone. They had decided the young man had drowned like the princess. Only the king and his courtiers remained on the bank, and they were all in deep despair.

Suddenly, the king saw his daughter, alive and well, in the arms of her rescuer, and his joy could not be described. He embraced his daughter, and shook the young man's hand.

News of the princess's return from her watery grave spread through the city like wildfire. People rushed to the river in their thousands to gaze upon the princess and the man who had rescued her.

The king said that the young man must live in the palace. And he gave him a reward three times as great as he had promised.

That night, as the young man climbed into his silken bed, the flea tickled him behind the ear, and said, 'Do not stay here more than two days. You are rich now, and there is nothing more for

slipped into the yard and from there into the house.

'Look at the door on the right,' the flea whispered. 'There is a golden key in it. Shut the door and put the key in your pocket. Then the old fairy cannot get out. The princess is imprisoned in the room to the left. Open the door with the silver key and go into the room.'

When the young man turned the golden key in the lock there came a noise like thunder from inside and the walls shook. He put the key in his pocket and went to the other door. He opened it with the silver key, and saw the princess. At first she was startled, but when she heard why the young man had come, she sprang from her bed.

'Come with me quickly,' the young man said. 'We must get out of the gate before the bears eat all the honey.'

He took the princess by the hand, and passed the bears unseen. As he shut the gate, the flea whispered, 'Call the nosebag back!'

you here. There are still many adventures before us. The king wishes to give you his daughter in marriage, but you are still young, and should not marry yet. Let us rather wander the world until you are older and wiser!'

Now, the young man was not too keen to leave the palace, but the flea had advised him so well in the past that he decided to obey.

The king and the princess begged him to stay with them. But he would not be persuaded, and off he went.

Of course, like any other rich man, he could have travelled in a comfortable coach, and put up at the best inns. But he was in no hurry, and the nosebag provided him with food and drink, so he set off on foot, in search of his next adventure.

The next day, he was resting by the roadside when he heard the flea whisper, 'They are coming after you to take your bag! The three artisans told the folk in the city about its powers. Now, some of the wicked men are after it. You must cut a stick that will fit into the bag. Drill a hole at the end of the stick and fill it with lead. Then you will have a valuable weapon!'

The young man cut a stick, hid it in the bag, and went on. He walked for two whole days until he came to a dark forest. Suddenly, a dozen men came out from behind some of the trees, and leapt upon him.

And the flea whispered, 'Call on the stick for help!'

The young man did this — and oh, the wonder of it! The stick jumped out of the bag and began to beat the robbers so soundly that they made off as fast as they could!

The young man wandered on, until, one summer's evening, he arrived in a large village. The boys and girls were on swings, making music and dancing in the green meadow to the sound of merry tunes.

The young man gazed on them wistfully, and felt like dancing too. As he watched, his flea-companion whispered in his ear, 'We have come here at the right time. At long last, my evil enemy, the Black Magician, has fallen into our hands! I shall tell you what to do; but don't make any mistakes! He must not escape us. Study the girls, and find the one who wears a many-coloured ribbon around her neck instead of beads. Ask her to dance, waltz her round and round, and when she grows dizzy, take the ribbon from her neck, but see that it is pulled to pieces!'

The young man entered the circle and found the girl with the many-coloured ribbon round her neck. All the boys were begging her to dance, for she was tall and pretty and curly-haired.

The young man grabbed hold of her and begged her for the next dance, and she agreed. Faster and faster they danced, and the young man waited his chance and pulled at the brightly-coloured ribbon. There was a noise like thunder and the girl vanished!

The startled onlookers then saw an old man with a grey beard running towards the deep forest, and another tall man pursuing him!

Darkness fell, the incident was forgotten, and the young people began their merry-making again, as if nothing had happened.

The young man watched the merry-making a while longer, before he began thinking of finding somewhere to stay for the night. He walked away from the village until he heard footsteps behind him. He turned and saw a stranger.

'Wait for me, brother, and we shall go together!' said the stranger. 'I am myself again, and you do not recognize me. But I am still in your debt. First, you released me from my long imprisonment in the stone. Today, you have helped me to overcome the Black Magician. Now I need no longer hide in your pocket as

a flea. Or, indeed, masquerade as a manikin!'

The magician then told the young man how he had captured his enemy in the forest, and had tied him up securely. Now he could not escape, for all his powers lay in the many-coloured ribbon.

All that remained was to discover where the Black Magician had imprisoned the three young princesses he had pledged himself to rescue.

'When we find out where the princesses are,' he told the young man, 'you will be rich and famous beyond your dreams.'

After their talk they revived themselves with food from the bag and went to sleep. In the morning, they set off into the forest where the Black Magician lay bound, but all the young man saw was a poor old man, his hands and feet so securely fastened that he had no chance of freeing himself.

His friend called out, 'Stick, out of the bag!'

The stick leapt out of the bag and began to beat the Black Magician on the back and shoulders. In the end, the wicked magician promised to tell them where he had kept the three princesses captive if only the stick would cease to punish him. This he did, naming the exact spot where they would find not only the princesses but their treasures as well. He revealed that the beautiful princesses had been asleep for a hundred years or more!

Then the young man's companion said to him,

'You will be my prisoner until we find the princesses. But I will not leave you here. You might be set free from your bonds by someone who did not know how wicked you are!'

He picked up the wizard as though he were a feather and carried him to a deep gorge, where he left him.

'You will stay here until we return,' he said.

Then the magician told the young man where they must go to. The princesses were hidden in a far-off place which they could only reach with the help of the bag.

On the magician's command, the bag turned into a trough with room for the two of them. They could either sit or lie in it. Wings sprouted from its sides, and as the two friends took their places, it flew up into the clouds, and made off southwards. They did not have to worry about food, for there was plenty in the trough.

The trough flew without stopping, day and night, for more than a week. Finally, the magician ordered it to descend to the ground.

Now they were in a scorching desert close to a pile of ruins. The magician changed the trough into the nosebag, fastened it on the young man's back, and said, 'It is several days' walk to our goal, but I cannot go there.' And he began to scrape the sand beside one of the ruined walls. Soon he revealed a trap-door, and the travellers opened it. Beyond the dark entrance, steep stairs were visible. The magician then caught a large blue fly hovering above his head, placed it in a box, and told the young man to hide the box about his person. Then he continued speaking, 'When you find the three princesses, you will be asked who is the youngest. Open the box and let out the fly. It will settle on the youngest princess!'

The young man approached the trap-door, peered down into the darkness, and thought, 'Come what may, down I go!' And he set off boldly down the steps.

As he went down the steep steps, they seemed endless. He grew tired and hungry, and at length he sat down and had some food. Then he set off again. Down and down he climbed, until finally he saw light ahead. Sometime later he found himself in a green valley and there, in the distance, stood a fine palace. The young man set off towards it, and as he drew near, a small, grey manikin came out of the palace, and said, 'Go on, go on, try your luck! If you can guess which sleeping princess is the youngest, take her by the hand, and she will come to life. But if you guess wrongly, you yourself will fall into a deep sleep.'

The young man thought of the little box containing the blue fly as he followed the manikin into the palace. They passed through several rooms until they came to the room where, on silken beds, slept three beautiful girls. They were as alike as three peas out of the same pod!

The young man stared at them. But he could not decide which of them was the youngest. His only hope was the fly, and he opened the box. The fly flew out, circled round and round, and settled on the girl who slept between her two sisters. The young man went to her, took her hand, and proclaimed, 'This is the youngest!'

As he spoke, all three princesses came to life and rose from their beds. The youngest put her arms round the young man's neck and said, 'Welcome, dear sir! You have roused us from our long, enchanted sleep, and broken the Black Magician's spell. Now we must escape from his underworld.'

The steps down which the young man had climbed had disappeared. But a tunnel under the palace led them, at last, into green meadows. The sandy desert and the ruins he had expected to see had gone. In their place, there was a great city and a fine palace. As he gazed about him in wonder, his old friend suddenly appeared.

'Come with me,' he said.

And he took the young man to a shady pool and told him to look down into its clear waters.

The young man obeyed; he looked into the water and saw himself reflected there. But he could scarcely believe what he saw, for it seemed to him that he was dressed like a prince, in a handsome suit of brocade and velvet.

'Where did such magnificent clothes come from?' he gasped.

And his friend told him, 'They are my final gift to you. Your fortune is now made! In a few days, you will marry the youngest princess, the king's daughter, and in time you will become a king yourself. Are you content with the fortune I promised you?'

'You have rewarded me richly!' cried the young man. 'And I thank you from the bottom of my heart!'

A few days later, the wedding was held in the royal palace. And after a year, the young man, who had saved the manikin, taken the advice of a flea, and boldly faced all manner of dangers, became king of a mighty land!